EXOUSIA

BECA LEWIS

PERCEPTION PUBLISHING

ISBN-13: 978-0-9885520-6-7

CONTENTS

ONE

Emily Sands thought she had seen nothing more beautiful than the view from the hill. It was a view she had visited almost every day for the past year. A sight she dreamed about practically every night.

To get to her favorite spot on the hill, she'd park her car at the bottom of the rise and hike. In the rain and snow she often slid down as much as she moved up, but the view was always worth the effort.

It was the middle of February in Pennsylvania, so Emily had dressed for the cold. It had snowed the day before, leaving about a foot of snow on the ground. But with chains on her boots, the trek up the hill hadn't been as hard as the first time she had tried to climb it in bad weather.

Emily was not a fan of cold, and given the choice of hot or cold, she would choose hot anytime. However, she had learned that good things come from the cold and the winter season. It was a time of retreat, of planning, of preparation. And she was doing all three.

Emily thought that February was both the worst month of the year and the best. It was still winter, but as the season wound down, instead of snow sometimes there would be brown mud and chilly winds. Those were the days Emily liked the least. On the other hand, spring was right around the corner, and that vision was on everyone's mind. No matter where you went, someone would be talking about the weather and the coming season of green and growing things.

During her weekly grocery shopping trip, Emily had struck up a conversation with a friend about picking out dahlia bulbs for planting in the spring. Within minutes, four other women had joined them talking about the wonders of dahlias. If it wasn't dahlias, it was tulips or roses. Browsing through bulb and seed catalogs was a favorite February pastime in the village of Doveland.

For Emily, winter had been full of a different kind of browsing. She had been blueprint browsing. She had taught herself to use Google Sketch-up and drawn a version of what she was going to have built in the spring. This year, instead of a garden, she was going to plant some buildings. At least that was the dream, one that had been with her as long as she could remember. If all went well, this was the year it would come true.

As she gazed out over the snow-covered hill that she had just climbed, she thought about another reason to put up with the cold and snow. She loved to look out her window in the morning and see which animals had crossed through her yard during the night. It was incredibly exciting to see the visible tracks left behind by creatures who at any other time of the year were mostly invisible. In winter, she could see where they had been and where they were going.

Still standing, and looking down the hill that she had just come up, she could not only see her zigzagging footprints but also the tracks of the six deer she often encountered and the fox who sometimes allowed Emily to see her. Yes, winter did bring many blessings, she thought.

It was hard to tell that it was midday. The clouds hid the trek of the sun across the sky. Emily could never understand why some people thought that only sunny days were beautiful. She loved cloudy days and the feeling of being embraced by the sky itself.

Emily swung her backpack off her back as she sat down on the flat rock that jutted out from the hill, brushing the snow off before sitting. Six more weeks and spring would be here, and the snow would be mostly gone. Better than that, another few months and she would be building on this piece of heaven.

Nothing about her dream had been easy. Well, nothing about life had been easy. However, as a young girl, she had been given a gift that had saved her life. Now, she was only months away from giving other children that same gift.

Opening her backpack, she took out a sandwich and a jug of hot water. There hadn't been time to eat before coming out to the hill. Working part-time while teaching classes in the space she had rented in town kept her busy. But her schedule enabled her to carve out the time to visit this place and watch it change with the seasons.

Today, the bare tree limbs stood out in stark contrast to the snow and gray clouds. It was like looking at lace growing into the air. Every squirrel's nest was visible, sitting high in the branches. The bones of the tree were beautiful. In the summer, it was hard to see the structure of the tree beneath the leaves.

It reminded Emily of watching her dancers in their practice clothes that showed every movement and line of their bodies. She preferred that view, although audiences loved the costumes as much as people love leaves on trees.

At that moment, the sun made a surprise visit streaking through an opening in the clouds and sliding across the white landscape. Its warmth probed beneath the surface where all the green and glory of summer were still a few more months away.

Below, in the village of Doveland, the bells in the chapel rang out the hour. They were a recent addition, gifted to the church from the Anders family. Hank's family.

Emily knew she would be seeing a lot of Hank Blaze in the coming months. He was going to build her dream for her. As soon as the ground was soft enough, he and his crew would be out on the hill digging foundations. She had visited him a few times out at Melvin's place in Concourse to talk over her plans, and they had become good friends in the process.

All of it was a new beginning for her, and she hoped for the children of Doveland. Sitting on her rock imagining her dream, a deep thrill ran through Emily, bringing with it a heady rush of joy.

What Emily didn't know was that beneath the ground lay not only the seeds of plants and grasses that were waiting to sprout in the warmth but a secret that had been buried for over forty years. A secret that would tear the town apart. A secret that threatened to destroy her dream. It was only a matter of time. Spring was coming.

Two

Melvin Byler's living room had seen better days. Filled with mementos and decades-old furniture, it was stuffy but comfortable. While waiting for Melvin to wake up so they could have breakfast together, Hank Blaze sat in an old chair, the springs of which had also seen better days, staring out the window at the snow on the ground. He was tired of winter. He had big plans for the coming year, and he was itching to get them started. At the same time, Hank was grateful for the downtime that winter offered. It gave him a chance to look over his life and decide what he wanted to do with it. Grant was dead. Hank was free.

For the first time in his life, Hank felt safe enough to plan a life that was not haunted by his past deeds. He knew he would never forget what he had done, or what was done to him, but now he had a chance to make up for the past.

As he watched the wet snow fall and coat the tree limbs so that they looked as if they had icing on them, Hank ruminated over what had happened last summer. Many good things. Ben's christening. Pete and Barbara Mann moving to town and running the Diner. Grace Strong and Mandy Minks opening the coffee shop and bookstore called Your Second Home.

Hank had also discovered the generosity of the town of Doveland. Members of the community had rebuilt Melvin's barn after Lenny had blown it up to divert attention from what he had planned for Jay Kalin's birthday celebration. Jay was Hannah's "past-dad," as she called him because they remembered each other from their past life. However, the party had turned into a tragedy for Jay and Hannah.

Hank was haunted by the memory of Jay stepping in front of a bullet meant for Hank. He vowed that Jay's sacrifice would not be in vain.

Upstairs, lying in bed, Melvin was doing the same thing as Hank. Reminiscing. Although Hank had stoked the fire, the house was still cold. He was taking advantage of the fact that Hank had moved in with him after Jay died. He could wait until the house warmed up before heading downstairs, something he had never been able to enjoy before.

The loss of Jay had brought Hank and Melvin together. Melvin hadn't minded the barn being destroyed, but he grieved for his friend, Jay. Although Jay had only been in his life for a few months, it had changed everything. Melvin had stopped drifting through life until his time to die so he could see his wife Sally again. Instead, with Jay, he had looked forward to every day.

However, even in the midst of his grief, Melvin couldn't help feeling happy for Jay. In the end, Jay had overcome the temptation to take revenge on Hank for what he had done to Jay's family in his past life. Instead, Jay had saved Hank's life by sacrificing his own. He had shown the world the good man that he always had been. His goodness had just been buried under all that anger.

The fact that Melvin knew that Jay had been reunited with his wife Maggie, also helped ease his heart a bit. Melvin knew that Jay, Maggie, and Sally most of all, were waiting for him. He hoped that they were enjoying themselves in the meantime. He intended to do the same.

Nope, the barn blowing up was a blessing and Melvin had kept the promise to himself to write to Lenny in jail and thank him for sparing his house. He had never heard back from him, so he didn't know if Lenny actually got the letter. It didn't matter. He had thanked him.

Yes, Lenny had done Melvin a favor. After Jay's funeral, the town of Doveland held a barn-raising event for him. It was Hank who had made all the arrangements for the construction. Melvin knew that Hank was trying to make up for Jay's death and doing something tangible helped. But Melvin knew that Hank desired more. He wanted to settle down and do as much good as possible in the hopes it would erase some of his guilt and pain.

So Melvin asked Hank if he would like to move to the farm. It didn't take long for Hank to say yes. Hank thought he did it to keep Melvin company, but soon learned he had done it for himself. They were the perfect fit. Both of them were quiet, private men, but in need of good company.

As the leaves dropped from the trees in the fall the two of them would often walk Melvin's property talking over their lives. Sometimes Hank would bring Hannah out to the farm for the weekend. Hannah's mother, Ava, was happy to let her go. She knew that it was the three of them that needed the most healing and that doing it together would make it easier for all of them.

During the winter, with a storm raging outside and the wood-stove blazing away, Hank, Hannah, and Melvin made their own little world. Sometimes they played games. Sometimes they read books to each other. And as time passed, and their hearts had healed a bit, they started making plans.

They had spent many evenings bent over the old kitchen table talking about what they would like to do. It was Hank who brought up the idea of providing a space where kids could come out to learn the construction or farming trade with Melvin and Hank as their guides.

Hank decided to design it as if he were a boy in trouble. What would he want? Hank knew what he would have wanted because he had been a kid in trouble. But he never found a place to get help. Instead, he was on his own until Grant saw him on the streets. Hank had already thought of himself as a bad person, so it was easy for Grant to convince Hank to let him be his mentor. The problem was, Grant had no desire to turn Hank into a good person. Instead, he taught him the hidden ways of an evil man.

Hank didn't want other kids to suffer under someone like Grant. He wanted to offer something better. Not pity. Not punishment. He wanted to give them a way to find themselves.

Not all the kids in trouble came from bad families. In fact, most of them didn't. But the pressures in school to take drugs and join gangs existed even in the small towns in the country.

So the three of them enjoyed their time together as they schemed and planned. They had the perfect property to use to put the idea into action. Melvin's farm. Melvin's new barn would be the beginning.

Hank spoke to the police departments in both Concourse and Doveland and explained what they wanted to do. The police in both towns liked the idea and agreed to help them by pointing out some of the kids who were in the greatest danger.

However, the kids didn't have to be in trouble to come learn with Melvin and Hank. Everyone was welcome. What wasn't welcome were drugs or violence. Hank knew that learning how to say no to those things was a matter of education and of building up a purpose big enough so that they could not be tempted. They needed a community and connection.

They wanted each child to become their own authority. Each one of them would be given the opportunity to experience the possibilities that life had to offer. Construction and farming were the skills that Melvin and Hank knew. They would use that knowledge to share life skills that would translate into whatever the kids chose to do.

In spite of all their planning and the healing it was bringing, sometimes at night, Hank would scream in his sleep, lost in a nightmare. Melvin would wait in his room to see if Hank would wake himself up from the dream. If he didn't, Melvin would gently wake Hank and remind him that he no longer lived the life governed by someone who had authority over him. That nightmare was over.

That part was true. However, a new nightmare was just beginning.

THREE

Grace Strong and Sarah Morgan sat comfortably beside each other on the church pew. For seven months they had spent hours every morning sitting together, side by side. Sometimes weeping. Sometimes praying. Sometimes whispering together.

Both of them knew that it couldn't continue forever. In fact, Sarah and Grace knew that the time had come for them to rejoin the circle of life going on all around them. Seven months ago they both had to make a decision. It had been a painful one for both of them. Each had to let go of the love of her life.

It had been hardest for Sarah, and both of them knew it. But Sarah hated the moments when she became angry with her friend, Grace. She would feel the wall of anger building and then it would become reinforced by the guilt she felt for feeling that way in the first place.

All her friends, even Grace, told Sarah it was normal to go through this stage. But that didn't make it any easier for her when she realized she was angry at her best friend and at her husband, Leif.

Rationally, Sarah knew that there hadn't been any other choice for Leif. And that was another reason Sarah would get mad. She would think how selfish it was for Eric to ask her to give up her husband so that Eric wouldn't have to die. What right did he have to ask that? He knew what Leif would say.

He knew that Sarah would agree that it was the right thing to do. But if Eric had just not asked, then only Grace would be grieving her husband's death. Sarah would be comforting her and then going home to her Leif. She could almost imagine the conversation. They would have said, "Poor Grace, what can we do for her?"

Instead, Sarah and Leif had done the ultimate something for Grace and Eric. They had given up the rest of this lifetime together.

Eric had asked Leif to take him to the Forest Circle, and they had agreed that since Leif was the one who knew how to do it, he would have to go.

So even though Sarah would sit on the bench beside Grace every day, both of them mourning, it was Sarah who was also trying not to be angry and guilty because she was angry.

Grace, on the other hand, although not angry, was overcome with guilt. She had helped Eric ask Leif, knowing that Leif would say yes, and that this would deprive her best friend of the physical presence of the love of her life. Grace often wondered if that made her a monster.

Before Suzanne Laudry had returned to the Forest Circle she had told Grace that it wasn't true. Grace wasn't a monster. She was a woman following a chance to keep Eric in her life rather than losing him. Perhaps she would find him again in another lifetime, but that was never guaranteed.

Leif too had assured Grace that he thought that there was a more significant reason for Eric's request. He didn't know what it was yet, but time would tell. This way, he and Eric both would be around to watch over them. The rest of the Forest Circle had work to do in other dimensions, but Eric and Leif could stay close.

Over the past seven months, Grace and Sarah had worked hard to overcome, or at least accept, the feelings they both had and to try not to let them come between them. They knew the more significant bond that they had together was the one of loss. In the end, it would make their friendship stronger than ever.

Sarah did have an advantage. She and Leif could still talk. Sarah could see him, and he visited her as often as possible. Sarah knew that if she was ever in real danger, she just had to reach out to him. But there were times in the middle of the night or in the garden when the physical missing of him was so powerful that she would find herself wailing in her sleep or dropping to her knees sobbing over the loss.

Grace didn't have that luxury, and Sarah never talked about it with her. There was no need to made Grace feel worse than she already did. For Grace, Eric was gone almost as effectively as if he had died. Grace had tried over and over again to see Eric. She could feel him near, but she longed to hear his voice and see his familiar form.

Nothing had worked. Sarah thought it was time to give Grace some relief and a little pleasure. Because what Grace couldn't see was both Leif and Eric sitting beside them.

Sarah knew she should be grateful for the fact that she could see Leif there with her. But she couldn't hold his hand. She couldn't snuggle against his back at night. She knew she was going to miss those things when she had agreed to this plan. She just didn't know how much.

But it was time. She and Leif had talked it over the night before. By not letting go completely she was keeping him from doing his work. He wasn't going to be gone all the time. He just couldn't stay in Doveland with her any longer.

So Sarah turned to Grace to tell her, but as usual, Grace already knew. "I know, Sarah. I have to let him go. I just wish I could learn to see Eric the way you do when he and Leif visit."

Sarah smiled at her friend. They both had changed since Leif had taken Eric with him to another dimension instead of letting Eric die.

"We could try something if you are ready, Grace. Both of them are here now, but you're right, we have to let them get to work. However, it may be possible to set up a channel through me for you to see Eric when he visits. Would you like to try?"

There was no need to wait for Grace to answer, her face told it all. Sarah reached out and held her hand and opened herself up to Grace as much as she could manage. Then Sarah drew a line in her heart to Grace and then to Eric. She hadn't tried to connect them before because the anger and guilt had been blocking her from opening her heart. However, Sarah knew that it was time to let all of it go, and give Eric and Grace the gift she was capable of giving.

"Oh, I see him," Grace whispered. "And hear him. He just told me how much he loves me."

"I know, Grace," Sarah said. "The only bad thing about doing it this way is I have to be here with you two. But I think in time you will do this yourself. I'll try not to listen."

But it was impossible not to. Sarah's heart broke all over again as she heard them talk about their love for each other. When it was time, Leif gave her an air hug and an air kiss, and she let go of Grace's hand, and the door closed.

"They're gone?"

"For now. But we have work to do ourselves. Are you ready?"

For an answer, Grace stood as tall as her short stature would let her, brushed off her slacks, grabbed her bag and headed out the door of the church.

"Meet me at Your Second Home after lunch," Grace called over her shoulder. "I have an idea."

Sarah waited a few more minutes before leaving. She knew what needed to be done. Now that Grace was ready, it was time.

FOUR

Hannah sat on her bed staring at Jay's picture. She knew that her mom was hoping that she would start to forget her past life, but Hannah knew that would never happen. It wasn't that Ava was trying to make her forget, she just thought it would be easier for Hannah if she did.

She is probably right, Hannah thought. But she doesn't need to worry because remembering doesn't haunt me like it did my past-dad, Jay. It's more like a book that I can pick up and read whenever I want to, but it remains closed unless I open it.

Still, Hannah was grateful to Melvin for thinking about taking a picture of Jay for her the morning of his birthday. The morning he gave his life to save her Uncle Hank. Now she had a picture of him to keep forever. He looked just like she remembered him from both lifetimes.

She gave the picture one last look and put it back on the table beside her bed. It stayed there along with a photo of Evan—her dad in this lifetime—her mom, and her new brother Ben.

She missed her adoptive grandfather, Eric. He used to pick her up and take her to school every day. Now she rode the bus. That was fun though. She was making new friends. Besides, riding the bus she heard all the news about what was going on in town.

If she could, she sat beside Lex. She liked him as a friend, but it was his brother, Johnny who she was interested in and this was a way to stay close.

Johnny had been in trouble last summer for helping Grant, but now he was working at the Diner after school. Hank said Johnny would be in the first group that he and Melvin would work with as soon as spring came around.

Hannah knew that she didn't miss Eric as much as Grace did though. Because even though he couldn't drive her to school anymore, given he wasn't physically present, he still waited with her for the bus, and she could see and talk with him. Grace still hadn't figured out how to do that.

Grabbing her book bag, Hannah hurried out the door to catch the bus and to see Eric. She stopped in her tracks when she saw him. Something was wrong. This morning he looked sad as he waited for her. Sometimes Leif came with him, but today it was only Eric.

"You have something to tell me, don't you, grandfather?" Hannah said.

Eric moved closer and knelt down in front of her. Well, not actually knelt down because his knees weren't touching the ground, but he got as close to eye level as possible.

"Little one, you know I could spend all day here with you, but Leif and I have to be doing other things now. So, I can't be here every morning. I will come when you call, though, because you and Grace hold my heart in your hands."

Ava, looking out the window at her daughter staring at something directly in front of her and knew that Hannah saw something Ava couldn't see. She guessed that it was Eric.

When tears started running down Hannah's face, Ava made herself not move, in spite of her own breaking heart. Sarah had told

Ava that Leif and Eric wouldn't be around as much as before, so she figured that was what was going on now between the two of them.

Ava longed to be able to see what so many of her friends could see, but she was grateful that her heart was open enough to allow her to see the love that was passing from Hannah to Eric. Perhaps she couldn't see his form, but she could see their love for each other.

She waited. She knew that if Hannah wanted her to come, she would call her. She could hear her daughter's thoughts sometimes, and for that she was grateful.

She wasn't all that grateful though that Hannah could hear hers. Sometimes it was when she would answer, "Yes, pancakes would be lovely," when Ava had only thought about making them. It was the other thoughts she hoped Hannah didn't hear.

Hannah had promised not to listen in, but she was a curious child. Sometimes she might hear things that were not what a young girl, even one as wise as Hannah, should know.

At that moment, Hannah looked up and smiled at her mom standing in the window, and Ava knew that Hannah was grateful for letting her have those moments with Eric by herself.

The bus pulled up to the house. The driveway made it easy for it to drive straight up to the front door, and then curve back down to the street. It was safer than Hannah waiting by the road to town. All the kids waved at Ava and Ben standing in the window. Hannah gave one last wave before stepping into the bus, and the bus driver honked as the bus moved down the drive.

Ava always felt bereaved when Hannah left for school. Ben was going to be one year old in April, and she was ready to find something to do with herself. Up until now, Ben had taken all her time. And over the winter months, she had allowed herself time for thinking about and healing from the summer events. Now, she was ready to move on. She was bored.

Ava had never thought she would be just a wife, mother, and housewife, as much as she loved those roles. She wanted something more, even if she didn't know yet what it would be.

Sarah had hinted at something a few weeks before. Maybe she was ready to tell her now.

Spring fever in March. Or was it cabin fever? Either way, Ava was ready to get out and do something. She could feel something coming her way that made the hair on her arms stand up. Ava wasn't sure if she was excited or scared, but she was ready, whichever way it went.

FIVE

Craig Lester glanced around his small waiting room and felt a wave of contentment move through him. It was perfect. Well, not entirely perfect. There was still some work to be done to fix some of the problems an old building inevitably suffers. Besides, he knew that Mandy was preparing color and furniture choices for him. She told him that she wanted to keep the bungalow essence of the place while still bringing it into the modern age. Whatever she meant by that was okay with him.

Craig knew he would never be able to put all those ideas into words let alone into something called a color and style palette. But Mandy was over the moon excited to be given the opportunity to design another space. She had been practicing on anyone's space who would let her. The bunkhouse at Ava and Evan's house had a whole new look, and so did Grace's apartment. He knew that, given time, Mandy would be retrofitting every building in town with a new look. Mandy had discovered a passion. Designing.

Craig sat in one of the old chairs that he wanted to keep but knew Mandy would shake her head and tell him no. She would be right, too. For her help in designing his office, Craig said he was paying her. Even though Mandy told him she would be happy to do it for free for everyone forever, Craig wanted her to see for herself that she had a budding design career happening. It made him feel good to help Mandy find her perfect work.

The last year had been hard for Craig. But, he too was finding his work, now that he had moved to Doveland. His wife Jo Anne had been delighted to divorce him as long as the money flowed into her bank account every month. That meant he needed to keep working. But it was a payment he was happy to make. Jo Anne had put up with his craziness for years, so in this way, he could thank her for doing so. He knew she already had a new man in her life, so he wasn't expecting to be paying for too long.

The chair was comfortable, worn smooth by the many people who had sat in this waiting room during the last fifty years. The doctor who owned the practice had been working out of this space the whole time. It had history and Craig liked that feeling. When Craig approached him to take over his practice, it turned out to be perfect timing. He was happy to sell it to Craig for a reasonable fee.

Both of them knew that not all of Dr. Joe Hellard's patients would continue as Craig's patients. Many of them would not be interested in the more holistic practice Craig was planning on offering. Holistic and preventative. Craig felt his heart lift as he thought about it. Finally, he would be a family doctor, not a corporate doctor. That was a life he was happy to be giving up.

Craig had sold his practice in Rochester to a doctors group, and that money would fund a less lucrative practice in Doveland for many years. Other than paying Jo Anne, Craig wanted to live a simple life in Doveland which wouldn't take much money. He planned to live above his practice, at least in the beginning. It made for a fast trip to the office.

Joe Hellard and Craig had become friends as they made the transition. Craig had been assisting Dr, Joe for the past six months, and they had both agreed that Joe would stay on as a consulting physician for another year.

Fifty years of practicing in the same small town had earned Dr. Joe respect from almost everyone in Doveland and Concourse. Craig knew he was a lucky man to have decided to become a village doctor at the same time Joe decided to retire. Craig loved the synchronicity of it.

Craig wondered if he would find someone to take over the practice when he was ready to retire. In twenty years perhaps someone else would be looking over the waiting room the same way he was, wondering what secrets it had to tell.

• • • ● • ● • ● • • •

A car door slammed, and Craig heard Mandy call out, "Hey, in there! Help!"

Craig hurried out the back door of his office and found Mandy struggling with carrying too many things at once. She had two shoulder bags slung over her shoulder, a backpack, and a cardboard box in her hands. Laughing, Craig grabbed the box and the shoulder bags and shut her car door with his foot.

There was a hallway that led from the back parking lot through the offices. Patients would be coming in the front door, not the back one. They would only go down the hall to the restroom or one of the examining rooms, or even the meditation room. Craig was going to have a rolfer and a chiropractor come into the office a few days a month. He was serious about having a full-service alternative practice.

"This is a dreary place, Craig," Mandy said. "Not only is it too dark, it feels dark."

"I see that it looks too dark, but why do you say it feels dark, Mandy? I don't feel that at all."

Mandy put down the backpack and stood in the waiting room. And waited. Perhaps she was wrong? No, as she stood there, she felt something strange. But since Craig didn't sense anything, maybe she was imagining it.

Besides, once she was done making the place light, airy, and comfortable, she was sure that it would feel better too. However, it wouldn't hurt to smudge the place with sage.

"Okay, you are probably right. It's probably the physical darkness of the place that's getting to me. If you can okay the colors and fabrics, I can get started on the transformation. Are we doing your upstairs too?"

"Yep. Joe used it mostly for storage for the past twenty years, so it's going to take some work to make it look good. It's empty now. He took everything out last week. I've been camping out with a cot, sleeping bag, and hot plate since then."

"Hank's coming over to put in a small kitchen and update the plumbing and do all that stuff for you?"

"That he is," Hank said, coming through the back door.

"How come we didn't hear your truck?" Craig asked.

"I parked at Sarah's and walked over."

"Are you fixing up Eric's old place too?" Mandy asked,

It was an innocent question, but one that struck a nerve with all three of them. Mandy sat down in the old chair that Craig had been sitting on and Craig and Hank stood looking at the floor.

"I miss them both so much," Mandy said, brushing away the tears that threatened to spill over.

The ringing of Hank's phone broke the cloud of silence. He glanced at it, and seeing it was Ava hoped she would say something to cheer him up. He knew Mandy meant she missed Leif and Eric, but Hank had another sorrow. He missed Jay, too. It was the weirdest thing. When Jay died, it was as if at that moment he experienced an intense bond between them. Hannah told him later it was probably because they had always been connected somehow in every lifetime. Hank wished he had time to find that connection in this one instead of it being yanked away from him so violently.

Ava's voice was cheerful, and when she heard where he was asked him to put her on speaker. "Hannah wants Hank to come over for dinner since he is there with you two. Do you want to come too?"

At the sound of Ava's voice, Mandy brightened up and asked if she could bring Tom, and Hank asked if Melvin could come.

By the time the conversation was over, Ava had invited everyone. Mandy went off to find Grace and Sarah, and Hank called Melvin, Sam, Tom, and Mira.

Craig said he would be along soon. He had to lock up. After Hank and Mandy left, he sat again in the old chair and tried to feel what Mandy meant.

Was there a darkness in the room? Was he mistaken about Dr. Joe? No, he was sure that wasn't it. Probably it was because so many people had waited for the doctor for all these years, some of that pain and sorrow must have built up.

Mandy was right. He needed to smudge the whole building. He would do that tomorrow. Tonight, it was time for friends.

Six

D r. Joe Hellard stared at the pile of crap he had removed from
the storage room above his office. Fifty years of files. He was
tempted to start a bonfire in the backyard and take every box out
and burn it. It was hard to remember why he had kept them in the
first place.

He supposed it was because when he first started meeting
patients, he wanted to refer back to his notes as he worked with
them. What helped them? What didn't help? Over time, taking
notes became less necessary. Instead, Joe and his patients found
that his methods almost always worked, so he rarely looked at his
records. Once a year, he would drag a box or two up the stairs and
leave it there to get to someday.

It was someday now. Joe had just turned eighty. Most people
didn't realize he was that old. He still had his hair, although long
gone gray. Unlike many of his friends, he hadn't lost any of his
height. He wasn't that tall to begin with anyway. But he had
changed in ways he couldn't quite put his finger on. Perhaps he
just didn't care as much anymore.

Times had changed. Who was he kidding, everything had changed. The Doveland he had moved to fifty years before was not the same.

When he had first moved to town in the early Seventies, it was in recovery. Once a thriving farming town it had shrunk to just a few hundred people, and only a few farmers were left. Then the young kids, the boomer kids, began moving out to the country to get back to the land. Doveland was ripe for picking. The old farmers were ready to retire, and making a profit by selling their property was unexpected but welcome.

Some of the young people formed communes and worked the land together. They had their own rules and their idea of a personal community. Free love and shared families.

Doveland's long-time residents at that time didn't understand what they were doing. But the young people with their new ways spent their money in town, improving the town's bottom line and tax base, so they were begrudgingly accepted and mostly left alone.

However, some of the real old-timers, now long gone, didn't like those hippy farmers or commune groupies. They would sit on benches in front of the Diner during the day, and in the bars every night and complain about them. More than once Joe had stopped a bar fight and often worried that something more violent would take place.

The town's revival didn't last long. Within a few years, most of the young ones learned that farming and living off the land was much harder to do than they thought it would be. The winters could be brutal. When spring arrived, more than one farm would have been abandoned during the winter as the young ran home to mom and dad, or to a corporate job that paid well.

If someone was paying attention, they could get a lot of land for cheap in those days. They could wait until the bank foreclosed on the property and then buy it up for a song. Joe was one of a few men who took advantage of the glut of land on the market.

He did it quietly, and very few people knew how much property he ended up owning, both in and outside of town.

The problem was, Doveland never fully recovered after that brief boom of prosperity. It stumbled along doing its best to remain viable. But when the children of Doveland grew up, they almost all left for the city or warmer climates. There wasn't enough tax money to keep up maintenance of many of the buildings, so Doveland became just another small town, falling into disrepair.

Then a few years ago something happened. Joe figured that if you wait long enough, things will cycle around again. And that's what happened to Doveland. A new group of people decided to try the country. Not hippies this time. Mostly young people who were tired of the city and ready to live in a small town and either farm, cater to the farmer, or run a small business.

The internet gave people the freedom to run a business from their homes anywhere they wanted to live. Once a few people found Doveland, more people were attracted to it.

And then that group of friends of Craig's arrived. That changed everything.

Not only could Joe now retire, but he also had someone who would buy his practice. Joe wasn't hurting for money though. Being a doctor in a small town doesn't earn anyone much wealth. Instead, Joe had learned other ways to become wealthy while enjoying the amenity of small-town life, combined with trips to discover the glories of mother earth.

It had been a good life. In fact, he planned to continue to have a good life. But right now, he had to decide what to do about the records of that life. Maybe it was time to get a really good shredder and get started cleaning things up.

Slapping his hands on his knees, he stood up, stretched, and turned his back on the boxes to look out the window of the office in his home. It was a view he had enjoyed for years, but perhaps it was time to chuck the whole thing, sell his house, and move on.

He had already sold his property that bordered the road out to Concourse to Craig's friends. They had some crazy idea of making a bike path from Doveland to Concourse. Joe couldn't understand why anyone would want to do that, but it seemed to be all the rage these days. Made no difference to him. A walk around the golf course was all the exercise he needed, and he certainly didn't need all that land anymore. He was happy to let it go.

Yes, it was probably time to let all of it go. Clean stuff up. That would be his motto for the spring. Hang around for a year to help out Craig and then maybe go live in that small town in Spain that he had stayed at years before.

Checking his watch, Joe realized he better get moving. There was a meeting of the rotary club in town. That woman, Valerie, wanted to talk about a fundraising event for the next solstice celebration. No one really knew how close that had come to being a total disaster last year.

Nope, Joe thought as he shrugged into his overcoat and grabbed the keys to his car. It almost was, but not this year. This year, if he had anything to say about it, there would be just a regular good old-fashioned small town celebration—his favorite kind.

Seven

I t wasn't unusual for everyone to gather at the Ander's home on the spur of the moment. Just a few miles outside of Doveland Ava and Evan's house had become the hub of what Hannah had started calling the Doveland Circle. The original Stone Circle had expanded to include all their friends and family, and they needed a way to talk about who they were. Their Karass was definitely growing.

Ava thought that their expanding circle was proof that people are drawn to each other over many lifetimes. But Ava knew that first people have to accept that there are many lifetimes, before they would begin to recognize their personal Karass.

The Doveland Circle had met so often everyone knew to bring food when they got together. No planning was involved. Each person either picked up something on the way or brought what was already in their house. Of course, Pete and Barbara brought food from the Diner, and Grace and Mandy brought deserts from Your Second Home.

Unlike some meetings called by the Doveland Circle to discuss a problem or decide on a project, this one was just a comfortable gathering of friends on a Friday night catching up on what was going on in each of their lives.

Although cold outside, inside with a fire in the woodstove everyone was warm and cozy. The friends sat in groups content to chat about nothing.

However, since Leif and Eric had gone, there was always a sad spot. Neither Sarah nor Grace had been quite themselves since summer and Hannah would often sit beside them and talk about school or things she wanted to do. Ava knew that Hannah was doing her best to cheer them up. At the same time, Ava knew that Hannah was also struggling with missing Leif, Eric, and of course her past-dad, Jay.

That's why Ava was pleased that during the height of the party, both Leif and Eric showed up causing everyone who could see them to babble with excitement. Those who couldn't see or hear them waited patiently to be told what they had to say.

Hannah and Sarah had discovered that sometimes if they touched someone who couldn't see the travelers from another dimension, that person could not only see the travelers with their own eyes but hear them too.

Everyone who couldn't see them directly hoped it was just a temporary problem. They hoped that over time they would learn how to see the travelers without assistance. More than anything, it was a state of mind and a point of view that blocked their abilities.

Nothing in the human experience made it impossible; it was only conditioned belief. *A hard one to get over, though,* Ava thought.

Leif and Eric didn't stay long. Although they had told some people that they wouldn't be around much, not everyone knew, and once Leif and Eric heard about the party, they thought it was an excellent way to tell everyone at once.

No one was happy about it, but everyone understood. Sarah wondered why it was so easy to understand and still feel so terrible about it at the same time.

After Leif and Eric left, Mandy broke the pall of silence that had fallen over the group by asking who wanted dessert. She had been trying out recipes for making sugar-free cookies and needed people to try them, and let her know what they thought.

No one needed a second invitation, and soon the room was buzzing again with chatter over which cookie was best. Everyone loved every cookie, although they each had a favorite, which pleased Mandy. She would have a choice of which kind to make each day.

Watching from the sidelines, Hank stood beside Ava and asked her if there was anything he could do to cheer Hannah up.

"I thought she might like to take some kind of lessons. Maybe music, or art, or even dance." Ava said.

"Dance? Did I hear the word, dance?" Hannah said from across the room. She skipped over to the two of them and grabbed their hands as she looked up at them. "I would love to take dance lessons. It was lovely watching those dancers at the solstice. Do you think I could do that?"

"Absolutely," Ava said. "I'll have to find out the name of that teacher and get you set up."

"Well, that's handy," Hank said. "I know her. Her name is Emily Sands. Emily hired me to help her build a summer camp for dance and art. For now, she is renting space in the town hall. Would you like to meet her and try out lessons?"

There was no need to hear Hannah's answer. Her face had changed into the bright face they knew before last summer.

"If you want to dance, Hannah, we'll make sure that happens for you," Ava said.

"Yep, I will take you to Emily's house after school on Monday. I promised to bring some plans by for her to look at, so that way we will take care of two things at one time," Hank said.

It was a happy Hannah that went to bed that night. She had continued the practice of kneeling by her bed each night to say thank you for the day. Recently her thanking felt forced, but tonight, the words of gratitude were heartfelt.

As soon as Hannah heard the word dance, something clicked inside, and she went from being okay in the world, to joyful. *Whoever this Emily is,* Hannah thought, *I am going to enjoy every minute of learning to dance.*

Hannah was not the only one who gave thanks that night. Everyone had seen the transformation and were overjoyed to see the light come back into her eyes.

Even Grace and Sarah seem better, Ava thought and breathed a sigh of relief. It looked as if spring would be not only bringing flowers and warm days but a renewing of life for all of them. It had been a hard seven months. They were ready for something good to happen, and no more surprise evil events. Was that so much to ask for? Ava didn't think so.

Evan walked everyone out to their cars and made sure that they were safely on their way before coming back inside. On the way to bed, he stopped in both Ben and Hannah's bedrooms and kissed them on their foreheads thinking that he was probably the luckiest man in the world.

In spite of everything, he was still the proud father of two beautiful children and the happy husband of the love of his life.

The problem was, he couldn't shake the feeling of foreboding that came over him when Hank talked about building the dance teacher's summer camp.

Shaking it off, he walked out onto the back deck and looked up at the star-laden sky. Although it was still cold, the snow had melted, and he knew that the daffodils had already started coming up. It was a new season of renewal. He was ready for it.

EIGHT

The wind grabbed the door and swung it open sending a sheet of rain into Your Second Home. It was Saturday morning so almost all the tables were full, and everyone turned to look at who had caused the disturbance and brought the cold into their cozy environment. Their expressions ranged from total exasperation to a smile of understanding. They had all done the same thing at one time or another.

Sam Long said "Sorry, sorry," as he shook out his hat and wondered where to hang his wet coat. Mandy put down her coffee pot on one of the few remaining empty tables and hurried over to help Sam with his hat and coat.

"We should've built a pass-through door, shouldn't we have?" she asked Sam, already knowing the answer.

"Yes, you should have, and a place to put wet stuff. You still could you know."

"How?" she asked.

"Well, Hank could push the doorway out. You are set back from the sidewalk far enough that the town will probably let you, and then you could turn the right-hand side of the store at the front into a kind of coatroom. You would lose one set of front windows, but it might be worth it."

Looking at all the people sitting with wet coats hooked on to the back of their chairs, Mandy agreed. She and Grace could talk to the permit department at the town hall and then arrange for Hank and his crew to do the build out. Mandy thought it would help Grace take her mind off of missing Eric.

"Are you ready to taste a lot of cookies and pastries?" Mandy asked.

"Absolutely. Keep the coffee coming, and bring another cup, Mira is meeting me here."

"She's already here, hiding in the back."

Breaking into a big smile, Sam walked back to join Mira, thinking that moving to Doveland and living with Mira was the smartest thing he had ever done in his life. Some days he missed the excitement of puzzling out a mystery. But the stress of hunting down Grant and Lenny had been the final breaking point for him. He had resigned from the FBI in the fall. They weren't happy with his leaving, and he had a hard time adjusting, but Mira had helped. They only let him go after he agreed to be called in as a consultant on a case by case basis. He hoped he would never get that call.

To give him something to do, Mira suggested that Sam go back into catering. Of course, it was a small town, so there wouldn't be that much work. So how about an internet business of some kind around his food? Or even write a cookbook? They decided to begin with the catering company in town and see where that took them. Catering business was what they were doing today. They were tasting Mandy's desserts that they would include on their catering menu.

The rest of the business would have to grow more slowly, but they weren't in a hurry.

Sam glanced around the room and realized he knew almost everyone. He loved that. Small town living where you know everyone.

However, Sam was not naive. He had spent too many years chasing down criminals who lived ordinary lives. Their neighbors never knew that the man they borrowed the lawnmower from also kidnapped young girls. Or the guy who worked at the grocery store ran a gambling ring. People thought that criminals had a face of a criminal, or you could tell they were lying by watching their eyes or their body language. Sam knew how untrue that was. It was almost always the person you least expected that had done the most serious crimes. Sam was glad those days were behind him.

In the corner of the room, Valerie Price and her husband Harold were sitting with another couple that Sam recognized from town hall meetings, although he couldn't remember their names. At first, Sam thought they were having a conversation but then realized that they were listening to Harold, who didn't even appear to take a breath as he spoke.

Tilting his head in their direction, he asked Mira, "Do you know Valerie and Harold very well? Harold seems to like to dominate a conversation. Is he that interesting? I worked with them last summer when we discovered it was their son Johnny who lit the fireworks at Grant's request, but other than that, I don't know them well."

"Speaking of Johnny," Mira answered, "I see him once in a while when I stop in at the Diner to see Pete and Barbara. It was such a nice thing for you to do for him. To give him a chance to work off what he did rather than go to jail.

"To answer your question, though, I know Valerie pretty well. She put together the solstice celebration last year. She is excellent at managing people and planning events! But Harold, I don't know him other than overhearing his stories when I go by their table. He seems to think he knows everything about everything. Not that he does, he just acts like the authority."

They both glanced over at the table again where Harold was still holding court. Mira caught Valerie's eye, and they waved to each other. Then Valerie went back to listening to her husband as if that was the most important thing she could be doing.

"Don't expect me to be doting like that, Sam," Mira said.

Sam reached over and squeezed her hand, "Thank you. I want you to become more and more your own woman, Mira, and I am grateful that you have chosen me to be in your life as you do that."

"Oh for heaven's sake," Mandy said, arriving at the table with a plate full of goodies. "Stop mooning around and start eating." Then she winked at Mira, who winked back. They understood each other. Mandy was just as in love with Mira's twin brother, Tom as Mira was with Sam, and they both knew it. In fact, the two of them had discussed a joint wedding. It wasn't official for either couple, but everyone knew it was coming.

At Valerie's table, Harold said something that caused the group to gasp and then laugh, and when Mandy glanced up, Harold motioned her over.

"Could you settle something for us, Mandy?" Harold asked and grabbed her hand. "Which of us is the most handsome?"

Mandy looked at the other man at the table, and then at Valerie trying to decide if it was a joke or not. Valerie's expression told her it was serious, but Mandy lightened it up by laughing and asking how could she ever choose. But since Harold was the more regular customer, she would pick him. It seemed to work. Valerie relaxed and gave Mandy a weak smile, and Harold asked for the check.

After they left, as Mandy wiped off their table, she found a piece of paper with her name on it. Unfolding it, she found a five-dollar bill and the words, 'thank you.' Wondering who wrote it and what that was all about, she stuck them both in her pocket.

The morning continued to be busy, and Mandy didn't think of it again until that night when she found the note while getting ready for bed. Tom was traveling, so she was alone. She took the paper out and puzzled over the writing. Who wrote it? What were they thanking her for? Mandy thought she would ask Valerie about it later and stuck it in the book she was reading so she wouldn't forget.

Mandy wondered how well she knew anyone in the village. Like Sam, she knew that what you see, is not usually what you get. She had been around too long, in too many ugly places to have forgotten that bitter lesson.

Her days as an escort for men for money were long gone, but her memories, though faded into the background, had taught her not to trust looks or charm. She also knew how hard it could be to discover the true essence of someone. Yes, she would have to talk to Valerie. How did she and Harold meet? What was that look on Valerie's face, anyway?

Mandy drifted off to sleep, hugging Tom's pillow instead of Tom, and wondering if something was going on that she needed to know about. She would talk to the women's group about it at their first meeting.

NINE

Grace looked around the room one last time. It looked different now. For almost a year it had been the room that she and Eric sat in every morning and talked, or read books together, sometimes stopping to read a passage to each other. She had decorated it with Eric in mind. It had been Mandy's apartment, but when she and Eric married they knocked down walls and built this room. A long room filled with light. If you wanted to, you could stand at the windows that looked out over the town square and watch everything that was going on in downtown Doveland.

On summer nights when the band played their concerts on the green, Eric and Grace would fling open the windows and listen while snuggling on the couch together. *We never had a winter together in this room,* Grace thought. Only married a few months and then he was gone.

Grace knew that Eric was sick when they married. But she had hoped against hope that he would be cured and they could live out the rest of their lives together. At least more than a few months. Instead, she had a ghost for a husband.

Well, it's better than never seeing him again, she thought. She saw him. Through Sarah. Or Hannah. But still, she saw him. Every once in a while.

He looked well and happy and, if she told the truth to herself, that kind of made her mad. She knew she shouldn't be angry. But still, sometimes the feeling was so intense it hurt.

Eric looked better. She looked worse. At least she felt that she did. Eric told her he looked better because as a dimension traveler they could wear bodies like coats. Clean them up, look good. Didn't she remember that we are not our bodies?

Of course, she did. It's just that right at that moment her body missed Eric's, and hers was old and getting older, and she hated every minute of it. Every minute. It wasn't like her to be so discouraged. She used to call herself a busy-body old lady, which was the truth. She still was a busy-body old lady, but now she was a sad and discouraged one.

Sarah said that what they were going to do would help. Grace was so discouraged she didn't see how it could. The only reason Grace agreed was because if Sarah wanted it, Grace was going to do it. Sarah had sacrificed for her, and she could never repay her, even if she only had a ghost for a husband. So did Sarah.

So with Mandy's help, she changed the room. If they were going to be meeting here, it had to turn into something that didn't remind her of what she had lost, but inspired her to begin again. Today was the first day of their meeting. None of them knew what would come of it, but Sarah said it was necessary to start somewhere.

They would start small. It would be Grace, Sarah, Mandy, Ava, and Mira.

Grace heard footsteps on the stairs coming up to her apartment. Downstairs was her beloved bookstore and coffee house. The stairs to her apartment were through a door in the back of the store. Only her friends had a key that opened the door to the stairs. At the top of the stairs was a landing and then the door to her apartment. It was perfect. Just what she had always dreamed of having. *Really,* Grace thought. *I am blessed. I need to get over myself.*

With a soft knock on her door, the four women stepped into the apartment.

"Oh Grace, this is lovely," Mira said, standing in the doorway of the newly decorated space.

"Mandy did it," Grace answered. "She's a wonder."

Mandy blushed and said, "Thank you. I can't tell you how much I love doing this. It makes me happy inside and out."

After hanging their coats in the closet outside the room, the four of them stood together looking at the two couches facing each other with a beautiful coffee table between them, placed perfectly for talking.

"Let's begin," Sarah said.

• • • ● • ● • ● • • •

Hank kept his word and picked up Hannah on Monday after school to go meet Emily. All day in school Hanna could barely stay still. She was used to people asking her to stop fidgeting, but today was worse than ever. Her teacher finally gave up and ignored her.

Hannah suspected that her teacher had the same problem and understood that something important was happening that day. Hannah's suspicions were confirmed when during recess the teacher came over to Hannah and asked why she was so excited.

When Hannah told her she was going to meet the dance teacher after school and start taking lessons, her teacher hugged her and said she understood completely. She loved to dance too. In fact, she was part of the adult students who took the class Emily taught in the town hall. Hannah thought that Ava and Evan might like those lessons, and promised to tell them about it.

In addition, her teacher wanted Hannah to show her what she was learning and asked her to be sure to invite her to the performances. Hannah had never considered that there would be performances. It both terrified and excited her, and the rest of the school day was a blur.

Hank said that Emily—Hannah was supposed to call her Miss Emily—taught the children's classes in the house that she was renting. He cautioned her not to get her hopes up. Maybe it wasn't what she wanted to do. But the moment Hannah walked in the door and saw everyone in their dance clothes, and the mirror, and the wood floor, and the barre on the wall, she knew she had found her place. It was like coming home.

Miss Emily was busy teaching a class of little children, younger than Hannah. Hannah thought they were adorable. They struggled with getting their feet in the right place but looked as if they were enjoying every minute of it. When they all sat down on the floor to do some stretches, Hannah did the same in the back of the room. It hurt, and it felt good.

After class, Hannah talked to Miss Emily for a while. Emily explained to Hannah that since she was starting a little later than many of her students, she would need to be diligent about practicing and paying attention. Hank waited patiently for the two of them, happy that Hannah was finding something that was moving her past what had happened last summer.

After they were finished talking and getting to know each other, Emily gave Hank a schedule for the classes that she thought Hannah might like. Hank thought that Ava and Evan would figure out a way for Hannah to take all of them if it made her that happy.

While Hank and Emily talked about when he would start construction out at her site, Hannah walked around the room touching everything.

Emily watched, recognizing the signs. Hannah was going to be an exciting student to teach. It was one more indication that moving to Doveland was the right choice for her to have made.

At first, the move was to find the answers to a family mystery. After a year of living in Doveland, she was no closer to the solution. Maybe she never would be. Now it didn't matter as much. Instead, she had the land where she could build her dream. Doveland was becoming the perfect place to live and teach. Answers or no answers.

TEN

Craig closed the door to the office, made sure it was locked, zipped his coat up, and started walking to his breakfast meeting at the Diner with Dr. Joe.

They had been meeting now early on Tuesday for over six months. It had started when he had first approached Joe about buying his practice. Their initial meetings had been filled with the tentative "test each other out" kind of conversations. Craig thought that Joe would bring folders and folders of information to their meetings to show him what kind of practice he had run for fifty years. But he never did.

Instead, he answered every question from memory. Of course, Joe had his accountant prepare all the numbers that they needed to agree on a price for the practice, but everything else appeared to be tucked away within his memory banks.

During those first meetings, Craig and Joe had discovered many common interests. The one that delighted Craig the most was that they both liked the idea of trying out alternative healing practices. Craig had spent too many hours as an emergency room physician to discount how important it was to take care of the body before something broke down and it became an emergency.

At first, they only touched on the surface of the different practices, but after many months of weekly meetings, they had started to get more in depth.

Craig was amazed at the amount of information that Joe knew. Without looking at notes, he could cite multiple incidences that proved or disproved the ideas and theories that they'd discuss.

Their discussions had prompted Craig to do even more research into other means of healing. One modality that he was exploring was the idea that it was always the mind that did the healing. It was what the patient believed happened, or would happen, that impacted the healing more than any medicine they could use.

However, every time he brought up the research, Joe would change the subject. Craig wondered if it was because he didn't believe in it, or that he thought Craig was not well enough versed in the knowledge of the practice. So he let it drop, and continued the research on his own. Craig decided he would give the discussion a try again in another month or so. Besides, he could always talk that particular idea over with his friends. They loved the subject!

Tuesday morning breakfasts were not always conversations about patients and healing. After months of being together, they had become more than an old doctor selling his practice to a younger doctor. They had become friends.

Craig and Joe discussed everything from politics to their favorite restaurants. They had both traveled the world, so those restaurants were often found in other countries. Craig discovered that Joe loved Spain as much as he did, and they talked about taking a trip there together one day.

This morning, they both arrived at the Diner at the same time, which made them both laugh at how in tune they had become with each other.

As they entered the Diner, Pete's new cook, Alex, greeted them. Right behind Alex was Johnny who had stopped in on his way to school. Craig was getting used to everyone knowing Dr. Joe. Joe had been the town's doctor for so long there was practically no one that he didn't know by name. If they were born in Doveland, Dr. Joe delivered them. If they lived in Doveland, he had taken care of them at one time or another.

Johnny wanted to ask Dr. Joe if he was coming over to dinner on Wednesday. He heard his mom and dad talking about getting a group together, and his name had been mentioned.

Craig thought that he saw a flicker of annoyance in Joe's eyes, but it passed by so quickly Craig decided that he probably imagined it. Besides, he had heard that Harold was what Ava called a conversation stealer, and Joe's reluctance to be part of that, was probably what he had sensed. Craig thought that if anyone should be talking all the time, it should be Joe sharing what he knew. Joe was an actual authority, a walking library of information.

However, Craig knew that Joe didn't like to show that side of himself much, preferring to remain the quiet, unassuming, but very effective doctor. Craig admired him for it.

After a few cups of coffee and Alex's famous omelet, Joe excused himself saying he had work to do, leaving Craig at the table nursing what he promised himself would be his last cup of coffee for the day. He wondered what he was going to do with himself the rest of the day.

Craig was seeing a few patients a day, even while Mandy was putting the last touches on his redesigned office space. Getting the practice going had been slow. Dr. Joe's patients were getting used to him. He didn't mind. It gave him time to learn about each patient and the town. The only drawback was sometimes he just felt bored.

Today there were no patients at all, so boredom and restlessness threatened to set in. All of which must have shown on his face, because it wasn't long before Pete appeared across the table from him and asked him what was wrong.

"I don't know. Maybe it's pre-spring fever. One day its winter, the next its spring."

"That's the end of March for you," Pete said. "Maybe we should do something new and exciting."

"And what would that be, Pete?" Craig laughed.

"Well, Barbara and I were thinking about going to New York City for a few days and taking in some Broadway shows. We'll get tickets when we get there. Wing it. We don't even have to drive. We can ride the Megabus into the city together. Have ourselves a little outing.

"Alex can take care of the Diner. Grace and Mandy will check in on him and Johnny. If you can reschedule a few patients, we could take off tomorrow."

Craig looked at Pete and wondered how he could have gotten along without him before. Until moving to Doveland, he had friends, but he didn't have friends like this. No other agendas but the one of friendship and kindness.

"Let me make a few calls, Pete. I'm in."

Alex beamed with pride when Pete told him that he was in charge. Yes, Alex said, he would have Grace check everything to make sure it was running smoothly. Yes, he would call in every evening to let Pete know how it was going and get any questions that he had answered.

Plans were made to pick up the Megabus in State College. It would take them directly into the city. Barbara booked them rooms in a hotel near Times Square. They would pick up tickets to plays once they got there. Winging it was what Pete said. Craig needed a brain break.

Craig hoped that it would be that easy. Something was bothering him, and he hoped getting over it was as simple as getting away.

ELEVEN

The library was just right, Emily thought. It was not too big, and not too small. It was Goldilocks size, just perfect. Old, but not dusty. Large windows let in light and air. But there was privacy and warmth to be found back in the book stacks where she sat at a small square table looking through old newspapers on microfiche.

She had traveled to the Allegheny department of records instead of the closest one in Concourse because she had already tried that library, too. She went looking for the past newspapers and records of the area in the 1970s, but there was very little to see in Doveland. Almost all the papers and microfiche records of the area before 1990 had been stored in a basement in the town hall, and during one extremely stormy season it had flooded and destroyed everything.

Since arriving in Doveland, Emily had tried to be inconspicuous about her interest in the past. She didn't want everyone to wonder why she was so curious about the 1970s because she didn't want anyone to know that there was an alternative reason for her coming to Doveland other than the story she told.

Most of the story was true. Emily's mother, Mary, had grown up in Louisiana. Her mother's sister, Jean, was ten years older. It was Emily's mother who told the story about Jean. In 1968, when she turned twenty-one, and Mary was only eleven, Jean had decided to travel the United States on her own.

Jean had been working what she considered a stuffy job as a secretary in a lawyer's office. It didn't take long for Jean to realize that office work wasn't for her. The lawyer's office was stinky and small, and no new ideas were allowed. She couldn't stand it. Jean told her family that while she was young, she wanted to explore the ideas that were being discussed among the young people of the day. How could she do that in that little town that never changed? She couldn't. Jean said she had to go.

The entire family objected. Emily's mother was inconsolable. Jean was her hero. She needed her. Mary begged and begged, but Jean was full of the idea of freedom.

Tired of arguing with everyone, one day Jean just left. The family woke up and found a note saying she would keep in touch and would send pictures of what she saw. Mary found a note under her pillow that night. Jean said that she loved her, and wanted to set an example for her of what was possible. Women are allowed to be free, Jean said. Along with the note she had left a four-leaf clover pressed in wax paper, saying it would bring Mary luck.

Jean kept her word. She mailed postcards from all over the United States. Her family was afraid to ask how she was getting around the country, or where she got her money. Jean said that sometimes she traveled with groups of people. Mary's dad said they were all called hippies. They were people who took drugs and danced with flowers in their hair.

That didn't help Mary at all. She feared for her sister, missed her terribly, and cried for her every night before falling asleep.

A few years after Jean left, she sent them a letter from a place she said was the perfect place to settle. In fact, that was what she was going to do. Settle down. Once everything was in place, she would come home for a visit, and tell them all about it. That was in 1973. They never heard from her again.

That place was Doveland.

Growing up, Emily heard very little about Jean. Her grandparents had passed away when she was young, and Emily never knew her dad. Missing Jean, her mom had looked for love with the young men in town. She didn't find love with them, but she did find joy in having Emily. The two of them had been close all the years of her growing up. But, they had never discussed the secret of Jean.

Emily knew that her mom had an older sister that had traveled the country. But if she wanted to know more, she was shushed, or her mom would turn away with tears running down her face. When Emily went off to college, for her mother, it brought back the memory of her sister leaving. So, finally, Mary told her more of the story, a tiny bit at a time.

The summer Emily graduated from college, a drunk driver crashed into her mother's car. Emily never left her mom's side as she slowly faded away. The day before she died, Mary told Emily the rest of the story. Jean had never come home. Did she stay in Doveland? Did she move away and not tell them? Was she still alive? And if she was, why didn't she come home?

Mary asked one thing of Emily. Would she find out what happened to Jean and when she found her, would Emily please return the four-leaf clover? She told Emily where to find it hidden in a special box in the chest at the end of the bed. The next day Emily's mom was gone.

Emily spent the summer going through her mother's things. She sold the small home they had lived in, and collected the money from the insurance policy that Mary had put on her life. It was much more than Emily thought it would be. In Mary's files, she found a note asking Emily to use the money to fulfill her dream.

Her mom knew what the dream was because they had talked about it many times. Emily realized that her mom had asked only two things of her, both of them based in love. Why not put them together, she had thought.

The story she told anyone that asked about why she came to Doveland, was that her Aunt Jean had passed through Doveland years before and raved about the area's beauty. Emily had come to see it for herself. That part of the story was entirely true.

What she never told anyone was that her aunt had gone missing in Doveland. If something had gone wrong while Jean was in Doveland, Emily didn't want to alert anyone to the fact that she was looking for her.

And that was why she was in the library looking through the microfiche at newspapers from the early 1970s, looking for anything that would hint at what might have happened. Anything that might point to where her aunt had gone, and why.

TWELVE

Melvin stood at his kitchen window holding his favorite coffee mug and watched Hank as he tinkered with the equipment that the two of them had invested in for Hank's construction company. What Hank had used before had belonged to Grant's company. However, when Grant died everything became part of the police investigation. That left Hank without a way to earn a living or do the work that he loved to do.

Hank had saved quite a bit of money over the years, and Melvin pitched in a little money along with providing the home base for Hank's construction company. That, plus a loan from Evan, got them what they needed. Hank and Evan settled on an agreement much like the one Evan had made with Pete and the Diner.

The equipment would also be used for the youth apprentice program. The first thing they planned to work on was the bike trail that Mandy had dreamed of doing the year before. Hank also wanted to work on building Emily's dance and art camp.

Hank told Melvin that if it didn't snow or rain in the coming week, he would begin grading Emily's land. Emily had come over the night before to check on the plans. As Melvin had watched Hank and Emily bent over the plans on the kitchen table, he thought that perhaps these were the best years of his life. He was surrounded by people who were filled with imagination and believed in possibilities. An old man with dreams was not something that he had ever envisioned for himself. He had thought he would simply fade away. Maybe even die in his chair and not be found for weeks.

No chance of that happening now, he thought, lifting his coffee cup to the heavens in thanks. But still, it was time to put his affairs in order. The last time he had visited Dr. Joe, he learned what he already knew. Things were slowly shutting down. There was no point in going back to the doctor's, even if it was to that new fella Craig with his fancy ideas. He was winding down just like an old watch.

Melvin had already transferred all his accounts, including his farm and house, over to Hank. All of it was done in secret with Evan's help. Melvin didn't want Hank to know. First, Hank would be upset that Melvin was thinking about dying, and second, because Hank would have tried to talk him out of it feeling he didn't deserve it. Melvin knew that Hank did. There was much to be done, and Hank would need all the resources possible to do it.

As far as Melvin's son, Melvin had left him a small amount of money set aside in a trust for him. But his son had no use for the farm and hadn't visited or been in touch with Melvin in years. Melvin had tried calling and writing, and other than a terse "hello," there had been no response. It's okay, Melvin thought. He felt no pain from their separation. His heart was full.

Melvin knew that he would see Sally soon, but in the meantime, he was planning on doing as much good, and having as much fun, as possible. He couldn't wait until the first kids started showing up with all their faults and hopes and dreams.

He would show them how to farm, Hank would teach them how to build, and between the two of them they would learn how valuable they were, and the possibilities the world was offering them.

• • • ● ● • ● • • •

It was a beautiful April day. The air was warm with just a hint of cold hidden in the slight breeze that blew across the hill and ruffled the hair that was sticking out from beneath Emily's baseball cap. She and Hank were standing on the rock that she had sat on so many times in the past few months, looking out at the view.

Emily had mixed emotions. She knew that once Hank got started the land would never look the same again. It would be the last time the hill looked untouched.

She and Hank had discussed the plans over and over again while sitting at Melvin's kitchen table. Sometimes, Hank and Melvin would come to town, and they would meet in her living room, but this was the first time she and Hank had stood together to see the land free of snow.

The stakes for each building had been laid out. They were not going to build everything at once. They would begin with a small cottage for her to live in and a building very much like Melvin's barn.

Inside the barn would be a spacious dance space, and running down one side would be smaller rooms for art and music. Maybe even a place for writing. Eventually, each of the arts would have its own building, but Emily wanted to be sure that she would have something finished by summer when she planned to have her first summer art camp or retreat.

She had started calling it a retreat because she had decided that it would become a year-round place to come. A retreat from the everyday world, and into the art of creating for all ages.

However, the essential part of the retreat would happen just above where they were standing. It would be a massive deck that jutted out over the hill. Emily could imagine the joy of teaching on that deck and the beautiful performances that they could have there. The audience would sit on curved seating built into the hill. A winding gravel walkway would bring them to the first building. Behind a stand of trees, they would tuck the parking lot so as not to spoil the view with cars.

For each building, they would have to level the land, which meant they would be moving quite a bit of dirt. Emily had plans to put that extra dirt into gentle rolling mounds where she would plant even more trees. Most of them would be behind the buildings and deck. She didn't want anything to block the view into the valley and towards Doveland.

Emily turned to Hank and said, "Have I said thank you yet for doing this?"

"Well, you are paying me!"

"Sure, but you have put so much more time and attention into this project than just a regular contractor might have done. You have made me feel that my dream is in safe hands."

Hank turned to look at Emily. If his life had been different, this young woman would have been what he wanted in a daughter. He thought that someday he might tell her that, but at that moment he just smiled at her, and said, "You're welcome."

Emily had brought a thermos of coffee for them. She put the small blanket she was carrying on the rock so they could sit to have their coffee.

"How come you don't have a southern accent?" Hank asked. "You said your family lived in Louisiana."

"My mom did, and so did I when I was younger, but when I went to off to college, I worked to get rid of it. Took speech lessons and everything."

"Why? I always think that southern accents are beautiful."

"Maybe. But the accent marked me as coming from the south. People have an idea what that means, and I didn't want those ideas to be attached to me. I wanted—want—to be my own person. Seen just for me. Clean. Does that make sense?"

Hank laughed. "Well, it's obvious you are your own person. And yes, I understand not wanting to be judged by things like how you talk, or look, or where you come from."

"Where did you come from, Hank?"

"From here. But I only came back here a few years ago. I spent most of my life roaming, and I am sure you have heard that I spent most of that time getting in trouble."

Emily laid a hand on his. "I haven't heard much, Hank. I probably need to get out in the community more to let people know about this dream of mine and convince them to send their kids here. However, I know what I have seen of you, Hank, and that is only good."

They sat quietly for a while sipping coffee and enjoying the peace of where they were.

"And you, Emily. Why did you choose Doveland?"

Emily sighed and wondered if Hank was the one she would tell the full story to, but she wasn't ready. Instead, she said "My mom's sister had told my mom about Doveland way back in the Seventies. When my mom died a few years ago, I was curious about what could have been so wonderful about the place."

"Have you answered that question yet, Emily?"

"This may seem strange, but as soon as I got here, it felt as if my Aunt Jean was still here. Of course, she isn't, but she must have left her love of the place here for me to find because I do see what she loved about it. It's beautiful. However, it's not just that. It's all of you. This community that you all are building feels like home to me."

Hank nodded at Emily, trying not to let tears form in his eyes. It was home to him now too, for the same reason.

Tomorrow they would start the process of transforming this piece of land. He would do everything he could to turn it into her dream.

There was only one thing that bothered him.

Emily had said that the man who sold the land to her said it had never been built on before. He wasn't so sure about that. And if it had been, why would he lie about it?

THIRTEEN

Every time she came back to the place she now called home, Sarah had to adjust her whole being just to be able to walk in the door. It wasn't the house's fault. It was a charming bungalow a short distance from the town square.

It was the house that Eric had rented when he first came to Doveland. After he and Grace married, he moved into her apartment bringing his few belongings with him.

It was the last straw for the owners. They wanted to move to Florida and were tired of always having to find a renter, so they put the house on the market.

When Leif decided that the right thing to do was to take Eric to the Forest Circle, Sarah bought the home so she would have a place to live in Doveland with her friends. She knew she didn't want to stay in Sandpoint without Leif.

While Sarah took care of selling the Sandpoint home, her friends did all they could to turn her new Doveland house into a home she would come to love.

Hank updated all the plumbing and wiring, made sure the roof didn't leak, and her friends had done the rest. They cleaned, painted, added more doors to the outside garden, and took down walls to make it a more modern space. They had even started a garden for her.

Sarah loved it. And she didn't. There was no forest outside her door. Instead, it was a small patio, just right for sitting with a friend or two inside her completely private backyard. There wasn't a lake view. Instead, it was a neighborhood.

It wasn't a big home; it was just a thousand square feet. Perfectly sized with everything she needed right at hand. Everything except Leif. Sarah knew that if she called him, he would come, but that wouldn't be fair to him. Although he would always be there for her, he had work to do now with the Forest Circle. However, to ease the transition for both of them, they made plans to talk every Friday night, at least for awhile. However, she loved that he would surprise her once in awhile and just show up.

Sarah knew she would get used to it, but it was taking much longer than she thought it would. Someone told her that the missing would never go away. It was something she would have to learn to live with, and that was what she was going to do. Live with it. Perhaps even live well with it.

No matter what, Sarah knew that it was time to get back into the world, or at least into the community. The idea to begin the meetings with the women had been Leif's. Probably it was an attempt to get her out of her thoughts and into something constructive. But the more she explored the idea, the more Sarah realized that there was a need for women to gather together to support each other. There was a need for women to take more authority within their own lives and their communities.

Preparing for the first meeting, Sarah spent time thinking about the meaning of authority. What made someone an authority? What was the responsibility of someone in authority? It seemed to Sarah that too many people claimed authority over others when they didn't have the right to do so. They wanted people to do things their way. If they didn't, they were wrong, and varying degrees of punishment would be utilized to bring people in line. To Sarah this wasn't authority, it was bullying, and sometimes it was tyrannical. True authority acted for the good of others.

During the women's group's first meeting in Grace's living room, Sarah had raised the subject, and they had spent quite a bit of time discussing it. During the discussion, Ava had looked up other words for authority and found the word Exousia, meaning the power to act, to have authority. They liked that it was a feminine noun and that its full definition talked about moral authority and influence, "of a spiritual power, and therefore of an earthly power."

Mandy's question about Valerie's husband, Harold, prompted more discussion. All of them had witnessed some of what they decided was a false authority. Sometimes it was just the way he took over conversations, and always had to have the last word, and sometimes it was something in the way Valerie looked when he was around.

Ava suggested that perhaps they could be a council of women who focused on the true meaning of authority—or Exousia. They all agreed that doing so carried a great deal of responsibility. But each of them decided that they were willing.

They agreed to meet at least weekly, either to just talk or to discuss anything specific that was bothering them. They'd start by acting as guides for each other, and perhaps that would expand into making more of a difference in the town that had been so gracious in accepting them.

That first meeting hadn't been all serious discussion. Lots of laughing and talking about gardens, and food, and what they were reading. In all, it had been a great start. Ava asked if they were going to have other women join them, and after a brief discussion agreed that they would. In time.

For now, it was only them. And one of the first things they would do was watch over Valerie. And Harold. Was he just a little too self-important, or was there something else going on? Because Mandy and Grace were still on the committee with Valerie for the next solstice ceremony, they promised to pay more attention.

It was an excellent first meeting, Sarah thought. She made herself a cup of coffee and settled into her favorite chair that looked out over her garden. The daffodils had just started to bloom. Spring had arrived. But instead of reading, she found herself lost in thought.

It wasn't just missing Leif that was bothering her. There was something else going on. It was times like this that she missed Leif the most. What would he say? Perhaps it was just spring fever that made her feel a tiny bit restless and worried. Time would tell.

In the meantime, she would pay more attention to what was going on around her. It seemed like a good recipe for moving on. Not forgetting, just moving on.

FOURTEEN

Clearing Emily's land was put off for another week. A snowstorm had rolled in covering the ground with three inches of wet, heavy snow. But it melted quickly in the warming spring air, and one beautiful April day Hank and his crew moved the equipment out to Emily's hill. First, they cleared a driveway up to the stand of trees where the parking lot would be. It would first be a staging area where they could park their machines when they weren't in use. When the construction was over, they would turn the staging area into the parking lot.

Hank's crew didn't have any of Grant's, or Lenny's, or even Sam's people in it as it always had in the past. This time they were his crew, just for construction, not for spying on each other. Hank's hand-picked team liked him. They had watched Hank turn from a hard-headed, withdrawn, and often terse boss, to one that cared about each of them personally. He promised them all work. If there weren't any jobs in Doveland, they would work in nearby towns like Concourse.

But this job was one they had all looked forward to over the winter. It was a beautiful piece of land, and they liked that they were going to respect both the contours of the property and the trees that lived there.

They also appreciated that Hank was going to feed them once a week using Sam's catering company. Sam was discounting the price, partially because Hank was his friend, but also because he wanted an opportunity to build his reputation and skill.

Because this was just a setup day, they had all brought their lunch. During the lunch break, the entire crew sat on the hillside looking across the valley. Some of them had moved to the area after being chosen by Hank to work with him a few years before. A few of them had kids in Emily's dance classes. The fact that they were part of the building of this new arts center made them heroes in their kid's eyes.

Emily sat with them, her long legs stretched out in front of her, her baseball hat keeping the sun off her face with a few escaped strands of long blond hair catching the wind. She kept trying to tuck them up into her hat, and they kept escaping. It made Emily laugh thinking that her hair wanted to be free, just as she did.

It was a momentous day, and she wanted to be part of the first turn over of dirt. As much as possible she hoped to be on the site every day. She planned to take pictures and videos and to document the process. Perhaps someday a film student would decide to turn her collection of videos into a real documentary. Emily envisioned one of her students writing the music for it, another editing it, and perhaps another doing artwork. She had big plans to go with her big dream. However, Emily hadn't forgotten why she was in Doveland, even though the fact that a childhood dream was coming true overshadowed its importance. She would get back to it someday. What Emily didn't know was that someday was just a day or two away, and would come in a form no one expected.

• • • ● • ◉ • ● • • •

That same day, Ava and Hannah decided to have lunch together at the Diner. The weather was beautiful, and it was spring break. It was a perfect day to do something different. Evan had work to do at home, so he was watching Ben. Ava said it was a girl's day out which Hannah thought was the best thing ever.

Hannah asked to go to the Diner because she said she hadn't seen Pete and Barbara for far too long, even though it had only been a week. Besides, Johnny was working there that day, and she had a teeny, tiny, crush on him. Hannah knew he was too old for her, for now. But she was counting on that someday he would see her as more than a little kid.

Plus, she reminded herself, she wasn't really just ten. She had memories of her past life, which made her much wiser. Those memories had faded a bit. Hannah knew her mom was happy about that, and honestly, Hannah was also glad that she couldn't remember things as well anymore.

She would never forget her past-dad and past-mom, but she lived in this lifetime with Ava and Evan, and she loved them with all her heart. Those memories, like all memories held to, kept her from living entirely in the now. Or that's what Sarah had said the last time they talked. Hannah figured that Sarah knew what she was talking about. She had to move on too.

When they got to the Diner, Lex was also there eating lunch with his mom and dad, Valerie and Harold. When they saw Ava and Hannah, they called them over to sit with them at their table. Hannah was glad. Lex was fun, and they did lots of things together, including going to dance classes at Miss Emily's.

Everyone at school knew Miss Emily even if they weren't taking dance classes from her. For one thing, the sixth-grade class got to take social dance classes from her as part of their school work. Not everyone liked it, but Hannah and Lex were looking forward to going next year.

Miss Emily and Valerie, who was the principal of the school, said it would help them all learn how to act with each other. Besides, they would learn how to dance, too, even if it was just the waltz.

Johnny took their order, looking nervous. Hannah figured it was because he was hoping to impress his mom and dad, but he did take the time to turn and wink at her, causing her to giggle. Valerie and Ava looked at each other knowingly. Hannah missed the look because she and Lex were talking about all the homework they had over the holiday.

"Hey, Hannah," Pete said coming out of the kitchen to hug Hannah. "Do you have room on the seat for me?" As they moved over to let him in, Pete asked Lex and Hannah if they were excited about the new arts center being built out of town.

Hank and his crew had been in that morning on their way to work and told him about what they were doing.

"Yes!" both Lex and Hannah said together.

"Oh, I missed that it was really being built," Valerie said. "I heard rumors about it last fall but didn't realize that it was actually happening. Where is she building it? Who's it for?"

Hannah couldn't help herself. She had to tell her everything. "It's for everyone, but mostly for kids. At least for now. Dance and art first, then Miss Emily says it will grow into all the arts. That is if she can get enough kids to come. Mom says I can definitely go this summer. It's going to be like camp only a thousand times better. At first, a bus will pick us up every day and bring us home at night, because this year she won't be able to build the places for us to sleep yet. Doesn't it sound wonderful? Lex can go, can't he?"

Out of breath, Hannah paused, and Valerie said, "I don't see why not. We'll have to see what it costs, but we'll work out something. A bus will pick you up? So this place is out of town?"

"It's going to be beautiful," Hannah said. "She is building a huge deck off the side of the hill. Where is it, mom?"

Ava laughed. "It's north of town about five miles. The land used to belong to Dr. Joe, but now that he is retiring he has been selling some of his lands. We bought some of it along the road going west so we could build a bike trail to Concourse."

Harold hadn't been paying a single bit of attention to the conversation. Instead, he was trying to catch the eye of other people in the Diner to see if he could have a conversation with them about something he was interested in. Harold loved his son, but dance? He wouldn't stop Lex but it didn't seem very manly to him.

However the words "Dr. Joe" did get his attention.

"What did you say about Dr. Joe?" he asked.

"He sold the land to Emily Sands for her art retreat," Ava answered. "It's about five miles out of town. Go north, and it's on the left. A pretty hill that looks back onto the town."

"And she's building something there?" Harold asked barely choking out the words.

"Honey is there something wrong?" Valarie asked looking at her husband who had turned completely white.

Harold didn't answer. He just got up and stumbled out the door mumbling something about forgetting he had an appointment.

"What was that about?" Pete asked.

They all looked at each other and shrugged.

"Probably did just forget something," Valerie said as Johnny brought their food to the table.

They all tucked into their food, pretending that nothing out of the ordinary had happened. Valerie resolved to get Harold to talk to her about it when he came home. She would have to be careful how she asked, and he probably wouldn't tell her anything, but she had to try.

FIFTEEN

I was chaos. Not at all what Emily had envisioned for the beginning of building her dream. In reality, there was no way she could have envisioned what happened. Not in a million years.

Emily wasn't the only one in shock. Everyone was. She thought back to the day before when she had turned over the first shovel full of dirt, when she and the crew had celebrated with a shout and hugs were exchanged. It had been a joyful day for everyone, the beginning of something beautiful.

For the past week, Hank's crew had been busy bulldozing a drive up to what would become the staging area. It would be muddy until they turned it into a regular driveway, but they needed a way up the hill. Even in its beginning stage as a slash in the dirt, it was beautiful, slowly curling its way up the rise.

Yesterday, they started building the staging area. First, Emily's shovel of dirt. Next, the dozer had to clear off the vegetation. That took all day.

Yesterday, when the clearing was done for the day, she and Hank sat on her rock and let the feeling of starting something beautiful wash over them. The crew had built a bonfire where they burned the cleared vegetation in preparation for digging deeper.

Flames leaping, reaching for the sky echoed Emily's joyful feeling of reaching for her dream.

That was yesterday. Joyful and celebratory. Today, Emily was sitting on the same rock, surrounded by chaos and fear. Nobody sat with her. This time she was alone.

Emily could see Hank talking with his friend Sam at the edge of the meadow, gesturing at the equipment. Even from this far away she could tell they were tense and worried. Who wouldn't be?

The bulldozer that had been leveling the ground for their staging area was sitting as if it was a massive dinosaur waiting for its next meal. Its bucket raised just a few feet off the ground. Emily could see something caught in the teeth of the bucket. She shivered at the thought of what it might be. The truck filled with the rocks that would be put down first as a base for the parking lot sat idle. The driver was leaning against the door, probably wondering if he should stay or go.

Someone had put a blanket over her shoulders, but even though the sun was beating down on her, she couldn't stop shivering. All she could think about was that her dream was now a nightmare. A nightmare that had just begun. There was a chance it would never end. Please, God, she said to herself, make this go away. She knew it wouldn't, and she hated herself for only thinking about her dream at a time like this. For someone else, this was going to be so much worse.

"Emily?"

Emily looked up to see Hank's niece, Ava, standing by her, a baseball hat on, squinting at the sun in her eyes.

"Hank called me. Do you mind if I sit down?" Ava said.

Emily nodded mutely and moved over a bit on the rock. Ava handed her a bottle of water, and said, "Drink this."

It was the voice of one who knew what to do, so Emily took a few sips of water. Although they were almost the same age, it was Ava who had the experience of taking care of children, and at the moment, Emily desperately wanted someone to take care of her. She barely knew Ava. Ava's daughter, Hannah, was in her dance classes, but it was usually Hank or Evan who brought her and picked her up. Once in a while, it was Ava, but Emily was always busy rounding up kids for the next lesson and making sure the children in the last class had their rides home, so they never had time to talk.

Ava put her arm around Emily's shoulder and pulled her close. With a slight hesitation Emily put her head on Ava's shoulder and let the tears run down her face. Although both women were tall and slim, Emily's blond hair was pulled back into a ponytail, and Ava had kept her dark hair at chin length after cutting it into a pixie a few years before. It was easier to take care of, and Ben found it harder to pull her hair when she leaned over to kiss him.

After a few minutes, Ava said, "Emily, I am going to take you to our home. You are going to stay with us for a few days while we figure out more of what happened here. Hannah will be delighted, and a few of my friends are bringing over some comfort food."

"What about my car?" Emily whispered.

"Hank will take care of it. He and Sam will come by later and tell us what is going on. We'll put you up in the bunkhouse so you can have some privacy. We'll stop by your house on the way so you can collect a few things."

Emily stood up reluctantly. This was her land. She was responsible for it. How could she leave and let other people take over?

"I know you are worried, Emily. But I promise you that Hank and Sam will not let anyone destroy your property. But there's probably more that's going to have to be done before they can stop, and I don't think you need to witness it."

As Ava led Emily to her car, she glanced back at Hank. He tipped his hat in acknowledgment. He knew what Ava and Emily needed, and he would take care of it. Ava felt a rush of emotion and tears forming. This was a horrible situation, but she knew that they had each other. For that, she was eternally grateful.

Ava also knew that the women's council was on full alert. She had called them on the way out to the site. Grace and Sarah would already be at her house, and Mira and Mandy would come later. Mandy needed to be at the shop until closing time, and Mira had been at Melvin's home, helping him with his vegetable garden when Ava called. Once Mira was finished, she would head over to Ava's. Besides, Mira thought she could ask Melvin if he knew anything about Emily's property that would be helpful.

Although the news of what was happening would probably be all over the town before evening, they didn't want to be the ones spreading it. They wanted to be the ones paying attention. Listening. Looking at patterns. Did anyone know about this? And if so, were they responsible?

So many questions needed to be answered, but for now, Emily needed the comfort of friends. It's time to welcome her into our circle, Ava realized. Although they barely knew her, Ava knew that Emily had been brought to them for a reason. Or perhaps, it was the other way around. They were there for her for a reason.

And I thought she was just going to be my daughter's dance teacher, Ava thought. *Apparently, it's more than that.*

As Emily huddled in the passenger seat, Ava started making plans. They would find out what had happened. She was sure of that. But she was afraid. What if the answers turned out to be something they didn't want to know? Something better left buried.

Ava shook her head. Too late. It was out in the open now.

Sixteen

The town was buzzing as if it had a current of electricity running through it, like lightning in the air. But, it wasn't a storm that was causing the excitement. It was something happening north of town. Police cars and ambulances had raced out earlier that day and not returned. The two-lane road traveling north out of Doveland was blocked off leaving just one open lane. Someone stopping at the gas station to get snacks and gas had said that even the Concourse police were heading up north. There was also speculation that the FBI would be returning to help find out what had happened.

Good for business, Tina thought and then clapped her hand over her mouth. God, she needed to clean up her act. She didn't really feel that way. It was a habit left over from years of survival. It would take some time to recover from what her husband Frank had put her and her children through.

In spite of the fact it felt heartless to think about making money in times like this, Tina Jacks had to admit that an increase in business would be very helpful just about now. It wasn't her fault something terrible was happening.

In the same way, it hadn't been her fault that Frank had turned out to be such a terrible and frightening monster. It wasn't her fault that they had to run and hide from him for so many years.

On the other hand, it was her fault she had married him, the jerk. They met in grade school. He was a jerk then too, but everyone told her that boys acted that way because they liked you. Whoever made up that bull crap ought to have known better. What a terrible thing to teach young girls. She would never, ever, say that to her daughter Lynn. She would never let her son Manny treat a girl that way. What an excuse. Because he likes you? No. Never.

Because if they were jerks when they were young, they most likely would continue to be jerks when they got older. And if they mistreated people when they were young, it was a strong probability that they would only get worse. Which is exactly what had happened. Frank was charming, when he was around other people and when he wanted to be. In private, he was cruel.

Tina hated that people believed that being charming was an indication of inner goodness. In fact, she could attest to the fact that often it hid an ugly way of thinking. She didn't want to make it an absolute since nothing was ever absolute, but when she met people who acted all nicey-nice and charming, especially men with their smiles and smooth-talking ways, she was immediately on high alert.

She had learned that all you had to do to discover the truth about people was to watch how they treated the "minor" people in life. People that they considered less than them. Of course, the fact that they thought anyone was less than them was a dead giveaway.

But sometimes it wasn't noticeable until they interacted with people like waitresses, or people of a different race, or religion, or gas station attendants. Like her. A gas station owner maybe, but she was a nobody. She was not worth a second glance or a kind word from people like that unless they wanted something from you. Tina had learned the hard way. If they could maltreat anyone, it would eventually turn on you. Bottom line.

She wasn't sure about the people of Doveland yet. Everyone seemed to be friendly enough. But once again, it sometimes took time to see the truth of someone. Besides, she had only been back in town for a few months. Hiding from Frank for years meant she didn't have any contact with him, so she had no idea he had gone to jail last summer.

Eventually, Valerie, that nice lady who ran the Bed and Breakfast Inn had tracked her down with the help of Sam. She knew Sam used to be in the FBI and that's how they found her. *Bet they'll be using him on whatever is going on now,* she thought.

Frank was in jail, never to get out again. That's what she prayed for every night anyway. Once she knew he couldn't get to her, she divorced him. Sam helped her get Frank to sign over the gas station to her as part of the divorce. She didn't know what he had said to Frank, but she was now the owner of a beat-up old gas station.

Since she knew next to nothing about gas stations or business, the first few months had been a disaster. Literally. But, she learned. One of the bank managers taught her about bookkeeping and checked on her every week to make sure things were flowing smoothly. She thought he was probably protecting his investment since she had to take out a small business loan to fix up the station. On the other hand, she was grateful they had taken a chance on her. Still wasn't sure why. Tina knew she was an unknown commodity.

And then there were those other women. Always checking on her. Sometimes bringing her food because she was constantly working and had zero time to cook for herself and her kids. There was a small house behind the gas station that they were renting, which was helpful because it was so close. But she had them do their homework at the station, sitting at the counter so she could see them. Plus, she figured that they might as well learn how to run a business while she learned.

What Tina wanted right now was to run across the street and ask one of those women what was going on. She could see Mandy still serving over at Your Second Home. But Tina couldn't leave the station, and there was nothing on the news yet. Maybe Mandy or Barbara would stop over and tell her. Tina hadn't been in town long before she realized that it was those women who knew what was happening. If she needed something, she only had to ask one of them. Usually, Tina was a little put out that they were always checking on her. Today, it was different. She wanted to know what was going on

At least she knew that Frank wasn't involved. He was long gone. On the other hand, who knew? Perhaps he had been smarter than she thought.

Nah, she thought, shaking her head. He was too stupid. Look how easily he had been caught. No, something unrelated to Frank was happening.

The bell dinged. A customer. It was time to get back to work. She'd find out soon enough. As long as it didn't touch her or her family, they would be okay.

SEVENTEEN

ank didn't show up at the house until after everyone had gone to bed. He had a key, so he let himself in. Ava had insisted that Hank keep his room in the bunkhouse so that he would always have a place with them. Hank had resisted her kindness at first, but realizing she would never give up, he had given in. Tonight, he was grateful for her stubbornness. He was dead tired, too tired to drive to Concourse. He had called Melvin to let him know where he was staying, and probably would be for a few days. He needed to be closer to the scene of the crime.

Another scene of the crime. How many times would he be present at a scene of a crime? Hank had thought that last summer would be the end. Grant was dead. Lenny was in jail. He was out of the crime game. He was out of the helping FBI game. He was done, or he had thought he was.

Perhaps it was his lot in life to never be done. The only thing that eased the pain was the knowledge that this time he had nothing to do with it. Well, other than digging it up. He didn't put that body there. Hank corrected himself—bodies.

Silently making his way through the dimly lit hallway in the bunkhouse, he thought about Emily waiting in her room to find out what had happened. He didn't want to be the one to tell her there was more than one body. It was terrible enough when they uncovered the one. Now it was a nightmare. A nightmare that was probably just beginning.

So in spite of thinking that he owed it to Emily to let her know, he decided against telling her now. Hank knew that sleep could be a great healer and he needed some healing time before the day began again, only a few hours away. Besides, once he told her, she might not ever get to sleep.

Lying quietly in bed, Emily heard Hank moving through the hallway. She knew it was Hank. He had called Ava earlier when they were still all up, sitting in the living room, shell-shocked with no answers. She hoped he would knock on her door and tell her, and at the same time, she prayed that he wouldn't. She wasn't ready.

Now that he was in the bunkhouse with her, Emily felt strangely at peace. Actually, she had felt surprisingly at peace from the moment Ava had picked her up. In spite of everything, surrounded by Ava, her family and friends, Emily had found herself relaxing.

Lying in bed, unable to sleep, Emily puzzled it out. The only conclusion she could come to was that for the first time she knew she wasn't alone.

Whatever was going to happen, she wouldn't have to face it by herself.

As she heard Hank softly close his door, she knew she could sleep now. As Emily drifted off, she had the thought that everyone should have that feeling at least once in their life. The realization that they weren't alone.

· · · · ● · ● · · ·

Evan heard Hank too. When he heard him walk around the back to the bunkhouse he knew that Hank didn't want to talk about it yet. Evan was okay with that. Hank needed to rest, even if he couldn't. Evan had given up trying to sleep. Instead, he lay awake thinking about the day.

When Ava had gone to get Emily that afternoon all they knew was that something terrible had happened out on the hill. Before she left, Ava assured him that Hank said everyone they knew was safe. Still, Hank wanted Ava to bring Emily home to stay with them for a few days.

Evan's job was to stay home with Ben and wait for Hannah to come back from school. Ava said she would call when she knew more. While Evan waited, he prayed that whatever was wrong was temporary, and the good would override and dissolve anything evil going on. When Ava called from the hill, she still didn't tell him what had happened. Ava said that Emily was in the car with her. But it was the faint quiver in her voice that told Evan she felt it was too distressing to talk about over the phone.

When Hannah got home from school and discovered that Miss Emily was coming to stay at her house, she decided that she was probably the luckiest girl in the world. However, when Evan couldn't tell her why Miss Emily was staying, Hannah knew another terrible thing had happened. Well, she knew what to do about that. She would wait to hear what it was, and then she would ask Leif to come talk to her. She missed Suzanne, but Leif did his best to be comforting. He just did it differently.

On the other hand, Hannah thought that Sarah might be calling him to her too, so perhaps they could talk to Leif together later when Sarah came over to the house. Hannah knew that would be what would happen because it always did when something needed to be discussed.

Hannah was right. That night almost everyone came over, and as usual, food came with them. In spite of the pall of what was happening, they tried to maintain a cheerful and optimistic point of view. Later, when Hank called and said he wouldn't be back until late, and that he wanted to talk to them in person, they decided to go home and get some rest and come back in the morning.

Sarah and Leif, who had shown up as Hannah expected, suggested that they take ten minutes and sit in silent meditation or prayer together. No one objected. Emily had never done such a thing before but was comforted by the thought that everyone was quieting their thinking and praying to surrender to peace.

Leif went with Hannah as she got ready for bed knowing that she was looking for alone time with him.

"Do you know what is happening, Leif?" she asked.

"Yes. And for now, we are not going to talk about it. What we are going to talk about is the idea of evil. Just for a minute. I know that you have already experienced what that looks like, but you have also experienced the power of good. Good is the side you always want to be on.

"However, we sometimes mistake something as good when actually it is evil. Either it is evil because people didn't know, or it is evil because someone knew what they were doing and did it anyway."

"Why do they do it anyway?"

"Well, that's the tricky question. I think we all do things we shouldn't because we rationalize that it's okay. Other people do it. The end justifies the means. Because no one will know. But that never changes the fact that walking with anything other than right intentions for all people all the time, is not good. And sometimes it is evil.

"So, you have to be aware, sweet girl. You have to pay attention to the why of things. Why are you doing something? Is it to help, but not harm? Is it because you have rationalized that it will be okay?

Is it because you want something and don't care what happens to anyone else to get it?"

"Why are you telling me this, Leif? Do you think that I have been doing wrong things?"

Leif sat on the bed the best that he could and said, "It's times like this that I wish I hadn't left so that I could hug you right now, Hannah. No, I don't think you have been doing wrong things. I just want you to pay attention. Sometimes grownups miss things that children see."

"I wish you were still here too, Leif," Hannah said, a tear running down her cheek. "Is what you did more good than the good of staying?"

"That's a hard question, Hannah. I can see how sad it has been for Sarah and you, and me too. But yes, I still think I did the right thing."

"You had a bigger reason than what felt good to you?"

"When you say things like that Hannah, I know you understand. Now get some sleep. There's school in the morning. There will be plenty of time to find out what happened."

As Hannah drifted off to sleep, she mumbled: "Only good has power...."

Leif smiled, and whispered, "Amen to that, little one. Amen to that."

EIGHTEEN

They chose a table in the back of Your Second Home. It was a rainy and sleety Monday morning in April, so Grace had the wood stove lit, making the room warm and comforting. Hank was grateful for the warmth because what they had to talk about was far from comfortable.

Sam had asked Craig to meet with them. He knew that Craig was not a pathologist, but Sam thought Craig could be very useful for the investigation. Although Sam was no longer with the FBI, when the bodies were discovered, Sam asked to be the point man for them in the research into what had happened. They were delighted that he asked and agreed that if the FBI needed to send a team, they would.

But for now, Sam was to help the local authorities with their investigation. Such as they were. It was a small police force, not equipped to deal with such a large scale murder. Which is what everyone was assuming they had on their hands. The police knew they needed help, and were grateful for any assistance from Sam. None of them were happy that once again, they needed to work together because of another tragedy.

And that's why the three friends were meeting. It had been three days since the discovery of the bodies. Up to this point, Craig only knew what Hank had told everyone at Evan's house on Saturday morning, the day after the discovery. It wasn't much. Craig knew he needed to get more details before he could be of any help at all.

However, he had already helped with one thing. When Sam told him the bodies had been sent to Pittsburgh because of the potential magnitude of their deaths, Craig asked who was doing the autopsies. It turned out to be someone he had gone to medical school with, so he contacted him and asked if he would make their autopsies a priority even though it was a weekend.

After almost promising his firstborn child, if he ever had one, they agreed. The three of them were expecting the report this morning, and Craig was hopeful that was where he could be of most help. Interpreting the results.

After Mandy delivered their coffee and scones, Craig asked Sam to run him through the sequences of the event. Sam deferred to Hank, saying Hank was there from the beginning. Would he tell the story of what happened?

Hank squirmed. He knew that he needed to tell what happened but every moment of it was pure torture. Not only because of his past, but because of what he had felt when he saw the bodies. But he knew it had to be done, so he began:

"We had scraped off the brush from the site for the landing the day before. So on Friday, it was time to prepare the bed of the site. To do that, we dug down about eighteen inches so that we could level the ground to get it ready for the rocks and gravel that go in next. Everything was going smoothly, but right before the lunch break one of the crew yelled at the driver of the bulldozer to hold up.

"None of us were really worried about it. This kind of thing happens all the time. Something gets stuck, there is a rock the driver hadn't seen, things like that. But it didn't take us long to realize that this time it was different because he was frantic.

"I was up the hill looking at where the house is going to be and had to run down to see what was happening. It took a full minute for me to actually see what he was pointing at in the ground. It was so incongruous that I couldn't recognize it."

"What did you see, Hank?" Sam prompted when Hank stopped talking.

"Sam, I have seen dead bodies before, you know that. I should have been ready for it if there is such a thing. But it was just a hand, a skeleton of a hand, reaching out of the ground. I couldn't believe that is what it was. I kept thinking, perhaps a wild animal had died there. But a hand? It had to be human.

"None of us moved for what seemed like an eternity. Finally, I grabbed my phone and began taking pictures. I asked the men to call 911, while I called you. We didn't move anything. Everyone has seen enough crime shows to know that rule. Then you arrived, and you know what happened after that."

"Well, I don't," Craig said. "Someone keep the story going."

Sam looked at Hank fiddling with the handle of his cup and realized he was done talking for the moment, so Sam continued the story.

"Hank did the right thing. He had everyone step back from the digging. The equipment stayed exactly where it had been, and he called Ava to help Emily who had seen the whole thing."

Hank broke in. "It was awful. She had been sitting on her rock watching and ran up to see what the problem was. It was her screaming that made me realize that it was more than an animal. One of the men went to her and caught her just as she fainted."

"I didn't know she fainted," Sam said. "Poor girl. So much at stake for her. And then to see a hand sticking out of the ground."

He and Hank exchanged looks, both remembering what Emily had looked like after seeing what had been uncovered.

Gathering his thoughts, Sam continued, "After Ava took Emily home, we started digging out the body. No one in the area had done anything like that before so we had to move slowly. As the day progressed, it got worse. We found other bodies. All of them about the same depth as the first. It was as if someone didn't feel like digging. It turned out to be a mass grave."

Sam stopped and took a drink of coffee. Sighing, he continued the story. "I called my old boss at the FBI, and he told me to supervise. We took pictures and videos as we worked. In total, we found four bodies. How long they had been buried, or who they were, we have no idea. We carefully wrapped them, included soil samples, and sent them to Pittsburgh to get answers.

"The local authorities went through the rest of the hill using sonar to see if there are any more bodies. Since nothing more was found, I think they will release the site back to Emily sometime this week. Assuming nothing else comes up before then."

"Does anyone have any idea of what could have happened?" Craig asked.

"None. We are having a title search of the land done which should help find out what used to be there."

Hank glanced up to see Dr. Joe walking towards the table. "Did you invite him, Craig?" he asked.

Craig shook his head, no, but stood to greet Joe. "I think you know everyone? he said.

Joe nodded and said, "I know you are busy with what is happening on Emily's hill, but I thought perhaps I could provide you all with a little information. I have lived in Doveland for fifty years. Perhaps I can be of help?"

A chair was pulled over for him, and Mandy came to take his order. Once she put his coffee on the table, he leaned in, and asked, "Okay. I am at your service. What can I do to help you?"

Nineteen

After she closed the coffee shop for the day to the public, Grace opened the back door for her friends. Mandy had kept the coffee on, and baked a sugar-free cake for the group. She was still experimenting with recipes, and the council of women was the perfect group to try out these alternative ways of baking. Some were delicious. Some were a disaster.

Grace hoped that the cake for tonight would not be a disaster this time. They would need something comforting while they met to talk about what was happening on the hill.

Sarah and Grace had debated whether or not to ask Emily to be part of the group. She was so new to all of it. Plus, no one but Hank and Melvin knew her beyond the fact that Emily was Hannah's dance teacher.

However, Hank spoke highly of her and was as protective as if she was a daughter. So, using Hank's judgment, they decided that they would make it a provisionary membership. She needed them, and it would be wrong to leave her out of something that could be so comforting and uplifting.

That brought into question if other women should also be invited to join the council. They decided that there were only two that could be considered at this time—Barbara and Valerie.

They didn't know either of them as well as they knew each other and Mandy, Mira, and Ava. They debated and thought it over for a while. In the end, they asked Barbara, but not Valerie. Sarah felt that Valerie might fit in, but a voice inside of her kept telling her it wasn't a good idea, so she obeyed that intuition.

That meant there were going to be seven of them. Grace could still fit them in her living room, but for this meeting, they decided on the coffee shop. With new members, they wanted a slightly more formal meeting. They needed to talk about what the council was about, what internal rules they followed, and what was expected when they were part of the group.

At first, Sarah didn't like the idea at all. She had been happy to keep the council smaller, with her close friends. But Leif had something to say about that.

After the visit with everyone at Ava's on Friday night, Leif had followed Sarah home. Actually, the word "followed" was the wrong word. He was already there when she got home as she expected he would be. Perhaps not having a physical body was helpful sometimes, Sarah had thought. As she added a few logs to the wood stove Hank had installed for her she also thought it might be nice never to be cold again since Eric and Leif didn't feel hot and cold anymore.

On the other hand, without a physical body, there was no hand-holding, no hugs, and no warm body in bed at night. The loss of not having Leif around physically had been painful.

However, that kind of thinking never made her feel better. So Sarah dropped it in favor of being grateful for having Leif around to talk to, and that's what they did.

They had a lengthy discussion about what was going on and her role in it. Sarah didn't want a role. She wanted to stay home with a good book, and have a casual council meeting once in a while.

Leif laughed at her, as she knew he would. Of course, that was ridiculous of her to think such a thing. All of the Circles knew they had to be of service. Now that Leif was part of both the Stone Circle and the Forest Circle he was the bridge and conveyor of messages, and everyone in both circles knew that Sarah had a role to play. She had to guide them, as she had promised the Forest Circle she would.

"Everyone needs a purpose higher than themselves," Leif reminded her. He didn't need to remind her. She knew that, but she was resisting it. It meant she was moving on. Leif laughed again, and this time she joined him.

"Yes," he said. "That is what we do. Move on, expand, grow, learn, and hopefully become more aware of the one authority of divine Love and good."

So, as the women arrived at the coffee shop, Sarah greeted each one of them with joy. They had each other. And they had a crime to solve. They would solve it differently than the men that were out working at the site. They were there to listen to what was really going on. They were there to make sure everything was uncovered that needed to be discovered. They were there to watch over and protect. That they could do.

After everyone sat down, the women took time to introduce themselves. Of course, they all knew each other. But for Emily, this idea of a gathering of women with the intention to be of service was entirely new. Barbara wasn't quite as new to the process. She had been part of the larger group, or Doveland Circle, for a while, according to Hannah,.

After introductions, Sarah set the ground rules. What was discussed in the council, stays in the council. Period. No one shares anything said in the council with anyone. That would leave them all free to say whatever they needed to talk about with the full comfort of knowing it was a safe place.

Ava asked about husbands and boyfriends, and even Hank and Melvin. Sarah knew this was tricky. She always talked over everything with Leif but didn't tell him things she knew had been shared with the desire not to be repeated. Instead, she gave overviews to him so he could provide insight to her.

Ava also trusted that Evan would be the same way. Grace and Barbara said the same thing about the other men. They could be trusted. At this point, Sarah began to realize why it hadn't felt right to ask Valerie. Even if the provision was that only general ideas could be discussed with significant others, it didn't feel safe that Harold would know what was happening in the council. The other men, yes. Harold, no.

So, they agreed that current husbands, and Hank, Melvin, Sam, Craig, and Tom could know generalities when they needed to know, but not specifics unless given permission by the woman in question, or all the women if it was a general piece of information. They also decided that they would act as a consulting counsel to any of these men if they came to them with questions.

Then they talked about Sarah's new favorite word, Exousia. They would not be a human authority. They would be a conduit for Divine authority as the word implied. That meant they would have to address their own motives and intentions continually.

It was going to be hard work. But each of the women felt the light of purpose burn within them as they discussed these ideas.

And then they turned to the task at hand. Emily and the discovery.

TWENTY

It took longer than expected to get the autopsy report back. It arrived Wednesday morning. Both Sam and the local authorities got a copy. Hank was still staying in the bunkhouse, so Sam came over to Evan's with the report, giving Craig a call along the way. They could have met at Craig's office, but all of them had remained cautious, perhaps overly cautious, after dealing with Grant and Lenny.

Sam knew that Evan still had the house swept daily for listening devices and cameras and a Faraday box for phones to be put in whenever they met about things like this. The house was the perfect meeting place. Hannah was in school, and Ben was napping.

Tom was out of town, so they put him on a Skype call. He could have remote-viewed in, but not everyone could see him when he did it that way, so it was more comfortable to have him on a call.

Recently Ava, Sam, Hank, and Craig had begun to be able to see Leif and Eric who were also there. No one was sure if it was because their minds had fully accepted that it was possible, or if Leif and Eric had decided to be seen. Perhaps it was because of the current situation. For whatever reason, everyone was happy about it.

Of course, there was no need to pull up a chair for them, but they did. It made everyone nervous to have Leif and Eric just hovering around. A pretend sitting at the table was much easier to deal with than their nonphysical presence.

Ava made coffee for all of the people who were physically present and served them the leftover cake from the meeting the night before. It had turned out to be delicious. All of the men knew about Sarah's council of women. They also knew that the women would, as they always had, guide them to doing the right thing. So the men asked Ava to stay and listen so she could tell the council what they had learned.

She wanted to be there, and she knew it was essential to understand what the report said, but it was painful to listen and to look at the pictures. She tried to be detached while hearing the information, but it was hard to do.

Sam laid the report and the pictures out on the table. He said that all four of the bodies were women. They were probably all between twenty and twenty-five. It would take a while to get DNA samples back, but they weren't holding out any hope of finding out who they were that way.

"Why not?" Ava asked.

"Because it turns out these bodies were buried back in the Seventies. At least forty-five years ago."

No one said anything as everyone thought over the ramifications of what that might mean. Did it mean that whoever killed the women kept on killing? Would they ever find the killer?

"Wait. This report says that there are no signs of how they died. How can that be?" Craig asked.

"That's one of the most puzzling parts of this. The women had to die of something. Unless the report is wrong, there is no sign that they were murdered. But how could it be otherwise? The women were young, buried together, and at about the same time," Sam said.

"And buried together in a shallow grave," Evan added. "If they died a mysterious natural death, why not report it to the authorities?"

"And why were they all up on that hill? Was there something there before?" Ava asked.

"Well, we do have a few answers about that, thanks to Dr. Joe," Craig said.

"He was the one that sold the land to Emily. It is part of his process of retiring. I know he sold the property that is enabling you to build the bike trail to Concourse, Hank. He said he bought the land on the hill in the late Seventies, so according to this report, the bodies were already there when he bought it. He never developed the property on purpose. He didn't want the town sprawling out too much. Plus he can see the hill from his home office window and liked looking at the view.

"But when Emily came to him and told him what she wanted to build and how she would preserve the look of the hill as much as possible, he agreed. He has a soft spot in his heart for the arts."

"So who did he buy the land from then? They must have been there when the bodies were buried. Maybe they would know how they died and why they were buried there?" Ava asked.

"Well, this is where it might get tricky," Sam said. "Most of the town records before 1990 were destroyed when the basement of the town hall flooded. Dr. Joe said he purchased the land from the bank, but no one who worked at the bank is still around here, and the bank records are going to be hard to find too since it has changed hands more than a few times.

"What Joe did say was that there was an informal commune up on the hill for a brief time. Finding out about that and someone who knows about it is a priority. Joe said he visited it a few times and gave talks on basic health care, but doesn't remember much more than that."

Hank had sat quietly listening and trying to remember something that Emily had told him. Finally, it came to him. "Emily told me that she originally came to Doveland because her aunt had sent them a postcard of the town and Emily thought it looked beautiful. She came here to see what it was all about and then stayed. Perhaps she has more information or could ask her aunt. Ava, could you talk to her about it?"

Ava nodded while wondering why Emily hadn't mentioned that in the discussion at the council the day before. "I'll arrange to meet her after Hannah's dance class."

"How is she doing?" Craig asked.

"We took her home yesterday, and she wanted to start teaching again. Said it would take her mind off of what happened, and get her back into believing that the dance camp will happen this year, even if only for a week."

"It's possible," Hank said. "If she wants, we could build the barn and probably a deck. She won't have a house there yet, but it would work for a day camp. As soon as the hill is released officially, we'll start building again."

"She'll be happy to hear that," Ava said. "I'll let you all know what she says about her aunt."

Ava was happy for Emily but wondered why she withheld that information. *Still doesn't trust us yet,* she thought. *Wonder why.*

TWENTY-ONE

Valerie was at her wit's end. Harold had become temperamental as he aged, but he was so much worse since the discovery on the hill. She sighed. She was getting too old for this. Well, maybe that wasn't the right word. She was getting too wise for this. Whatever this was, she was not happy.

She and Harold had met at work twenty-two years ago. Harold was a big shot in the company where she slaved away as an assistant to an assistant. Everyone got along with him. Charming and handsome and quite a singer, he always had a crowd around him at company gatherings.

She had noticed Harold long before they met officially. It was hard not to. He stuck out so much from everyone else. Besides, he was her boss's boss so he would often be at the department meetings where she would be sitting in the corner taking notes for her boss who hated going to meetings. Plus Harold was so much older than she was and at the time that made him even more mysterious. Forty and never married?

Valerie sighed again at the thought. Harold ran those meetings with a compelling combination of grace and authority. Harold always knew the right thing to say, and how to get people to do things for him. She marveled at his skill. At the time, Valerie was taking night classes to finish up her teaching credentials. It had been her dream to teach in a small town. Her parents had both been teachers, and she wanted to carry on the tradition. She had learned a lot about how to run her classroom by watching Harold run a meeting.

It was when her boss told Harold that Valerie was studying to be a teacher that Harold began to notice her. Harold told her later that he had always noticed her, but he was officially her boss and didn't feel right about asking her out. She was young. He was old and set in his ways. However, when he found out that she would be leaving to be a teacher he knew he couldn't let her go.

Valerie always loved him for that choice. She thought he demonstrated integrity. Later, Valerie wondered if perhaps he had been expressing his willingness to follow the rules of someone with more authority and not his own sense of what was right and wrong. She thought it was a subtle but profound difference.

They continued to date for another year, while he worked and she taught school. She loved the teaching but didn't enjoy the school. Too big, and too regimented, without enough leeway to help each student with what they needed.

When Harold asked her to marry him, she thought it was the best day of her life. By then he was forty-one, and she was twenty-five, ready to marry. A year later, the company moved many of their employees out of the country and offered those that didn't want to go a small settlement package.

Harold had a plan. Why not take the money, move back to his hometown, and open a Bed and Breakfast. He would do the work of running it, and she could teach school in a small town. He barely got the words out before Valerie said yes. It never occurred to her that she wouldn't like the place, or that she wouldn't get a job teaching there. It sounded like a dream come true.

The Bed and Breakfast Inn took a while to get off the ground. However, Harold turned out to be great at both the restoring of the building and the day-to-day business of running the Inn. They didn't have many visitors. Doveland wasn't a destination spot for tourists. On the other hand, they didn't need much money to live comfortably. Harold's natural gregariousness worked well in town and for their business. He also continued to do consulting work with people he had met in his last job. That helped with the money, and he could do most of the work from home. Once in a while, he would have to go out of town, but they just never booked the Inn during those times.

Johnny came along a year after they moved to town, but she never took time off. He was born in June, and she was back at work in September. Lex was a surprise, born eight years later. By then, she was the principal of the school and loving every minute of it. Everything was perfect.

Except that as the years went by, Harold's charm became more controlled. He was a good father, but at times was a demanding husband. He stopped listening to her and got mad at the smallest things. She overlooked it because otherwise everything worked pretty well. She still loved being a principal, and he did a great job of running the Inn.

However, when Johnny started getting into trouble, Valerie began to look at her marriage differently. Maybe Johnny was acting out because of the tension that sometimes happened in their house. She thought she kept Harold's abusiveness hidden, but she knew as well as anyone that children know much more than it appears that they do.

After Johnny was caught last year working with that evil man, Grant, things began to turn around for him. Sam gave Johnny a second chance, and Johnny was grabbing it for all that it was worth. It was his last year in school, and he would be heading off to college in the fall. Thanks to Pete and Hank taking him under their wing,

Johnny had discovered he could be his own person. He dropped his friends that got him into trouble and, if she was honest, stayed away from his dad as much as possible.

Had it really gotten this bad? Valerie wondered. *Was she like the frog in hot water, and hadn't realized that the situation with Harold had gotten worse because it had been a slow progression? Not slow anymore,* she thought. That's what had changed. Since the incident with Grant last year, Harold's rude, dismissive, and sometimes abusive behavior had escalated.

After rushing off from the Diner a week ago, he had returned angry and withdrawn. She tried to find out what was wrong, but he dismissed her saying he didn't feel well. And then, the day after the discovery, something had set him off, and he had slapped her. It wasn't the first time, but this time felt different.

Valerie was conflicted. Should she leave him? She was still young. She was only forty-six. She had a life in front of her. She had children to protect. Whatever was wrong with Harold would need to be over soon, or she would have to make a decision. It wouldn't be easy.

If she needed help, she knew she could go to Grace. Valerie had a feeling that Grace already knew what was happening but was waiting for Valerie to tell her. Grace was a busybody with a wise heart. Yes, Valerie decided. If I need to, I will go to Grace. She prayed that Harold would get over whatever was bothering him. She had loved him all these years, and she didn't want to stop now.

• • • ● • ● • ● • • •

At the gas station, Tina was praying that Harold would just pump the gas and go. Lately, she hadn't been that lucky. Tina was sure there wasn't a need to get gas as much as Harold did. Unless he was doing a lot of driving during that day, which of course was possible.

Tina wished that if that were true, he would keep on driving and never come back. Instead, he showed up and acted as if she should be glad for his presence.

Not on your life, buddy, she thought. *I know what a dark, angry person looks like. I already ran from one. I won't run from another.*

She wasn't lucky this time either. Harold finished pumping and headed to where she was in the small store. If the kids were home, she would have them take care of him, but they were in school. He didn't need to pay in the store. He could use the same card at the pump. No, he wanted to come in to flirt. If it was during the day, that's all it was. At night, he pushed harder.

Tina wondered if she should talk to Valerie about it. Did she know what her husband was doing? They always looked so lovey-dovey when she saw them together. But then Tina knew all about fake love.

TWENTY-TWO

Craig decided to walk to Dr. Joe's house. Before he and Jo Ann divorced, he had used walking as a way to get out of the house when an argument started. While walking, he discovered that he had time to think. Now it had become one of his favorite pastimes. Sometimes between patients, he would go out the door and start walking. Even a short walk around the block was helpful.

On longer walks, he would often see Emily Sands running. It would be a brief exchange as she was a fast runner, and he was a slow walker. He looked like he was faster because his long legs ate up the distance, but he didn't care how long it took him to get somewhere. He wasn't going anywhere physical. He was traveling mentally.

Walking not only calmed his thinking, but it also opened up channels for new ideas to come through. He had taken to recording the insights into his phone and then later putting them into a document titled, "notes from walking."

Some of the ideas just sat in that document, and others he implemented. They were often simple things like how to arrange the waiting room for the most comfort, or who in town might make a good part-time assistant. Other times, he would get an idea about what was wrong with a patient and after checking it out would discover that the thought that came to him while walking was often correct.

There were physical results too. One day, he realized that his knees didn't hurt anymore. Before he had started walking, they sometimes complained when he stood up or sat down, but it had been months since that had happened. And, as much as his vanity didn't want to admit it, he had become a bit overweight over the years. He was a big guy, so it didn't look bad on him, but then it didn't look great either. Without trying, he had lost pounds while walking and was now back to a weight that felt perfect for him.

There were some things that walking hadn't entirely helped with—yet. He had hope. He used to be so much more easygoing. Some people had called him boisterous. Somewhere that had just disappeared, and he wondered if it would ever come back. He doubted it. The divorce had sobered him up so to speak.

Perhaps that behavior wasn't me, and this quiet person is, Craig thought as he walked. He didn't think so, though. He felt that his happier side would appear again as time passed. Not the boisterous life of the party perhaps, but a wiser and more aware person was emerging. Craig thought he liked that person better.

However, the murders on the hill were not helping bring back his happy essence. The idea that something like this could happen was disturbing. It was tragic for everyone.

He thought of Emily and how disastrous this was for her. Even though Emily's dream would probably still be built, there would always be that memory of the bodies. He hoped she wouldn't give up her plans though.

The town needed her, and he thought that perhaps she needed the town. Sarah had told him they had invited Emily to the women's council. He was sure that was going to help if she would let it. He thought she had been running for a long time, and not just the physical running, either. Craig hoped that she would be able to face what she was running from. Perhaps the council would be able to help her.

Of course, the tragedy extended far past Emily or her dream, or even the town. Not only did they need to discover who it was that had committed these crimes, but they also needed to know how they did it. He assumed that they were dealing with four murders because of the circumstances. However, there was no evidence that they had been killed. All they had were questions. How could four young women die with no signs of how they died? And why hide their bodies?

Then there were the families of those women. They never knew what happened to their loved ones. Did they spend their entire life wondering and hoping and then losing that hope? Was there anyone still alive that missed them? Were they ever missed? If no one had missed them, it would be an even greater tragedy.

It was a puzzle, and walking was a great way to work out a problem. But today he was walking for another purpose. It was to meet with Joe and pick his brain. Craig had a copy of the autopsy reports and was hoping that Joe would be able to pull something out of them that would be useful. It would be at least another week before they had DNA results, not that he thought it would do any good. Still, it was a necessity, just in case.

Besides having Joe look at the reports, Craig was looking forward to the conversation. They had become good friends, exploring many ideas about healing. It seemed they agreed about many things, and even if they didn't agree, they both enjoyed the debate.

Craig would miss Joe when he was gone. That appeared to be happening sooner than expected. Dr. Joe had been planning to stay a year for the transition in patients, but now Joe was beginning to feel as if that wasn't necessary. Craig had picked up the information quickly, and most of Dr. Joe's past patients were happy with the quality of their care under the new doctor.

Craig could understand why Joe was just anxious to start a new life somewhere else. Who could blame him for that? He had prepared his life and his practice so that he could retire at a reasonable age and still enjoy himself. Who could fault that logic? Maybe he would visit Joe in Spain once he settled down.

Turning the last corner, he spotted Joe's house. No one would have thought this was a wealthy doctor's house. It looked like all the other houses in the neighborhood. Most of the homes had been built in the early 1900's and slowly updated as new owners took over. About ten years ago, Doveland had realized they had some beautiful old historical houses on their hands and that they were treasures that needed to be saved.

One of Joe's neighbors was a current patient of Craig's and had told him the story. The town council had gone to Dr. Joe and asked him to help with the restoration project since he lived in one of those old homes. Dr. Joe had asked what they needed, and after hearing the story, gave them enough money so that every family in his neighborhood was given the opportunity to have the outside of their homes cleaned up and painted one of the historically correct colors of their choice, for free.

He had also funded a grant that everyone could apply to that would enable them to fix up any age-related problems in their houses. They all took him up on it, and everyone in one of those old houses considered him a saint. Dr. Joe funded the trust every year, and they all knew that there was a provision in his will to keep it going after his death.

The homes on Joe's side of the street on his block all had back windows that faced out of town with an unobstructed view. There were no buildings behind them. Just an open field edged with trees—Craig suspected this was Joe's doing—so that they all could keep their view of the rolling hills.

As he walked up to the door, Joe opened it and beckoned him in, saying, "No I don't have that sixth sense some of you have, I just have cameras."

Craig looked up to see the cameras he pointed to, and realized there were cameras on all the houses on the street, something he had never noticed before.

Seeing his glance, Joe said, "Yes, I had them installed a few years ago. The cameras help everyone feel safer. It makes me happy because I enjoy helping people feel safe."

Craig stepped into the small entrance inside the door and handed his jacket to Dr. Joe to hang in the closet in the hallway. Craig had been here before, of course, many times. But every time he had the same feeling. It was a combination of warmth, safety, comfort, and something else that niggled on the back of his brain. He still couldn't place it this time either.

Oh well, he thought. *Not important, and if it is, I will figure it out sometime.*

Twenty-Three

Emily looked at her reflection in the mirror and decided she looked like death and then realized what she had thought and reeled back in horror. Death. Death looked a lot worse than what she looked like right now. At least she was alive, unlike the bodies on her hill.

But she looked terrible. The days had taken a toll. She couldn't decide what day had been the most horrible. Was it last Friday when the discovery shattered the joy of building her dream? Or the weekend at Ava's in the bunkhouse trying to sleep, to forget, to behave like a human while no one knew what had happened yet? Or was it when Ava brought her home, and then the silent hours by herself? Or was it the women's meeting where she should have felt safe enough to tell, but instead was terrified? The council was requiring her, well requiring everybody, to be honest. It sounded easy, but Emily wasn't sure if she could be. What if she was honest? What would happen? Yes, it was terrifying. During the meeting Tuesday night, she had been afraid they would know, but no one said anything.

Emily figured they couldn't tell there was sweat running down her spine the whole time, and her foot wouldn't stop twitching.

On the other hand, maybe they did know, but were being kind and were letting her work it out. Emily had never had a group she felt comfortable with before. She and her mother were a team. That had been enough. Or at least she had convinced herself that it was enough.

Now, she wasn't so sure what to do. Without her Mom, she no longer had a sounding board. She no longer had someone who took the time to listen deeply and then to assure her they would figure it out together. Hank and Melvin had been sweet, kind, and helpful, but it wasn't the same. Wonderful, but not the same. The idea that the women's council would be like that felt too unreal. Not possible for her.

Emily shook her head. She didn't know what to do; she was so disoriented. Yes, it was good to be home where everything felt familiar. Emily also knew that teaching would help. But now she was even more terrified than she had been at the first meeting because Ava had called and asked to spend a few minutes with her after Hannah's class this afternoon. What did Ava have to tell her? Why was she coming just by herself? Would Ava force out of her the secret she wasn't going to share with anyone? Was it a secret that should be kept, or was it time to let it go?

Either way, she had to look better than she did. Her long blond hair looked stringy; she had lost weight since the discovery, which wasn't a good thing. She was already thin, Now, her face was gaunt, with dark circles under her eyes, and everything about her looked dejected.

Checking her watch, Emily realized that she had time for a quick run, and a shower. Both of those things usually made her feel better. She had been down before and gotten back up. She could do it again! Turning from her self-examination at the mirror, Emily quickly changed from her ratty sweatpants into her running clothes. She slapped some sunscreen on her face, trying not to look in the mirror as she did so, grabbed a hat, stuffed her house keys into the running belt, and stepped outside.

Emily lived on a side street in Doveland. Old houses, but well maintained. She would have liked to run into the country, but today there was no time, so she was doing what she called her medium town run. She also had a short town run and a long town run. When she had plenty of time, she had explored some of the running trails in the hills and was looking forward to the bike trail being finished.

This medium town run took Emily through the back streets of Doveland, around the town square and then back to her house. As she ran, she was overcome with how much she loved the town. She waved at people she knew, and at Mandy, who she saw through the window at Your Second Home. She even waved at Tina, who owned the gas station. She didn't know her well, but she suspected Tina had secrets, too. It made them sisters of a sort.

Fifty minutes later, she felt more like herself. A shower, more makeup than usual, and she would look a lot better. She had made a decision. She would tell Ava what she wanted to know. Did she have any choice? It was either that or walk away. She had never walked away from a problem before, and she wasn't going to start now.

With a start, Emily realized she had made a decision. She opened her phone and texted Sarah. She had something to tell the council. Could Ava find out if the council was willing to meet with her?

Within seconds she had her answer. Yes. Sarah would take care of everything. Ava would pick up Emily, and they would meet in Grace's apartment above the shop.

Well, the die is cast now, Emily thought. She went to her files and pulled out what she had learned in her research. A picture of her aunt standing on the hill was in the front of one of the folders. She took it out and looked at it. The person was familiar. Not only because she had stared at the picture so many times trying to figure out what her Aunt Jean would look like now, but also because she saw that same person in the mirror every day.

She needed help to find Jean. The council was the place to get that help.

Emily tied up her hair into a ponytail and headed downstairs to her studio. The first of the kids would be arriving soon. She had a dance class to teach.

• • • • ● • ◉ • ● • • •

Sarah had spent most of the morning in deep contemplation as she had every morning since the discovery. Her desire was to lose her self-importance and to have a deeper understanding of what it meant to be the instrument of the Divine.

She did have an intent to go with that desire. She hoped to help Emily let go and trust the council, and in the end to discover and then heal whatever had happened on the hill.

It was tricky to have these intents and not try to say what she wanted the outcome to be. That meant she would be in charge, and that was the last thing she wanted. It was also tricky to "pray" for someone, but not invade their space and manipulate their thinking. It was vital to not impose her will and needs on to someone else.

Everyone had been aware of Emily's intense discomfort at the meeting. They all chose to let her be, not to ignore it, but to embrace Emily instead, hoping she would open up to them and trust what they had to offer. When Emily contacted her, Sarah bowed her head in thanks and then sent out a call to the council. Yes, everyone could be at Grace's that evening. What could they be doing that was more important?

TWENTY-FOUR

Hank needed to go to Melvin's house to get some extra clothes and see how his friend was doing, so he invited Hannah to go along with him. Since it was Friday night, Hank asked Ava if Hannah could stay overnight with him at Melvin's. He would bring her back the next day.

Ava thought it was an excellent idea. She knew how much Melvin and Hannah had taken to each other, and she was happy to get Hannah away from some of the tension going on in town. Plus, it would leave her free to go to the council meeting that evening. Evan was always happy to stay home with Ben. Ava loved how much fun they had playing together. She couldn't wait to see what they did together as Ben grew into a little boy.

At a year old, Ben was walking—barely. It was mostly stumbling from place to place. It was a job to keep track of him. Curiosity ruled every moment of Ben's life. It was both exhausting and joyful to be always watching over him. But Ben was sleeping through almost every night, which was a blessing.

Hank picked up Hannah from dance class, and then stopped by her house to get the suitcase her mom had packed for her, a casserole for dinner, and a pie for dessert. Melvin was a skilled cook, but his repertory was limited, so he was always grateful when Ava sent food. So was everyone else.

Hank had another reason for going home to Melvin's besides picking up more clothes and checking on him. He wanted to find out if Melvin remembered what might have been going on in Doveland forty-five years before. At this point, Hank felt that any piece of information would be helpful. When Mira had talked to Melvin the week before, the news was too overwhelming for him to remember anything.

Melvin was sitting on the front porch, waiting for them. Hank smiled at the sight of the old man. He had decided to pretend that Melvin was actually his father. Hank knew Melvin wasn't his dad. His dad was in the graveyard outside of town. However, by now Hank had learned anything was possible, and he chose to believe that Melvin was his father, perhaps in another lifetime, and found again in this one.

Out of habit born of experience, Hank grabbed Hannah and held on to her until he brought his truck to a stop. She had been known to be so excited about seeing Melvin that she opened the door as the wheels were still turning.

By the time he let go of her, Melvin was at the truck, opening the door and hugging her as she stood on the runner. If Hank was pretending that Melvin was his father, Melvin was pretending that Hannah was his granddaughter.

Hank's past was never far from his thoughts. He saw himself now as a good man steeped in the evil of his past. He would never be rid of it, but he had decided to soak up every piece of goodness in his life, and his niece's relationship with Melvin never failed to touch his heart. Not that he would tell anyone. He still had his stoic reputation to maintain.

That night after the two of them had tucked Hannah into bed and each of them had read her a story, they met at the kitchen table.

"How are you doing with the investigation, Hank?" Melvin asked.

"That's just it. There barely is one. We have no proof it was murder. We don't have any idea who the women were, and we have no idea how, or why, they were buried on that hill.

"I was hoping maybe you could remember anything at all from that time that may give us a clue, or at least point us in some direction. We heard that there might have been an informal commune out there during the Seventies. But that's it. Did you ever hear anything about that?"

On the wall, Melvin's old clock ticked as the seconds passed. Hank knew enough just to wait. He wanted to get up and get a cup of coffee, but instead sat as still as he could because he knew that any motion at all could be a distraction. So Hank waited and listened. And while the seconds ticked by, he realized how much he missed hearing his sister Abbie's voice.

He became so lost in his thoughts that he didn't realize that Leif had arrived in whatever magical way dimension travelers got around. He still couldn't see Leif as clearly as others did. He figured that it took practice.

He could see Leif enough to see that he was putting his fingers to his lips, and Hank knew enough to stay quiet. So they both waited, silently.

It felt like an hour had gone by before Melvin cleared his throat and got up to get coffee, although Hank could see by the clock that only a minute had passed. Either that or Leif had tinkered with time. Hank wouldn't put it past him.

Melvin couldn't see Leif yet, so he almost walked through him on the way to the coffee pot. Even though it wouldn't have made any difference, Leif still stepped out of the way, as he looked at Hank and laughed.

When Hank grinned back, Melvin asked, while his back was turned, "Whatcha grinning at boy?"

"Wait. How did you see me grinning?"

"You know about eyes in the back of your head don't you?" Melvin answered while grinning to himself, and then pointing at Hank's reflection in the microwave door. The microwave was a present from Ava so Melvin could quickly heat up the food she sent over. Hank installed it after taking a whole afternoon to rewire the kitchen in order to put it in.

Hank laughed. "Melvin, you old fool. You had me going there for a second. I was grinning at the fact that you almost walked through Leif."

Melvin spun around and said, "Hey, Leif," to the wrong corner of the room.

By then Leif was air sitting at the table, and Hank pointed to the space to let Melvin know where Leif had put himself.

"Go ahead, Melvin," Hank said. "I know you remembered something.

"Well. Something. I don't think it will be constructive, but I do remember a few young women coming out to the farm to buy some chickens from me. They said they were trying to be—what's the word?"

"Organic?"

"Yep. That's it. Organic. I had no idea what those girls were talking about, but I sold them some prime laying hens. They didn't want a rooster. Told them that if they let a few eggs hatch, they might end up with one though."

"Do you remember what they looked like?"

"Pretty. Long hair. Long dresses. Kinda naive. Really didn't know much about what they were doing. Sally—you know, my wife—spent some time with them teaching them how to take care of the chickens. There were two of them. The reason I think they might be from that group you are talking about is they said they were squatting on some hill near Doveland.

"Yes, it sounds like they might be part of that commune. Can't you think of anything else about them? Their name or where they were from? Did they ever come back?"

"They did. They must have done okay with the chickens, and they liked my wife, so they came back for a few more chickens. There were four women—well, young girls to me—that came that time. They told Sally that their little group was growing.

"I remember Sally showed them how she made bread over a fire. Still don't know how she did that. It always turned out tasty, but I never learnt how.

"That time, when they came, it was probably in the fall, cause it was getting cold and Sally was worried about how they would stay warm. They said that they had built a few shelters and would be okay. Don't see how. It gets to be freezing in the winter. Well, you know that, Hank. You grew up here."

"After that, did you ever see them?"

"Yep, now that I think about it, we ran into them in the grocery store in Doveland the next spring. They looked pretty skinny and miserable, but they seemed to have survived the winter. If I know my Sally, she probably slipped them some money to get food."

Melvin stopped talking and gazed into the distance. Hank and Leif gave him time. They knew he was thinking of his wife, and that there wasn't that much time until he would see her again.

"You know," Melvin said. "I think Sally was playing with her new camera that one time and might have taken a picture of those girls. If she did, the pictures are all up in the attic. Maybe Hannah and I could go through them tomorrow morning. Being a Saturday and all, she could stay longer."

Leif nodded at Hank and was gone. "That would be wonderful, Melvin. Now, how about a piece of Ava's pie and more coffee to go with it."

Hank knew he wanted to grab every bit of joy out of every moment, because if there really was a picture, someday he might find himself delivering sad news to someone who had been waiting for a long time to have answers.

He wasn't looking forward to that job, but Hank was looking forward to getting answers and giving names to those four young women. They deserved to be remembered.

Twenty-Five

In the light of a fading sun, Joe could see Hank's crew finishing up their work for the day. Hank had been there most of the day but had left early, probably to pick up his niece, Hannah, from school. Maybe, Joe thought, since it was a Friday evening, they were going to do something special together. Joe had heard from Craig that Hank and Hannah were very close.

The building on the land was quite a sight. Joe loved watching people build things, and even though the building was temporarily destroying his beautiful view, he wasn't upset. Even the low rumble of equipment that could be heard if the wind was just right, wasn't disturbing him.

Emily's idea of an art retreat or camp centered around dance made him happy. His wife, May, bless her heart gone for so many years, loved to dance.

"That's a good idea," he said aloud, even though there was no one there to hear him. Still talking to himself, he said, "Yes, I'll set up a trust for the camp, too, in your name. That should make you happy, right?"

Although Joe was talking to his wife, he was just pretending that she was there with him. Joe didn't believe in the afterlife. In some ways, he wanted to. Joe thought it would be lovely to know that the essence of yourself continued after death. That once dead you could still be happy and prosperous. But Joe thought that if he believed in a glorious afterlife, then he might have to believe that not everyone got there.

So, no, Joe couldn't believe in life after death. Although he was often called upon to support other people's beliefs in the afterlife because it was part of what he considered being a good doctor, he just couldn't get himself to accept it.

Getting up from his chair, Joe walked to the window and stood looking out at the hill. He figured that since they were building on the hill again, there were no more bodies to be found. In the middle of this terrible discovery, that was a reason to be grateful.

The autopsies that Craig brought to him were disturbing. There were no signs of how they died. Everyone was puzzled.

Joe was puzzled, too. Why were they buried on the hill? Why together? And of course, the other question, who were they?

Joe knew that was going to be almost impossible to solve. Too many years had gone by. Even if they were able to extract the DNA, they would have to have a relative that had DNA in the system within the last twenty years. So, unlikely. Too bad. He knew the families would want to know what happened to them.

What if he had never sold the land to Emily? Would the bodies have ever been found? He hadn't planned to sell that piece of property, and certainly, he hadn't intended to let anyone build on it.

Most of the land he had sold in the last few years had no-build restrictions placed on them. The bike path and the arts center were two ideas he liked, so he had approved Hank and Emily's plans to build.

But he detested housing developments and always said no to anyone that asked to buy his land for that reason.

Joe thought about how much more money he could have made if he allowed that kind of building. He could have even developed the land himself. But then that would be how people would have remembered him. What he wanted was to be remembered for the good he did.

Joe had delivered, or at least cared for, almost every person in Doveland, and a great many in Concourse. Joe believed that a man only has his reputation in the end, and he would do whatever it took to maintain the one he had spent his whole life developing.

He had done even more than the good people of Doveland knew he had done. Whenever he went away for a few weeks, he always hired a doctor to come to Doveland to take care of his patients. They were never without Joe's attention. They knew about his dedication to their health and well-being.

What the townspeople didn't know was that Joe had been attending private medical conferences when he went away. Special gatherings where alternative means of healing were discussed and practiced. Although Joe had been interested in mind-over-matter healing for years, it was only now becoming mainstream.

Joe had so much more he could share about his discoveries on the power of mind over matter, but he was tired. Retiring and spending time in warm climates was on his mind. Someone else would have to make the information public. It wouldn't be him.

Because, once again, his reputation was what mattered to Joe most. His patients didn't need to know why he was so successful at healing them, or the sacrifices he had made to become so skilled. They only needed to see the outcome. They were healed. By him.

Joe turned back to his files. Deciding which ones to keep and which ones to destroy was taking him much longer than he anticipated. He needed to make sure that he was making the right decisions.

Sometimes he thought there was no point in keeping any of them. Who cared what he did and how he did it? He was tempted to burn or shred them all.

He wasn't leaving for another few weeks, so he still had time to do that if it was necessary, or if it became easier than trying to divide them into keep-or-destroy piles.

Joe had been building a legacy his whole life. If his son ever returned, he would be returning to a town that loved his father.

Joe sighed. With all the resources he had at his disposal he never found his son, Edward. Only traces of where he had been. After his mother, May, died of alcoholism, Edward spiraled into a hatred of life that Joe couldn't stop. He left home when he was fifteen. A runaway. Joe had no idea if he was still alive.

Even if he was alive, it was possible that he would never come back to Doveland. If he ever returned, it would probably be long after Joe had gone. All Joe wanted was to be respected, and to hope that someday his son might find out that Joe was the town's hero.

In the meantime, he had work to do. With one last glance at Emily's hill, he turned to his desk and his papers. He had decisions to make and time was running out in which to make them.

TWENTY-SIX

Just before Ava pulled her car out of the driveway onto the road to town, another car pulled in. She backed up until she was parallel to the other vehicle. Ava opened her driver's side window so she could say hello to the car full of men heading up to the house. "How long did it take for Evan to text you and tell you I was going out?" she asked.

"Hey, don't blame Evan, it was him," Craig said, pointing to Sam sitting beside him in the passenger seat.

"Sam texted Evan and the rest of us as soon as he heard about your council meeting tonight. Guess he didn't want to be alone."

"It was just Sam that didn't want to be alone?" Ava asked.

Craig looked down sheepishly. "Okay, it was all of them. With all the women not home on a Friday night, it seemed like a perfect night for some game watching and beer drinking!"

Ava laughed. She knew that the beer drinking would probably be mostly coffee drinking and the game watching would probably be a talk session. But, she went along with the pretense of it anyway.

In the back seat of Craig's car, Pete winked at her, and Tom, Mira's twin brother, gave her a mock salute.

Ava was glad to see that Tom was back in town. Sure, the murders happened a long time ago, but until they found out who had done them, she was happy to have all the men paying attention.

"Okay, boys, have a good time. I left food in the refrigerator for all of you."

As Ava pulled out, Sam said, "Hey, how did she know we would be here?"

Tom snorted, "Still don't know much about women yet, do you, Sam?"

"Obviously not," Sam said. "Heck, I could have brought food. Didn't think of it."

"I rest my case," Tom said.

"What case is that?" Sam asked as he pulled up to the front door.

"Sam, between you and my sister, in your house, which one of you takes care of the practical things of running the house, at least most of the time? Which one of you makes sure you eat and look nice when you go out the door?"

"Point taken," Sam laughed, along with most of the rest of the men in the car.

Pete just smiled to himself. He used to take that kind of thing for granted. Now he made sure he was doing at least half of those practical things for his wife, Barbara.

Tom looked back at Pete as they stepped out of the car, "Okay, I take it back. At least one of us is wiser. Pete, we need to take lessons."

"Not going to dispute that, young Tom," Pete said.

Evan opened the door just in time to hear what Pete said. "Not going to dispute what?" he asked.

"That Pete has a lot to teach us all about how to be a good man for a good woman," Craig answered.

"Great. Get yourself in here and start teaching. Ava left us food."

All the men started laughing, leaving Evan to wonder what was so funny.

"Tom slapped him on the shoulder. Come on. We'll tell you over a beer."

This time they all laughed and trouped into the house bonded by all that they had gone through and the knowledge that there was more to come. They knew they would need each other to get through it.

· · · ● · ● · ● · ● ·

This time the council met in Grace's apartment. When Sarah had arranged the meeting, Grace told everyone that she was making food. She admonished them not to eat before the meeting.

Since Eric had left to go to the Forest Circle, Grace had lost weight for the first time in her life. She didn't do it on purpose. She had just lost her appetite.

When she looked in the mirror, she no longer looked like a short, stocky old lady. Now she was just a short, tired-looking old lady. She didn't like the look.

Although Grace had long ago resigned herself to the fact that she was now called elderly, it didn't give her an excuse for looking so drawn and thin.

Too thin, she decided. So for the meeting, she cooked up a big pot of pasta, some garlic bread, and brought some of Mandy's cookies up from the coffee shop. Mandy hadn't bothered to go home. Instead, she stayed in the coffee shop to clean up and prep for the next day.

"What is that delicious smell, Grace?" Barbara asked as she came in the door, unbuttoning her peacoat. It was Pete's. She often borrowed it. Pete would grumble about it missing when he needed it, but Barbara knew that secretly he was delighted to have her wear it.

Barbara had changed since moving to Doveland with Pete the summer before. She freely admitted that the move had been a godsend for her. Barbara had often dreamed of a life with friends that understood her, and something to do that made getting up each day worthwhile. Now she had both.

When Evan and Ava offered to help them buy the Diner, it was a miracle. A prayer come true. The offer had saved her from what she saw as a slow death. A life lived without ever becoming herself. Although it had taken them a few months to get into the swing of running a business, Evan had provided them with plenty of help. It pleased them both to know that just over three more years and they would own the Diner completely.

But, it wasn't just running the Diner that was the miracle. It was all the people who came in to eat. It was all the people in the community that supported it. And most of all, it was the circle of friends that Pete had met and then introduced to her.

Barbara had discovered something about herself. She was surprised and delighted to find out that she loved to be around people. All those years sitting at home taking care of kids, and waiting for Pete to come home from his latest trip, had made her think she was a loner.

What a joke, she thought. Thankfully, it wasn't too late to use her newly found people skills. Now that she was an official member of the council, she was determined to engage with the council to the best of her abilities and then do the same with the community, and with every moment of her life. She wasn't going to say no to new experiences. She would embrace them.

"Wow, Grace, you weren't joking about cooking tonight, were you?" Mira said, as she hung up her coat by the door. "That garlic bread smells heavenly."

"No kidding," Ava added, as she and Emily filed in behind Mandy. "Thanks for letting us know so we didn't stuff ourselves before getting here."

Grace bustled over to give a hug to Ava, and then Emily, who gingerly returned it. Grace knew that hugging would surprise Emily, but she wasn't going to stop being a hugger just because someone hadn't learned how to enjoy it yet.

Sarah was last in the door. It was unlike her. But she was also finding her way back to being part of everyday life. Grace had noticed that Sarah was also too thin. That day in the church they had both agreed that they needed to snap out of it. This meal was another step in that direction.

Because it was spaghetti, which could be messy, Grace had set the table for the seven of them instead of eating off of plates in the living room. For the next hour, they ate and talked about the small details of their lives. Sarah smiled, and touched Grace's hand as she whispered, "This was such a good idea, Grace."

They both looked at Emily sitting between Mira and Mandy. At first, Emily had acted stiff and afraid, but the laughter and food had seemed to help make her feel more at home. She and Mandy had just succumbed to a giggle fit that had them both choking on their water.

Mira looked up and caught Grace and Sarah's eye. No words were needed. Understanding passed between them. Emily was now a sister and would be treated that way.

After everyone was thoroughly stuffed, and groaning with pleasure, they moved into the living room. Grace and Sarah were hoping Emily would be more at ease in that setting.

Emily, realizing that the time had come, started to close up again. But Mandy grabbed her hand and pulled her aside before they sat down.

"I know you don't know these women well, Emily, but trust me when I tell you that they will understand whatever you need to say to them. Nothing will change the way they treat you or feel about you."

Mira stepped up beside Emily and added, "No kidding. You wouldn't believe what a mess I was a few years ago."

Emily looked at the two young women who seemed so in control of their lives and said, "Really? You aren't just making that up are you?"

"Heck no," Mira said. "Seriously, someday soon the three of us will hang out together, and we'll tell you our sad tales. Now, though, we want to be here for you."

"Okay," Emily said as she came back into the living room and sat in the middle of one of the couches. "It's time to tell you why I really came to Doveland. I don't know if it has anything to do with the women on the hill, but I'm terrified that it does. I didn't want to tell you because once I did, my fears would become real."

Emily looked at the six faces looking back at her, every one of them entirely focused on her and what she was going to tell them. All of them with kindness in their eyes.

She sighed and began, "I came here looking for my Aunt Jean. She disappeared from Doveland sometime in the early Seventies."

The implications of what Emily said hit them all at the same time.

"Okay, dear. Tell us the whole story. Let's see where it takes us," Sarah said. "No matter what happens though, Emily, we will be here to help you get through it."

She nodded. She was beginning to believe that with their help, she could do whatever needed to be done,

TWENTY-SEVEN

The boys at Evan's were in the middle of a particularly interesting discussion of the physics of the sport of curling when Sam got a text message from Mira.

"Boy's night is over for you, Sam. Come to Grace's. Now." He stared at his phone as if he wasn't sure that it was his. Mira had never written anything like that to him before.

"You look a little perplexed, Sam," Evan said, "Something up?"

"I guess you could say so. I've been summoned to Grace's place. I don't appear to have a choice."

"Maybe it's something to do with the case. I know Emily was going to be at the meeting tonight. Do you want to use the truck? That way everyone else can stay."

Sam nodded yes. He knew where the keys were kept so within five minutes he was on his way to Grace's house in Evan's truck, having texted back to Mira: "Your wish is my command."

Mira met him at the bottom of the stairs, her face flushed. "We have something that we think you are going to want to hear."

Sam was glad Mira came up the stairs with him because on entering the living room he was completely overwhelmed by the energy and focus of all the women seated there. He had been hanging out with most of them for a few years, but in a moment of clarity, he realized he had been taking them for granted all that time.

When they were in a social setting, they blended in with whatever needed to be done. Now, together, in this setting, they were women with a purpose. It felt like walking into a force field.

It was so overwhelming that a part of Sam wanted to turn around and run out of the room. Maybe if he did, he could go back to not being aware that the women were chameleons. On purpose.

But Mira had a firm grip on his arm, so he had no choice but to go forward. She steered him to an empty chair and then went back to her seat. All the women turned their full attention to Sam, scaring him even more.

Get a grip, he told himself. *I know all these women.*

However, they were so intense, and the energy in the room was so powerful he couldn't think what to say. In all the years of his work with the powerful men at the FBI, he had never felt so out of his depth. Finally, he blurted out, "What?"

Mira started laughing, and then the rest of the women joined in. Sam's discomfort was so out of character they couldn't help themselves. Finally, Sarah took pity on him and got him a glass of water. Putting her hand on his back as she handed him the water, she leaned over and whispered in his ear, "We are the same women you have known for years. Look again."

He took the water, amazed that his hand was shaking, managed a small smile for Sarah, and looked back at the room. There they were. His friends. The intensity had either never been there, or it had been withdrawn. Sam realized that if he tried to pretend that it had never been there he was a fool. He had seen something, and it scared him. At the same time gave him a feeling of hope he had not experienced before.

If these women were on the side of good, and were willing to use that hidden power, and do it together, well, everything just might turn out to be not only okay but would be beautiful.

Taking a deep breath, he said, "Okay. Thank you for asking me here, and giving me a taste of what you are all about, but that can't be why I was ordered by Mira to get here, now."

Sarah answered him, "No. It wasn't. Emily has something to tell you, and we think you will want to act on it quickly."

Emily went through her story as succinctly as she could, then she said, "We think you could test my DNA against the women buried on the hill. If one of them is my aunt, that would be a big step to finding answers, wouldn't it?"

Sam didn't answer. Instead, he took out his phone and made a call to Craig. Could Craig get his friend in Pittsburgh to run a fast DNA sample if he got it to him either tonight or the first thing in the morning?

While he waited for the answer from Craig, Sam went to speak with Emily. She was still sandwiched between Mira and Mandy on the couch, slumped back on the cushions looking exhausted. Mira got up to open a space for Sam to sit beside Emily. Mandy joined Mira in the kitchen with the rest of the women who were helping Grace clean up.

Sam tucked one of his long legs up onto the couch so he could face Emily. He took one of her hands and whispered, "Emily, I know this is hard for you. But if it is your aunt, she will be so proud of you for having the courage to search for her and to face what you might discover. I thank you for coming forward and sharing your story."

Emily lifted her light blue eyes and stared at Sam for a long moment before saying, "No. I think I am the one who should be saying thank you. Looking for my aunt has brought me all this. So, no matter what you find, I am already better off than I was before."

They smiled at each other. Sam's phone rang. "Yes," Craig said. "If we get it to him tonight, he can run it before the office opens tomorrow."

"So, I need to go now?" Sam asked.

"Yep. And I am going with you. We can stay over and wait for the results. I am taking everyone home. Meet me back here, in an hour?"

Not having a proper DNA kit with him, Sam took samples of Emily's hair and had her spit into a small glass jar. He hugged everyone and said, "Thank you," saving his longest hug for Mira, whispering in her ear that he loved her.

Just before going out the door, he paused and looked back into the room. They all still looked like his friends, the intensity gone.

Maybe I imagined it, he thought. Halfway down the stairs, he thought he heard laughter as he felt a rush of energy on his back. *Nope. I didn't,* he decided. *It was real.*

Twenty-Eight

Hank spent Saturday morning getting boxes out of Melvin's attic. It wasn't easy. The stairs to the attic was a ladder that pulled down out of the ceiling in the upstairs hallway. Hank had to repair the ladder before he was willing to go up it. Once he got up the ladder, he discovered that the light bulbs didn't work. After he replaced them, he wished he hadn't done it because the new light bulbs revealed layers of dust and a jungle of spider webs. Within minutes, Hank was sneezing and coughing.

Hannah and Melvin had offered to help, but Hank told them absolutely not. Only one person needed to be this filthy and uncomfortable. Besides, Ava would not be happy if he brought Hannah back covered with dirt.

Because it was impossible to discern what was in each box, they decided to take everything out of the attic and bring it downstairs. Melvin said it was time to put his affairs in order anyway, and he didn't want Hank having to do it after he died. Neither Hank nor Hannah was happy when Melvin talked about his death, but they knew he was right. It was something that had to be done sometime, and it would be easier with the three of them. Besides, they wanted to find the picture that Sally took.

At first, they thought they would bring the boxes out of the attic as they were, but when Hank picked them up, they started to fall apart. Hannah came up with the idea of putting everything in big black plastic bags and handing them down that way. It turned out to be a brilliant suggestion, and once they got into the rhythm, it moved fairly quickly.

Hank would drop the box with all its contents into the bag, step down the ladder part way and lower the bag to the floor, then head back up to get another box in a bag. Once the bag was on the floor, either Melvin or Hannah dragged it down the stairs into the living room. The bags were sturdy, so they weren't worried about tearing them as they pulled them. They had to do it that way. Neither one of them could pick up the bags.

A few hours into the project, Hannah came up the ladder and stuck her head into the attic and told Hank that she didn't think Melvin should do any more dragging or going up and down the stairs. She hadn't wanted to say anything in front of him to embarrass him, so could Hank give Melvin something else to do?

The next time Melvin came up the stairs, Hank asked him to make lunch. They would take a break and then go back to it. During lunch, they came up with a new plan. Hank would continue to clean the attic and Hannah and Melvin would start going through the bags that were already down. Once the attic was empty of boxes, they would take the whole mess over to Hannah's house where more people could help go through the bags with them. Otherwise, it would take forever.

Hank checked with Ava. She said it sounded like a great idea. She would have her friends come over the next day for a bag party. For reasons Hank couldn't understand, the words "bag party" made Ava start laughing. She was still laughing when she hung up the phone.

Shaking his head in confusion over women and their sense of humor, he confirmed the arrangements with Hannah and Melvin, and they went back to work.

By mid-afternoon, Hank had finished with the attic, and Melvin's entire living room was wall to wall black plastic bags. Hannah and Melvin had managed to look through only a few of them. Now they had two piles. A pile of trash, and a much smaller collection of things Melvin wanted to save.

It would have gone quicker, but Melvin kept finding things he wanted to tell Hannah about, and she was wise enough to let him. Besides, she loved his stories and learning about his life. While he talked, she had an idea and asked him if she could use her phone to record him. Melvin barely looked up from the pile of papers he had on his lap and mumbled, "Of course."

When Hank came down from the attic for the last time, Hannah told him her plan. She had asked her mom if Melvin could stay in the bunkhouse for a few days so that he could help with the search. Although the project had started out as a search for the pictures his wife took in the Seventies, it had turned into something more. Melvin was reliving his past, and Hannah thought it would be wonderful to collect his stories.

Hank told Hannah it was a fantastic idea. Melvin liked the idea, too. He packed a tattered suitcase with some clothes while Hank filled the back of the truck with black bags. What he couldn't get in, Hank said he would come back for later.

On the way home, they stopped at an office supply store and got see-through plastic bins for the papers and items that Melvin wanted to keep, and another big box of trash bags. Melvin burned his trash behind his house, but Doveland had stopped the practice so they would need lots of bags. The old-timers still snuck in a fire once in a while, but Hannah knew that Evan would not agree to breaking the town's rules.

By the time they got back to Doveland, it was late afternoon. When Ava saw how dirty the three of them were, she sent them off to the showers before they could sit down for dinner.

While the three of them cleaned up, Evan started moving the bags and the plastic bins into one of the spare bedrooms in the house. They would bring them out into the living room as they worked on them.

During dinner, Hannah told Melvin she wanted to continue to record some of his stories, so he wasn't going to be able to go through the bags unless someone else was there with him, preferably her. But Hannah understood the need to find the pictures. So, while she was in school, would he make sure someone else was working with him to do the recording?

Melvin reached across the table to hold Hannah's hand. "You and your family have brought me more happiness than I thought possible," he said. "The day your past-dad, Jay, walked into my yard my life changed. I have no idea why you want to hear an old man's stories, but I'll love telling them."

After dinner, Ava showed Melvin the little kitchen in the bunkhouse and told him he could stay as long as he wanted to. Then she hugged him and told him to get some sleep. They had a big job to start in the morning. Those black bags weren't going to sort themselves.

TWENTY-NINE

"I thought Sam and Craig would be back yesterday," Grace said. Hannah and the entire women's council were sitting on the floor in Ava's living room going through the bags with Melvin. Melvin decided that being the focus of seven beautiful women was the best thing ever. He hoped that Sally would forgive him for loving their attention so much.

They had made some progress. Sarah had set up a system. All the plastic bins were labeled using blue painter's tape and a sharpie. That way they could easily peel and stick until they had it right. There were boxes with just pictures in them filed by the year, and then there were boxes of things Melvin wanted to keep.

There was a pile of things Melvin wanted to go to the Salvation Army and another pile of bags of trash. The women sorted as they worked. They only added items to the trash pile after they had Melvin's approval. Once the original bags were empty, and everything was sorted using Sarah's system, they could go through each plastic bin again if Melvin wanted to double check what he was keeping.

As Melvin pulled out something that was important to him, they took turns asking him what it was, and either recording what he said or writing it in a journal. He couldn't understand why they were making a fuss about his stories, but Hannah insisted on it, and he was going to do what she asked, no matter what it was.

As Ava grabbed another bag, she answered Grace's question. "They called yesterday and said they were staying in town for a few days. The DNA wasn't ready. So, they decided to check in on the research being done on Grant's past."

"Why Grant's past? He's dead. What more do they need to know?" Mira asked. "Just thinking about him gives me the creeps."

"I know. Me too. But we all need to know who else Grant had been working with, and what he was doing. Sam says that the FBI has no idea where he initially began. Did Grant train with someone, or did he just become who he was on his own? Grant kept very few written records. He must have stored most of the information in his head.

"Anyway, as they find a name or a place they start tracking how it is connected to Grant. I'm terrified that they are going to find more people like Grant and Lenny and then we will be afraid all over again," Ava said.

"But, dear," Grace said, as she gently touched Ava's hand, "Not knowing about evil doesn't keep us safe."

"No, it doesn't, even though it feels like it," Sarah added. "It's essential that we look for and remove evil wherever it is hiding. Whether it is inside ourselves, our communities, or the world. Because when we don't do this, evil grows bolder. It claims more authority, and when we don't challenge its authority, it gets more and more sure of itself.

"We have to remember that it doesn't have any authority at all. Although it tries to convince us that it does."

"I like that word you used the other day, Sarah," Grace said. "What was it, again?"

"Exousia. The power to act. Spiritual authority. That's the only real authority and power."

The women all stopped what they were doing, and without planning to, nodded in unison, as one.

Melvin looked around the room. "Wow. You women are something else!"

"Tell me about it," Hannah said, and the room erupted with laughter.

Sarah smiled to herself. If they were able to keep laughing, they would always be safe. She and Leif had talked long into the night after the council meeting on Friday. They both agreed that whoever buried the bodies on the hill was still around. And now that people were looking for answers, that person was going to do whatever they could to stop them from finding them.

Sarah doubted it would be visible evil. Otherwise, they would have given themselves away years before. That made them even more dangerous.

Grace looked over at Sarah, and they smiled at each other, both of them understanding that they could no longer stay in grief. They needed to guard and protect.

Hank took in the smell of breakfast at the Diner. He hated to admit it, but being around all those women sometimes was just too much for him. Give him coffee and a plate of eggs at the counter of a good old-fashioned diner anytime. Especially one with friends, he thought as Pete slid onto a stool beside him.

· · · · ● · ● · · ·

"Man, it's good to see you, Pete," Hank said.

"You, too! You look a little worn out, old friend. The women keeping you busy?"

"Been keeping us both busy," Hank said, gesturing at Evan as he came in the door.

"Wow. This feels good," Evan said, as he took the stool on the other side of Pete. "Just guys. Having breakfast. I miss it."

"And you wouldn't trade any of what you have for this," Pete added.

"True," Evan said, "But it's nice to have a timeout. So now that we have established that it's good to have a guy's breakfast together, do you want to sit here and eat, or talk, too?"

"Eat," Hank said.

"Talk," Pete added.

"Yeah, both," Hank said after thinking about it. "The hill thing is getting to me. Not just the discovery, but what it means. And I know this is probably me being paranoid, but I keep thinking that Grant had something to do with this."

"How could that be?" Pete asked. "He wasn't around here in the Seventies, was he? And even if he was, are those the kind of murders that he did?"

"Well, that's the thing. We don't know where Grant was in the Seventies. But, you're right about the murders. We still don't know if they were murdered since there is no evidence of how they died. If it was Grant, though, he wouldn't have been so subtle. There would be some kind of trauma to the bones somewhere. He liked the feeling of violence. That leaves a mark.

"And that's what I mean about me being paranoid. There is absolutely nothing that would account for Grant having anything to do with those bodies."

Evan looked up from toying with his food. "You know, Hank, I think you might be right. There is evidence that Grant knew this area at least thirty-five years ago."

All three men looked at each other as they realized what Evan said was true.

"The fire," Hank said.

"The fire," Evan nodded.

"Grant had you set fire to that farmhouse. I know he told you to burn down the wrong farmhouse to make you feel guilty so that he could control you, but doesn't that mean he had contacts here somehow? Otherwise, why here? Why that farmhouse? Was there another fire or murder here at that same time? Not one he had you do, but perhaps he did, or had someone else do for him?"

"It makes sense," Hank said. "Terrible sense."

"How will we find out?" Evan asked. "All the town records were destroyed in that flood."

Pete chewed his lip as he thought about what he was going to say. "Okay, I don't think I'm betraying anyone because I know Emily has told the council about her aunt. Did she mention that she thought there were more Doveland town records in the county records housed in Pittsburgh? Perhaps she would know where to look."

Hank took out his phone and called Ava and asked for Emily. A few minutes later, he hung up and said, "Emily said she could go with me tomorrow. Either of you want to go, too? Perhaps we can meet up with Sam and Craig while we're there."

"I'm in," they both said.

Hank wasn't sure if he felt better or worse. But he knew that knowledge was always a good thing, even if it was painful and terrifying at first. Hank hoped they didn't find anything that tied Grant back to the bodies on the hill, but at the same time, Hank hoped they did.

It would at least answer why he had started to have nightmares again. Maybe one day they would be over. However, he wasn't counting on it. Hank figured it was something he would have to live with for the rest of his life. There are worse things, he thought. *Like being alone and afraid.* He looked at his friends sitting with him and knew that no matter what, although he might be afraid, he would never be alone again.

And as Johnny came in the door to help Alex with breakfast, Hank added to himself, *and I will do whatever I can to make sure other kids don't end up afraid and alone, either.*

THIRTY

The next morning, Ava hugged Hannah as she went off to school and kissed Evan as he and Melvin headed out to pick up Hank, Pete, and Emily to go to Pittsburgh. Melvin wanted in on the adventure, and they figured more people to look up information was a good thing. Besides, Melvin had been living in Concourse when the bodies were buried. Perhaps he would remember something by looking through the old newspapers.

After everyone was gone, Ava stood in the middle of her living room. Bags and boxes were everywhere. Nothing could be done with them until Melvin returned. She sighed and turned away, looking for something to do with herself.

Yesterday, the house was full. Today it was empty. Well, not empty. Ben was there too, but Ava wished there was someone to talk to about what was going on. Or about anything at all. As if reading her mind, Sarah popped into the kitchen, unannounced.

"Sarah, you scared me. You haven't done that astral projection thing in so long I almost forget you could do it."

"Well, I almost forgot, too. It was much easier when Leif was around. He basically just dragged me along. I've been practicing doing it by myself though. It looks like it finally worked."

As Ava picked up the dish towel she had dropped when Sarah arrived, Sarah added, "Sorry about that. I didn't mean to pop in without warning. I'm still not good at being graceful at this."

Ava waved her hand at Sarah's projection and said, "Maybe it was my fault you ended up here. I think I'm looking for company."

"Me too," Sarah answered. "Let's meet at the coffee shop. I could use some company, too."

"I'll be there in twenty," Ava started to say, but Sarah had already vanished. "Yep, you do need a little practice, Sarah," Ava laughed to herself.

Ava called Mary, the woman she often used as a babysitter, and asked if she could watch Ben for a few hours. Getting the okay, she grabbed Ben's baby bag with extra clothes, diapers, and food and headed into town. Mary lived on the way, so within the twenty minutes she promised herself, she was parked in front of Your Second Home.

Grace saw Ava first. "Wow. I'm glad you are here. Where's Ben?" Seeing Ava's guilty face, she added, "Oh, don't worry. I can see him another time. It's good to have you all to ourselves."

Grace went off to get Ava's favorite coffee and croissant as Ava found Sarah and Mandy already sitting at a back table. "Mira's coming too," Grace announced as she plopped herself into an empty chair.

"Already here," Mira announced, coming through the back door.

"This feels great. Just coffee and girl talk," Mira said after getting her own coffee and a cookie.

The five of them looked at each and burst out laughing. "Seriously, girl talk, Mira?" Ava said. "Do we know what girl talk is?"

"Hum," Mandy said, "I think we would talk about boys, I mean men, cooking, and shopping?"

The five of them were silent, waiting for someone to say something about those subjects and then started laughing again.

"I don't think we're good with girl talk," Mandy said. "Perhaps we could try something else. Like, what's going on with the investigation?"

All five leaned forward, ready to talk, when Valerie practically stumbled in the door. Grace was at her side within seconds, holding her hand and asking, "What's wrong, Valerie?"

"It's Harold," she whispered.

Grace led Valerie to the table. Mandy had already gotten up to get her a glass of water, which Valerie tried to pick up, but her hands were shaking too much to hold it.

Grace and Sarah pulled their chairs close to her while Mandy rubbed her back. Mira went up to Grace's apartment and got a wool shawl, which she draped over Valerie. After a few minutes, Valerie stopped shaking so hard. She took a big gulp of water and looked up with tears running down her face.

"Okay, Valerie. We are listening. What is going on? What about Harold?" Sarah asked.

With a lot of prompting and patience, the five women finally got a sense of the story Valerie was trying to tell. Valerie first told them how she had met Harold at work twenty-one years before. Valerie told them how Harold had made her feel that she was the most important person in the world to him. Valerie described the first few years of their marriage as being filled with love. When Harold suggested moving to his hometown of Doveland, she was overjoyed. She had always wanted to raise her children, and teach, in a small town.

But not long after moving to Doveland, Harold started to change. It felt like a slow leaking away of the man she married. He was replaced by a man with very little patience and a lot of anger.

At first, Harold directed his anger to the world outside of their family. They didn't like his complaining about other people and worried about his impatience with them, but the family felt safe from it. He was good with the boys. For a time.

Then Harold started picking on Valerie about her work. Valerie explained that she loved being the principal of the school, but it took up almost all her time and energy. By the time she came back from working all day and then helping Johnny and Lex with their homework, she was exhausted.

Harold became increasingly irritated. He complained that he was running their bed-and-breakfast all by himself. When she reminded him that it was his idea, and they could do something else, it only made him angrier.

"But no one knew about his anger, though," Valerie said, "Because when Harold is in public, he is so charming. He knows all the ways to make people think he is a wonderful man."

When Valerie saw the women look at each other, she added, "Oh, I thought you might have noticed something. But, really it wasn't too bad, and I thought I could live with it. Now, I don't think I can. Now, I am afraid of him. Even the kids are scared of him."

Valerie looked at her hands clutched together so hard that her knuckles were white. "Maybe they have always been afraid of him, and I just didn't notice. Maybe that's why Johnny was acting out last year."

"Did something happen that made it worse?" Sarah asked.

"Yes. It got worse the day we heard Emily was building the art center. Then, when they found the bodies on the hill, he never stopped being angry. He shakes when he is talking. Like holding in rage, or fear. I don't even see the man I married anymore. I think the Harold I knew might be gone. Lately, the kids and I have felt as if we are living with a powder keg. All of us have constantly been afraid that Harold could blow up any time.

"Today was the last straw. He got a phone call. He listened. He didn't say anything at all. Then he hung up and started throwing things and screaming. That's when I ran over here. I was hoping someone would be here and could tell me what to do. I am so glad the boys are in school!"

Finally, after telling the whole story, Valerie started sobbing.

"Would you like to go upstairs to my apartment and rest for a bit? You are safe there, and we will be here when you are ready," Grace asked. When Valerie nodded her consent, both Mandy and Grace were needed to help Valerie up the stairs because Valerie was shaking so hard.

"I can't believe she kept that all to herself," Mira said to Sarah after they were gone.

"It's the way of the world. We think no one will understand. Or if we tell someone else it makes it more real," Sarah answered.

"Perhaps we should have stepped in earlier. We were lucky. It sounds as if Harold didn't do any harm to Valerie and the boys. We need to tell Sam about this. And perhaps the local police."

"The police? Once we do that her family will be split apart. Perhaps this is something we should find out more about first?" Mandy said. "Although I agree. We need to tell Sam."

"And find out where Harold is now," Sarah added.

THIRTY-ONE

Harold knew he was in trouble. Something was terribly wrong. *I need to control myself,* he thought. After Valerie had run out of the house, Harold had panicked. What if she was going to the police? What would he tell them? He waited an hour, ready to explain that his wife had anxiety attacks. He knew they would believe him. As a teenager, he had learned the skill of saying what people wanted to hear. It had helped him in his business dealings, but it was useful everywhere. He knew how to direct people's attention and have them see what he wanted them to see. It was surprisingly easy when he was calm and in control. Which he hadn't been lately.

He was lucky Valerie loved him. But he had grown sloppy around her, letting her see the rage that often threatened to escape from his body. He had let down his guard, and his charm around his own family. It was a huge mistake. And one he better fix immediately.

When he and Valerie were first married, he thought he loved her for real. Yes, he had charmed her at first, having chosen her as the one to have his children. But it wasn't fake love. It was the best love he had, and he gave it all to her. Harold actually thought that he might have found the woman who would satisfy all his needs, and for the first time in his life, he relaxed his guard over himself.

After the first few years of a happy marriage, he decided he wanted to go home. As a boy, he loved living in Doveland. Then, right before he went away to college, things happened. Bad things. So bad, he thought he could never return. In fact, until he met Valerie, he was always in a preparation mode for running. After waiting all those years for someone to come after him, and no one did, he decided to take a wife and settle down. He felt safe.

However, he didn't escape his need for manipulating people. He got a thrill making people think and do things entirely different than they usually would. He enjoyed how many things he could get away with because of his ability to misdirect and manipulate their beliefs. He did it just for fun.

He never thought of himself as an evil person. A slightly bad one, but only by mistake. A mistake he didn't make. Mistakes other people made. Thinking about it now started heating him up again, so he stopped. He needed a diversion to calm himself down.

That woman, Tina, might be someone he could have fun manipulating and charming. He could confuse her so that she thought that she wanted him. Harold knew she didn't. He saw how nervous she was around him. Probably ruined by that bastard husband of hers, Frank Jacks.

What a dumb jerk Frank was, getting caught like that. Harold thought. He would never be that stupid. Inside, a little voice niggled at Harold telling him that he had been that stupid. He had let his anger out. It was dangerous. He needed to contain and control his temper.

Harold stood in front of the hall mirror and zipped up his jacket, studying his reflection. He also needed to be more careful with himself. Not just with his mood swings, but other things too. When had he gotten that belly? Yes, he was still ramrod straight. He was still tall and handsome, as Valerie used to say. Even though his hair had turned gray and wispy, she continued to love him. Surprising, considering how sloppy he had been with her lately.

Harold studied himself in the mirror. Something was off. His brown eyes were too intense. If he was going to visit Tina, he needed to soften them. And his face. Too severe. Relaxing the muscles around his eyes, Harold practiced smiling. Better. Breathe in. Breathe out. That was better. Harold could almost see the visible changes take place as he watched himself in the mirror.

Yes, that phone call had frightened him. No, if he were going to be truthful, at least with himself, he would have to admit that it terrified him. What would they find in Pittsburgh? His image tensed again. Not good.

Harold talked to himself. Even if they found something, it didn't mean anything to him. He had nothing to do with those girls dying. Harold was confident that although he had let himself get out of control a few times, he still knew how to project authority and trust. Do it, he commanded the image. Calm down. Be strong. Project authority and confidence. It worked. He still had it.

Smiling at himself in the mirror, Harold sucked in his stomach and promised himself he would take Dr. Joe's advice and start walking or maybe even start working out. This thing about those women would blow over, and he could move on. He was only sixty-two. So many more years to enjoy. He just had to get control of himself. He needed a little practice.

Tina would be the perfect person to practice his return to glory with. She needed a man in her life, and he intended to be that one. Yes, she had rebuffed him the other day when he tried to talk to her. But, he hadn't been himself. He had gone over to see her when he felt angry. He had been too pushy. Today, he would walk over with softness in his heart. She would fall for it. They always did.

For a brief moment, Harold wondered what happened to Valerie, but since she hadn't come back, and the police weren't at his door, he figured he was safe for now. He promised himself he would be the perfect husband again for her. Bringing attention to himself right now was not wise.

In the meantime, he would woo Tina. One last glance in the mirror assured him he had everything under control. He would walk around the block and arrive at the gas station from the back.

No point in being noticed for something as light-hearted as a little dalliance with a lovely young woman. The kids were in school. Valerie wasn't home. The timing was perfect.

· · · ● ● · ● · ● · · · ·

Tina watched with disgust as Harold opened the back door of the gas station. Because of him, she had installed cameras everywhere. Harold had scared her the last time he visited. He had tried to make her believe that she would want someone like him.

She had been taken in by Frank and his sweet talk, and later his anger had chained her to him. But now she was no longer a scared woman.

Although Harold was better at the charm and manipulation than Frank could ever dream of being, she knew the moves. There was no way she would surrender her mind and will to someone like him again.

The door creaked, and Harold paused, wondering if Tina had heard. He didn't know that she was watching him on her computer screen.

I should have locked the back door when I took the garbage out, she told herself. *I know better.* But it was too late. Harold was already at the station. She had a choice. Call the police, or deal with him herself.

She chose the latter.

Thirty-Two

While Valerie rested, the women planned. After a brief discussion, they decided that Grace would pick up Hannah, Johnny, and Lex from school. Valerie had called the school earlier in the morning and explained to her secretary that she wouldn't be in that day, she wasn't feeling well. Her secretary had assured her they would be fine. As hard as Valerie had been trying to hide it, her secretary had a good idea about what was going on in Valerie's home.

The women decided that it would make sense that Valerie would send her best friend, Grace, to pick up the kids after school. Johnny could drive, but they still weren't letting him take a car to school. Valerie said that he had to prove that he learned his lesson. It wouldn't be long, though. She was proud of Johnny. He was working with Pete and Hank, and they both had only good things to say about his work ethic.

While Grace went to pick up the kids, Ava would take Valerie to the farmhouse. She would set up Valerie and her two children in the two extra bedrooms in the house. It would feel like old times with the bedrooms and bunkhouse almost full.

The two groups in Pittsburgh called the women while they waited for Valerie to wake up. Sam, Craig, and Emily were on their way home with information that they wanted to share with everyone. Evan's group also called to let them know they too were on their way home. They had decided that instead of trying to read everything there, they made copies of all that they could find about that time in Doveland. That way everyone could go through it together.

That was the plan.

Until, once again, someone else stumbled in the door. This time, it was Tina.

· · · ● ● · ● ● · · ·

She had to admit it. Harold scared her. However, there was no way she was going to let him know it. Instead, Tina grabbed a wrench she had been using to tighten the pipe under the sink and stood in front of the cash register, holding it high, standing tall and pretending to be unafraid.

"What's this, Tina?" Harold said in a voice that felt oily and slimy to her. If Tina had been someone else, that voice might have worked. She was immune to it.

"This is me telling you to back off and leave me alone," Tina replied. "Either go away, or I will call the police."

Harold laughed. "If you were going to call the police, you would have done it already. Besides, what are you going to tell them? That I threatened you? With what?" He looked up and waved at the camera, and Tina put the wrench down. She was the one who would get in trouble if something happened. He knew the camera was there. She was safe. Or as safe as she could be with a snake.

"Look," Harold said, "I just wanted to apologize for coming on so strong last time. And I probably shouldn't have come in the back door. It just seemed like you would appreciate it not being so public that I came over to see you. I didn't mean to come on to you, anyway.

"It's just that day I wasn't doing well. Valerie and I had a little squabble, and I was feeling low. You are a beautiful woman, Tina, and I was nursing my wounds, entertaining thoughts I normally would never think," Harold paused and gave Tina a pleading look.

"I'm sure you understand. You and Frank must have had some rough times. You probably looked at other men when you and he fought.

"Anyway, I just wanted to apologize. Say I'm sorry. Perhaps I could make it up to you somehow.

"Maybe we can have coffee sometime. Just talk. I know a bit about business. Perhaps I could help with repairs, or help fix up the station. I have to do that all the time over at the Bed and Breakfast. They don't call me handy Harold for nothing."

Tina had no idea that anyone called him handy Harold, but so far, he hadn't said anything that wasn't true. When she and Frank argued she often wished for someone to talk to that would understand, and here Harold was looking for the same thing.

"Okay," she said. "Why not? If you have time now, it's not busy. Do you want coffee now? I was planning to have one myself."

Harold smiled and nodded. "That's perfect, Tina. I appreciate your help. Lately, I haven't been feeling quite myself."

Tina got Harold a coffee, the one she knew he liked. He had been making it a point to come in every morning for coffee on his way to wherever he went. Although Harold was only apologizing for being pushy the day before, he had been making eyes at her for months. She had mostly ignored him until the other day and then got scared because he reminded her of Frank.

However, this morning, he was calm. Why not have coffee with him? Tina poured his coffee from one pot, and hers from another.

"What do you mean, you haven't been feeling quite yourself?" she asked.

"Tired. More tired than usual," Harold answered and sipped his coffee. "Probably just the stress of what is happening on the hill. I hate seeing the town I love upset."

Tina listened as Harold chatted on and on about his life. She knew he loved to talk. All she had to do was nod and listen. Finishing with his coffee, he stood up to go, swayed, moaned, grabbed the table and collapsed onto the floor.

"Harold," Tina screamed. "Harold, what's wrong?"

When he didn't move, she knew she had to get help. Everyone had told her to learn CPR, but she never had. She could call someone or run across the town square to the coffee shop. There was always someone there. It would be faster.

Not wasting her breath screaming, she ran as fast as she could and stumbling in the door, yelled, "Call the doctor!"

The women looked at each other as they rushed to help Tina. Craig was out of town. They would have to call Dr. Joe. Grace dialed while Mandy and Mira raced to the gas station with Tina, and Sarah headed upstairs to get Valerie.

Sarah couldn't help thinking that something more significant than just Valerie and Harold having a fight was going on. She wished Leif were there to help her figure it out.

When she reached Valerie, Leif was there waiting for her. Although he couldn't hug her, he could make her feel warm and protected. Eric was there too.

"It's more than it looks like, isn't it?" Sarah asked the two of them. "Yes," Leif answered, "it is."

THIRTY-THREE

It was a somber group that sat around the Anders' living room that night. Stacked in the corner were the bags and boxes from Melvin's attic. Nobody felt like dealing with them. The files that Evan's group brought back were waiting on the dining room table, unopened.

Harold was in the hospital. Tina, Valerie, and Craig were with him. Mandy and Mira had taken Tina and Valerie there before coming back to the Anders'. Grace had picked up Tina's children, Lynn and Manny, along with Valerie's, and brought them all to the house.

While the grown-ups sat quietly in the living room, all the children were with Hannah in the family room watching TV. That was not something they normally allowed Hannah to do, but everyone knew the children needed a distraction.

Ava had provided them with popcorn and drinks, and they seemed happy enough to sit watching a movie Ava had chosen for them. Ava knew her daughter well enough to know that she only agreed to the TV to help the other kids. Hannah was already tuned in to what was going on and would have preferred to be with the grownups.

Then there was Sam's revelation. One that everyone had suspected, but finding out it was true had reduced Emily to a puddle of tears. She had cried the whole way home from Pittsburgh. Now she was sitting beside Hank, who had a protective arm around her shoulder. Everyone knew that Hank had adopted Emily as one of his own, and that knowledge was the one bright spot in the room.

"I wanted to know, didn't I?" Emily said. "I came here looking for my Aunt Jean. However, I think I was secretly hoping that she was still here. Maybe she changed her name. Or found love and moved away. But it makes more sense that none of that happened. She would never have abandoned my mother."

A fresh set of tears rolled down her cheeks, and she accepted a Kleenex from Mira, who was sitting across from her beside Sam.

"I know I look weak and sad. However, inside I am furious. What can I do to help find out what happened to her? And the other three women? Now that we know one of the bodies is Aunt Jean it should be easier to find out who the others are, won't it?"

Sam nodded. "I think so. If we can find a picture of your aunt in these bags with the other women, it will go a long way to helping to find them. So, searching the bags and the files are a priority."

"They are that, Sam," Sarah said. "However, I think we need to know more about what happened with Harold. Do you think they are connected?"

"I don't see how," Sam said, but seeing her face, he added, "And yet, I think you are going to tell me that they are."

"Well, for one thing, we know that Harold got increasingly agitated when he found out that Joe had sold the land, and that Emily was building on it. Why would that be unless he knew those bodies were there?

"Was Harold afraid they would be discovered? Since that night, Valerie said he has become more and more upset. Valerie said Harold received a phone call this morning that made him so mad she was terrified. Would it be possible to find out where the call came from?"

"It makes sense that he might know who did this. After all, he is from Doveland isn't he? He would have been a young man when this all happened," Mandy added. "But it's a leap to think that he did it. Isn't it?"

"Yes, but perhaps not that big of a leap to make. You two have made a strong point," Sam said. "Yes, I can get someone looking for where the call came from. I'll let the police know what you told me. I am sure they will want to question Harold as soon as he can talk."

Evan's phone rang and everyone turned to see who was calling. "Okay, Craig, I'll put you on speaker."

"Sam and I are planning to come to the hospital, Craig," Evan said. "It turns out Harold might have some information about the women from the hill."

"Not going to happen, buddy," Craig said. "He's going to need to recover first. He can barely breathe, let alone speak."

"What's wrong with him?" everyone said at once.

"Don't know. No one knows. Dr. Joe was here until a few minutes ago, and he is stumped too. Harold didn't have a heart attack, which is what we first thought. Joe suggested that it could be a poison of some kind, but that will take time to discover."

"Right now, a few police officers are getting statements from Tina and Valerie. Once they are done, I will take Tina home and bring Valerie back to the house in an hour or so."

"Wait," Grace spoke up. "Can you put Tina on the phone for me?"

Grace took Evan's phone, turned off the speaker, and waited until she heard Tina's tentative voice.

"Dear," she said, "you've had quite a shock today. Why not let Craig bring you to my house, and you can stay over with me tonight?"

Looking at Ava, who nodded knowing what Grace would say next, "Ava says the kids can stay here for the night and go to school in the morning with Hannah."

Grace listened and then said, "I'm not kidding, Tina. It won't be a bother at all. I could use the company."

When Grace hung up, everyone started laughing. "What?" she said, bewildered at the reaction.

Sarah stood and hugged her. We're laughing because it is lovely to see you being yourself again, Grace.

"An old busy-body?"

"Yes. And we love you for it!"

· · · · ● · ● · ● · ● · · ·

Joe sat alone at his desk, his favorite drink in his hand. Scotch, just like his father. They both chose scotch in times of stress. However, today sipping it wasn't helping at all. Harold's illness had shaken him to his core. It surprised him. He didn't know he would take it so hard. Perhaps it was the many memories of Harold as a young boy. Harold's father had died when Harold was a toddler, and his mother had no idea how to raise a son on her own. So Joe watched over him. It was easy to do. After all, he was their family doctor.

He watched Harold grow from a timid child into one who knew how to get what he needed using his charm and ability to discern what other people wanted. By the time Harold entered his teens, he had started coming to Joe for more than his health needs. Harold admired Joe. He wanted to learn what he knew. It was a beautiful time for them both. Harold was the perfect pupil. He soaked up everything Joe taught him.

And then something happened. Something neither one of them saw coming. As a result, Harold decided to go away to school rather than staying close by. Joe knew it was for the best, but that didn't change the pain he felt when Harold left. They kept in touch for a while, but eventually all that they had meant to each other faded away.

Joe figured that Harold felt that he had outgrown him. He heard that Harold had become a successful businessman. Then, almost twenty-five years later, Harold showed up in Doveland with a wife and a child.

Once again, Joe was part of Harold's life, but it was as if they had never been friends. Joe was simply the doctor for Harold's family. He even delivered their second child, Lex. Joe had hoped that he and Harold would connect again, but something about Harold had changed. He had a wall up around him that hid the essential parts of himself. He was even more charming, but Joe could tell it was only on the surface. Underneath, Harold was boiling with anger.

Joe wasn't surprised that Harold collapsed. He was a heart attack waiting to happen. That's what everyone had thought at first, but it wasn't a heart attack. Although they didn't know what was wrong, Joe was sure they would find it was a poison of some kind.

Perhaps Valerie or Tina would be blamed for it. The police would eventually find out what Harold had been doing with those two women. What would happen then? Maybe they would call on Joe to help with the investigation into what happened. He was looking forward to it.

Joe was reasonably sure that Harold would not survive this attack. Tomorrow he would revisit Harold. Joe wanted to be there for him. He was there at the beginning; he would be there at the end.

Thirty-Four

Ava had asked everyone if they would help finish the bags on Tuesday. She was pushing the process for two reasons. Of course, they needed the picture for the investigation. But they also needed to finish because Melvin had told her that he wanted to go home. He hadn't realized how much he missed his farmhouse until he had spent these few days away from it.

Melvin was very grateful for everything that people were doing for him, but the solitude of the country was calling him. Hank understood completely. As much as he loved Ava and her family and all her friends, he too was a loner like Melvin, and Ava's house was filled with people. It was too much.

So he begged off from helping with the bags explaining that he needed to be out with his crew on the hill. At this rate, they wouldn't get any structures done at all by summer. Besides, a construction crew without a foreman was dangerous. He had put his best man in charge, but it wasn't the same thing. Hank needed to get back to building things where things were easier to understand.

Well, he thought, *on the other hand, it was the construction that started this whole thing.* But Emily had a beautiful idea in mind, and he was anxious to help her see it come to fruition.

Then Tom said that he had to go out of town again to take care of some business with his group. He shared with Ava that every time he left town, he wondered if this was what he wanted to be doing with his life. His friends were doing something important too just by staying in Doveland. Besides he missed Mandy. He made her promise to keep him up to date with what they discovered. Ava hugged him and told him that she was sure he would choose to do the right thing.

The crew at Ava's became even smaller when Craig said he couldn't help. He had to take care of patients. He had been neglecting his practice and needed to catch up.

Sam couldn't help either. He needed to stay at the hospital in case Harold woke up. He didn't want the police asking Harold questions without him being there.

Mandy wanted to help out with the bags, so Grace said she would run the coffee shop.

Although Emily wanted to be out on the hill with the construction crew, she knew she had to help with the bags because she might recognize her aunt when no one else would. So she canceled her classes for another day and gave up the idea that she could spend time with the trees on the hill watching her dream be built, and prepared herself for digging through the bags at Ava's.

Knowing that Grace would be at the coffee shop, Emily decided to stop at Your Second Home on her way to Ava's. She wanted to bring coffee and pastries to share with everyone as they worked. Emily had another reason for stopping in, though. She wanted to thank Grace for all her help.

When Emily walked into the coffee shop, she found Tina sitting at a little table in front of the window staring at the gas station.

Emily sat down for a minute to talk with her, but instead, the two of them just stared out the window.

After a few minutes, Tina said, "I feel as if I have lost something important."

"Is it something you can describe?" Emily asked.

"Me. I think it's me that I have lost. I married Frank. Lost myself there. Then I came to Doveland to run the gas station since it was all that he left for me. But why? This isn't me either. I didn't grow up wanting to run a gas station."

"What did you grow up wanting, Tina?"

"And that's the thing. I don't remember. But I know it wasn't that," Tina said, pointing across the street.

"Or even this. The town. Did I want to live in a small town? I don't think so. I like people. Lots of people. Things to do. Places to see by just walking out my door.

"Here I see the town square, some houses, and pretty countryside. Nice. But I don't think it's me."

Emily put her hand on Tina's arm. "If it's not you, give it back. Or give it away. What makes up Doveland is what I have been looking for, but I understand the pull of what you are describing."

Emily paused in thought and then asked, "Can you sell the station?"

Tina jerked back in surprise. "I don't know. How come I didn't think of that? Do you think I could?"

Emily smiled at her. "Yes, I think you could. And I think we could find someone to help you do that. Plus, the women's group is skilled at helping people find what they really want to do. Why don't we ask them?"

This time, Tina's eyes filled with tears. "They would help me?"

Emily felt like crying, too. She had the same reaction when Sarah and her council said they would help her. "Yes. I know they would."

Grace had come to stand beside the table while they were talking. Neither of them had seen her, so they were both startled when she said, "Yes, Tina, dear. It would be an honor to help you."

Tina looked at Grace and Emily and said, "Well, then. I better get my butt in gear and get over there and get that station looking like a place someone would want to buy. Maybe I could hire Hank to help me?"

"Great idea," Grace and Emily said together. Tina hugged Grace and thanked her for the restful evening at her house, and then headed across the town square with a lightness to her step neither of them had seen in her before.

"She's going to need more help than she thinks," Grace said.

"What do you mean?" Emily asked.

"Sam called earlier. The police have decided that Harold was poisoned and they are going to be looking closer at Valerie and Tina. Valerie, of course, because they were having problems and she had access to many ways to accomplish it. Tina because Harold was bothering her, and she served him drinks every day."

"What? Neither one of them could have done such a thing. Could they?" Emily added, thinking that she was much too naive of the ways of the world. Perhaps she had missed something.

"No. I don't think either of them could or would," Grace answered. "And yet. Poison. They look at women first. If not them, then who?"

• • • • ● • ◉ • ● • •

Emily arrived at Ava's house feeling as if her skin was being pricked by hundreds of tiny pins. First, there were the bodies on the hill, her hill. And now, they think that either Valerie or Tina might have hurt Harold. No, she wasn't buying it. Maybe she was young and naive, but she thought she could feel the hearts of those two women. They weren't killers.

After sharing what she learned at Grace's to the small group of people gathered in Ava's living room, she added, "And, I think Harold's illness is tied up with the bodies on the hill."

"I agree," Mandy said. "So let's dig into these bags and see what we can find. It would be best if we could get done with them before the kids come home from school."

"Amen to that," Mira said. "Ava, how can you handle all those kids at once anyway? Makes me kinda glad I don't have any."

"Well, first, Lynn and Manny will be going home to their mom's. Only Lex will be here because Johnny is helping at the Diner after school. So just three kids. Not so many at all. Easy."

Ben took that moment to start running through the sea of bags grabbing papers and throwing them about the room.

"Okay, I take it back. Not all that easy. But I love it anyway."

"Sam is glad he doesn't have kids either?" Ava asked.

"I think so," Mira answered. "So far he seems okay not having any. But then he hasn't asked me to marry him either."

All the women and even Evan and Melvin started laughing.

"Geez, what's so funny?" Mira demanded.

Everyone just kept laughing, so Mira dismissed them all with a wave of her hand and started on the nearest bag.

"Fine, then," she said, but her red cheeks gave her away. She knew why they laughed. Of course, they would marry. She loved Sam. He loved her. Nothing could get in the way of that.

"Okay, Aunt Jean," Emily said as she opened the closest bag to her. "I know you are in these bags somewhere. Let's find your picture."

Evan wasn't going through bags. He was going through the files they had brought home from Pittsburgh the day before. He was confident that between the bags and the files, they would find something that would help them discover what happened to the women on the hill.

He felt someone looking at him and glanced up to see Eric and Leif winking at him from the corner of the room. No one else had noticed them, not even Sarah. They were gone in the blink of an eye, but he knew what they were telling him. He was right. There were answers here, and he intended to find them.

THIRTY-FIVE

They gathered around the table, bumping each other trying to look over Evan's shoulder at what he was holding. Huffing in frustration, Evan closed the file with a bang. "Sit. You're making me crazy," he said. "I promise to share all of this with you. But we're waiting for Sam and Hank. I want to talk about this together."

Ava, Mandy, Mira, Sarah, and Emily reluctantly obeyed. They were the only ones paying attention. Melvin was snoozing on the couch, Ben was napping in his room, and Hannah and Lex had not returned from school. Valerie was at the hospital with Craig, watching over Harold.

Evan had said, "Wow," about fifteen minutes before and the women had stopped working to find out what he had found. They had been annoying him with questions ever since.

They were growing even more impatient and were ready to do whatever it took to get Evan to talk when they heard the beep of cars coming up the driveway. Evan sighed, thinking it was the perfect example of being saved by the bell. Being the lone man trying to hold back determined women was not a comfortable place to be.

"Okay," Hank said, coming in the door, almost forgetting to take off his muddy boots until he saw Ava frowning at him. Sam took his shoes off too. They weren't dirty, but everyone knew the rule at Ava's was to remove shoes before coming into the house. She provided a closet where everyone could hang their coats and a shoe rack that was packed with family and guest shoes. Wearing good socks was something to remember if there was a possibility of going to Ava's.

Sam saw Mira waiting for him at the table and almost had to put a hand out to steady himself. She still did that to him. He was sure she would his entire life. No shoes was a rule in her house too. Now that he thought about it, it was a rule in all the women's homes.

It both pleased and worried him to realize that he was a man trained to be in charge and he really wasn't. Apparently, none of these men were either. They all had stocking feet.

Hank tried again, "Okay, what's so all-fired important that we both had to leave what we were doing?"

"Sit down, Hank. And you too, Sam. Evan is about to tell us. There's coffee in the kitchen if you want it, and since we've been waiting for you already, a minute longer won't make any difference," Ava said.

Hank sheepishly filled his coffee cup and got one for Sam before finding a seat at the table. The women had already scooted down so Sam could sit beside Mira. That meant Hank found himself beside Evan at the head of the table.

What Emily hadn't told anyone yet was at the same time Evan had said, "Wow," she had pulled out a picture that looked like her Aunt Jean with three other women. She was waiting to hear what Evan had to say first. Then she would share her news.

• • • • • • • •

Both Craig and Valerie got up when Dr. Joe came into the room, to shake his hand and thank him for coming. Craig had finished with his patients for the day and had arrived an hour before to keep Valerie company. Harold had shown some signs of recovering, and they both wanted to be in the room if he woke up.

Craig and Valerie had barely spoken during the hour. Neither knew what to say. Craig felt as if he should comfort Valerie, but he had no words of encouragement other than the standard statement that sometimes patients naturally recovered with no physical explanation. He didn't see any reason this couldn't happen in this case.

Valerie smiled a wan smile at him when he said that. She knew it didn't mean much. For the past day, as she sat with Harold holding his hand, Valerie had been contemplating what married life had been like with him. She hadn't fully admitted to anyone how difficult it had been at times. But then something would happen, and he would be sweet and loving again, only to turn back into someone else for no reason that she could see.

She hated seeing him lying there, and at the same time she felt the most peaceful she had in many years. Craig sitting in the room with her felt strangely comfortable. Neither of them had words to say. But it didn't feel as if they needed to fill the gaps.

Valerie was grateful that Dr. Joe was taking such a keen interest in Harold's case. He had stopped by the night before and stayed with Harold while she went home to shower and change clothes.

The house had been peaceful too. No children. They were safe at Ava's. And there was no Harold to be displeased with her. Guilt washed over her for feeling that way, and as if he sensed her mood change, Craig reached over and squeezed her hand. Once again, no words had been exchanged, but she felt as if she had been told to let that guilt go.

So when Dr. Joe walked into the room, she was once again happy to see him visit Harold. Valerie knew that at one time in his life

Harold had been mentored by Dr. Joe. He never talked about it, she just heard it through the small town grapevine. She had tried to ask Harold why they weren't friends anymore, and he said that they were.

Valerie supposed that was true. After all, Harold had not resisted when she had chosen Joe as their doctor rather than going to the clinic in Concourse. When Dr. Joe delivered Lex, he was kind and gentle. He always had the right words to say to make her feel better.

She thought that it was lovely that Dr. Joe was still there for her and Harold. She knew Dr. Joe would say the right things to her again, and do whatever he could to help Harold.

"So let's see what's going on," Joe said, checking Harold's chart at the foot of the bed. He wasn't Harold's official physician, but everyone at the hospital knew him and listened to what he had to say.

"It looks as if he is stable. Why don't the two of you get something to eat, and I will watch over him. I'll text you if there are any changes."

"I could eat. I'm sure you could too, Valerie. Besides, getting up and moving will feel good."

"You promise to let us know?" Valerie asked, as they started out the door.

"Absolutely," Joe answered.

He waited for a beat to make sure that Valerie and Craig were gone. Then Joe sat down in the chair vacated by Valerie and leaned over to the bed, taking Harold's hand. "Okay, my old friend. Let's have another chat."

THIRTY-SIX

Melvin breathed a sigh of relief. He was home. Hank had dropped him off and then headed back to Emily's hill. He said he would stay and keep him company, but Melvin shooed him away. He needed some time to himself.

The first thing he wanted to do was work in the vegetable garden. It was warm enough to work the ground and get it ready for planting. On the way upstairs to change his clothes, Melvin stopped in his living room. Last Friday it had been filled with black plastic bags, and now there was a small, neat pile of see-through file boxes, each one labeled with what they contained. He imagined he would be spending some tearful and happy times going through the boxes on his own and remembering the past.

"Thank you, Sally, for taking pictures of those girls," he whispered. "Even when you're not here, you are saving the day." Melvin glanced at his watch and saw that he had a few hours until the lawyer man came out to see him. Melvin hadn't told anyone about this appointment. He had hinted at what he was going to do, but he wanted to have it down in writing and filed away before telling Hank. Melvin didn't plan to tell his son. Instead, he would write a letter and have it included in the file the lawyer kept. No point in having angry words with him now. Melvin wanted to have pleasant, if only surface, talks with his son. That hadn't happened lately, but it was possible.

After listening to what Evan had found in the files, Melvin realized that he might know more than he had thought about what had happened. It was a long time ago, but pieces of the puzzle were starting to come together. However, when he tried to remember, it would slip away from him. He was hoping that now that he was home more pieces would come together for him. Once his memories were clearer, he was going to tell someone. But not before. If what he was remembering was right, it would be dangerous to tell the wrong person.

Melvin also realized that even if he told the right person, he would probably still be in danger. That's why he was going to be prepared. Just in case.

As Melvin headed upstairs to change his clothes, he whistled a song he and Sally used to sing together. He was sure he heard her whistling along with him. The edges of this world and the next were beginning to blur for him. He couldn't wait too long to remember. No matter what way he looked at it, there was only so much time left.

• • • • ● ● ● ● • •

It's hard leaving Melvin alone, Hank thought to himself as he drove down a back road to Emily's hill. He had discovered the back way a few weeks before. It meant he didn't have to go all the way to Doveland and then out to the hill. Instead, the road jutted to the north and came out on the road that led out of Doveland a mile from Emily's hill.

It was a dirt road full of bumps, but Hank loved knowing alternative ways to get places. Old habits of being invisible still were part of his being.

Hank promised Melvin he would be back in time for a late dinner. In fact, he told him that he would bring dinner with him. Maybe fried chicken from the Diner. Pete and Alex had finally come up with a recipe that they loved, and it had become an instant hit.

Hank understood Melvin's desire to be alone. He had the same wish for himself. Even though they both lived in Melvin's house, they never got in each other's way. When they wanted company or conversation, they knew where to meet. They would look for each other first at the kitchen table, or if it was a nice day, they would check the porch swing. Otherwise, they moved in harmony, but not in the same place. It was a talent that Hank appreciated in Melvin.

It only took twenty minutes to get to Emily's hill using the shortcut. A rough ride, but worth it to Hank. The bulldozer drivers were in the process of clearing the land for the dance barn. After that, the concrete for the foundation would be poured. While it cured, the bulldozers would go back to working on the driveway and parking space.

Then the framing crew would come in to the frame the barn. Even though Hank had seen it done hundreds of times, he always admired how a skilled framing crew could frame an entire building in just a few days.

While the crews were at work in the barn, Hank would have the bulldozers clear the place for the house and the dance deck. Emily wasn't counting on them being done in time for this summer session, but at least she could see where they were going to be.

However, Hank thought it might be possible to get the deck finished. He hadn't told Emily yet. If he did manage to get the deck done, it would be better to be a surprise rather than a disappointment if he couldn't. After finding out for sure that her aunt was one of the bodies buried on her hill, Emily didn't need any more disappointments in her life at the moment.

Evan's discovery and Melvin's picture with Emily's aunt and three other women had set in motion new searches. Sam was taking the picture to his friends at the FBI where it would be distributed through their network to see if anyone recognized the faces in the photo. Even though it had been forty-five years, everyone held out hope that they would find out who they were.

If you have lost someone, you would never stop looking, and you would recognize them no matter how old the picture was. That's what Emily assured them. After all, she hadn't even met her aunt, and yet she knew the face from the photographs her mom had shown her.

The information that Evan had discovered in the files meant a different kind of search. What worried Hank was the question that if the killer was still alive, would he panic once the search became public? What would he, or she do? Would they run, or would they kill again?

Hank shook off those thoughts and turned to what was right in front of him. They had to wait for those answers to those two puzzles. In the meantime, he would focus on what he could control. He would build Emily's dream.

THIRTY-SEVEN

He wasn't getting any better, and no one knew why. There were moments when Valerie thought that Harold was recovering. He would start mumbling, and her heart would race as she leaned over to hear what he said. But the mumbling would stop, and he would fade back into a sleep so still, it was as if he was in a coma.

It had been two days since he had collapsed, and nothing had changed. Craig had stayed again with her most of the last night, but left early in the morning to get some sleep before seeing his own patients. He promised to check in with her during the day.

Valerie expected Dr. Joe to stop by at any moment. She thought it was so kind of him to keep checking in. One time, Valerie had returned from getting coffee and heard Dr. Joe whispering something to Harold. Valerie smiled at that. She did the same thing. She read Harold stories and reminded him of their life together. She also whispered words of encouragement and love, hoping he could hear.

The police were still circling around both her and Tina. Valerie knew it was only because they had no answers, other than the suggestion that Dr. Joe had made that Harold had been poisoned.

It was the one thing that bothered Valerie. Why would he suggest such a thing? Didn't he know it would put suspicion on the women in Harold's life?

Yes, she had known about Harold always stopping off to see Tina. She didn't believe that anything would come of it. In her heart, Valerie felt sorry for Tina being bothered by him. Although she and Tina barely knew each other, Valerie was sure that Tina was not responsible for her husband's illness.

Was someone responsible? Or was it something that just happened without a cause? Lying in bed, Harold looked more peaceful than she had seen him look in years. It would be wonderful if he would open his eyes and look at her the way he used to, Valerie thought.

"Please, Harold," Valerie said, leaning over and kissing Harold on the cheek. "Please come back to me. Tell me what's wrong."

When there was no response, Valerie closed her eyes and laid her head on his hand, and fell asleep. Dr. Joe found them like that an hour later.

Pausing in the doorway, he decided he would come back later to have his talk with Harold. He knew Harold was listening. All he had to do was believe what Joe told him. Then, all would be well.

· · • · ● · ● ● · ● · ·

Sam asked Hank if he could meet him at Your Second Home. Sam liked it there. Grace and Mandy had made the coffee shop the perfect meeting place. It was cozy and comfortable, but most of all, conversations didn't carry. And the conversation he wanted to have with Hank was not one he wanted anyone else to hear.

Well, he thought. *Of course, Grace and Mandy would hear because they hear everything. Hiding anything from them was useless.*

When Sam walked in the door, Sam saw Sarah sitting at a back table reading a book. It made him think that somehow he had been set up. Did Mira suggest that he meet Hank here, or was it his own idea?

Either way, he was going to carry on as if he had come there by his own volition, have his private conversation with Hank, and assume that they would hear anyway.

Sam chose a table on the other side of the room from Sarah, after waving to her. Mandy brought him his favorite coffee and pastry and asked him if anyone was joining him. As if she doesn't know, Sam thought to himself.

"Hank's coming. Could you see that no one sits too closely?" he asked. "I want to go over some details of the investigation with him."

Mandy smiled and answered, "Of course." She took Hank's order as he passed her on his way to Sam's table, and patted him on the arm as she did so.

Sam watched her and shook his head, thinking that it was a good thing the women were all on his side.

After Mandy served them, Sam pulled out a file and slid it across to Hank, but kept his hand on it and said, "Before you look at this, I want to ask you a few questions."

Hank glanced at the file. It was a regular manila file folder with nothing marking it as anything significant. He pushed it to the side and started eating his pastry. He had had these kinds of conversations before with Sam, and they often turned into something that made him not want to eat. He wanted to make sure he got a bit of pastry and a sip of coffee before it began. Swallowing coffee and his bite of pastry in one gulp, he said, "Sure. What about?"

Sam answered him with one word, "Grant."

"Not him again! When will this ever stop?" Hank said, pushing his pastry to the side. He knew he wouldn't be hungry after Sam started talking.

"Sorry, Hank. But this is important."

"But, he's dead, Sam," Hank replied.

"Yes, but something has come up, and you might know more about it," Sam replied.

"When will that man stop haunting me?" Hank asked. "First he rescues me from the streets. Helps me grow up. Treats me like a son. But instead of teaching me how to be a good man, he teaches me how to be evil. Encourages it. Promotes it. Then I find out he made me do things on purpose that I have grieved about all my life, just to keep me under his thumb. And then, finally, Jay, my supposed enemy, takes a bullet for me so I can be free. All that, Sam. All that."

Hank looked down at the table and took a deep breath, "But I guess after all that I'm still not free from that disgusting man because here you are again asking me about him."

Sam, wisely, didn't say anything. He could never truly understand how Hank felt. Hank's life was so different than his. But Sam didn't know anyone he respected more than Hank. Hank had survived his childhood, and even his adulthood and turned his life around for love. Love of his niece, Ava, and now his family and friends.

It was a long silence, but finally Hank breathed out and said, "Okay, Sam. What do you want to know?"

THIRTY-EIGHT

She waited for tears. Nothing happened. None came. Maybe she had run out of them. Maybe her heart had died. Maybe she had never lived with love at all. Surrounded by all the women of the council she felt comforted but empty. Was that a contradiction? Valerie wondered. Could you be empty and comforted at the same time?

Her brain would not shut down. Thoughts of all shapes and sizes tumbled through her mind. Just like a clothes dryer with a glass door, one thought at a time would pop up to be seen and then tumble back into the mix.

Her heart might be closed, but her mind just kept running and running with nonsense. Valerie wished she could turn everything off. Pull a plug somewhere. She wanted to make it go away. She wanted to go home. No, not home. She wanted to go some place else, anywhere else. She wanted to crawl into bed and stay for the next year.

They had already taken Harold away. As still as he had been the last few days, she knew the minute his spirit had slipped away. One minute a person was lying on the bed. Then, within a split second, it was just a shell. It wasn't Harold anymore.

In some ways, Harold felt more present now after dying than he had been the last few days. Maybe the last few years. *It's just after-shock,* she thought. Harold was gone. She was alone. She had no answers. For anything.

Why did he die? Was it her fault? How would she take care of the kids? What would she say to them? So many questions. No answers. And for God's sake, what did Harold mean? She had finally understood one of his mumbles. Right before he died, he had said, "Tell them I'm sorry." She tried to get him to tell her more. But those were the only words he had spoken.

Who was "them?" What was he sorry about?

Craig had been at the hospital when Harold died. Dr. Joe had visited with Harold an hour before. Valerie caught Joe doing that whispering thing again. But by the time they declared Harold dead, Dr. Joe had already reached home. It was Craig who directed her through what needed to be done and then brought her to Ava's where all the women were waiting for her.

Somehow, they knew she didn't want to speak. They took turns sitting with her, but when she couldn't bring herself to talk, Ava led her to the bedroom she had been using and told her it was hers for as long as she wanted it to be. The kids would be taken care of when they got home. Just rest.

The bed was turned down. The blinds were closed. Just what Valerie needed. Oblivion. Ava helped her to the bed, took off her shoes, and covered her. And then gently shut the door as she whispered they would be there when Valerie needed them, but in the meantime, take all the time she wanted.

A small clock by the bed told Valerie it was one in the afternoon. Harold had been gone for just three hours. So many years of her life had been about Harold and Valerie, and now she was only Valerie. Would she be able to stand on her own?

Before drifting off to sleep, she thought she saw a small light in the corner of the room at the ceiling. Must be my imagination, she thought. But with the light came a feeling of wellbeing. Not what she expected to feel, but she welcomed it and closed her eyes.

· · · ● · ● · ● · · ·

Dr. Joe was in his home office when he heard the news. As a favor, a nurse he had known for years called and told him. It was a return of a favor that he had extended to her years before. She would never be able to repay him, so making a phone call didn't make a dent in what she would do for him.

Although he expected the news, what he hadn't expected was the well spring of emotions that arrived with the phone call. He was barely able to say "thank you" before he choked up and hung up the phone. Joe knew that holding back emotions was never healthy, so he let himself—at least for the time being—feel all the emotions and distress of losing Harold.

As a boy, Harold had so much promise, Joe thought. He let himself revisit the many days and hours they had spent together. Harold was like a sponge soaking up every bit of information that Joe had to offer. For all those years, Harold had been like a son to Joe. It had been especially true after Joe's wife died and his son ran away.

The thought of losing his son, Edward, brought a fresh wave of emotion, and he reveled in it. He let the emotions of love and loss sweep him away. Joe wasn't worried. He knew where all the tree branches were that he could grab onto in the stream of grief to bring himself back from the edge.

He would come back from the waters refreshed and energized. He knew he was a great healer because he was able to feel all those emotions, learn from them, and let them go. Then he could relay those emotions to others. He could empathize.

Joe was trusted, respected, and loved. Joe had no idea how anything could be better than that, although a bit of companionship would be welcome. However, after all these years he had learned that companionship brought another problem. The decision on how much to share. While he had been learning about emotions and control, Joe had learned not to trust. He had secrets much too dangerous to share with an ignorant world. And sometimes, in gratitude for companionship he had shared too much. The ramifications could be terrible. So he learned to live without that one element of life. He had everything else under control.

However, as a doctor, and discoverer of healing methods, Joe had a burning desire to share what he knew. When he was young, Joe thought he would tell everyone about his discoveries. Joe wanted to shout them from the housetops. But his life had taught him to be cautious.

Instead of telling everyone, he told only a few. Some of them understood. Most of them did not—or thought him a fool. It took a few disasters before Joe learned that it was best to trust only a few people with a little bit of information. And no one with all the information.

When the timer went off on his allowed time of grief, Joe's weeping stopped, and he felt refreshed. A new day in his life had arrived. Joe smiled with a renewed sense of purpose. Although he still felt the internal weight of what Harold had done, he could forgive him now. Joe knew that forgiveness was a vital part of a healthy mind and body.

Joe allowed himself to feel the disappointment that Harold had not learned how to follow everything that Joe had taught him. But Joe knew that Harold was at peace, and that made him happy. He had done his best. What Joe could do for him now was to write the best eulogy he had ever written. Joe loved writing them. Each time he got better at it.

Valerie hadn't asked him yet, but he knew she would. She would have no energy, or emotional or mental capacity to do it. Valerie would be relieved that someone had done it for her and that such a good friend of Harold's had been the one.

THIRTY-NINE

Now what? Sam asked himself as he stood in the midst of the gathering of friends in Ava's home. He looked around the room at all the earnest faces. It was a group of people that had gone through so much together the last few years. Tom, Mira, Ava, Evan, Craig, Sarah, Mandy, Grace, Hank, Pete, and Barbara all smiled back at him. The Stone Circle was the core of the group, but the group had grown. It was truly a Karass. A circle of people who knew each other. Who remembered?

Even him. Sam had begun to feel the truth that these were people he had known before. They were familiar. They had always been familiar. Sometimes when he met new people now, he felt right away that he knew them already. It didn't mean they always became friends or he liked them. It was an awareness that they had met before in a different life. Or, perhaps, as Leif would remind him, a different dimension.

Sam had begun to see the pattern. For that, he was grateful because he no longer felt like a stranger in a strange land. He amended that thought. It was still a strange land. And although the group in Ava's living room was one that he admired and loved, he didn't feel that he entirely fit into it, yet. *Maybe I will be more of this group soon,* he thought, looking at Mira sitting by his side. She smiled back at him, and the world righted itself a bit.

What Sam had learned was that he didn't know as much as he used to think he knew. He was learning that he didn't need always to be right. Or always the protector. Now he knew and could admit that he needed help. And right now, to be specific, he required this group's assistance. He had a suspicion, but he had to test it out first. Was there anyone in the group who would not understand why he was asking them, and not the police or FBI? Did he understand?

"That's a serious thought to be having," Leif said in his ear. Sam jumped. He had finally been able to see Leif and Eric when they arrived, but they always seemed to surprise him. When he glimpsed Leif's face and the twinkle in his eye, Sam knew they were doing that on purpose.

Of course, their arrival interrupted the meeting for a few minutes. Everyone could see the two of them now, and each time Leif and Eric showed up, joy filled the room. Hannah sometimes started crying with happiness, even though Sam suspected that Leif and Eric visited her on the sly more often than she told them.

Sarah and Grace looked radiant whenever they saw their husbands. *Perhaps it was getting easier for them to adjust to not having their physical presence. On the other hand, if Mira wasn't here to hold, how would he feel?*

Even though there was no real need for it, a chair was brought into the living room so Eric could sit beside Grace. And everyone slid over on the couch so Leif could sit beside Sarah. It was an illusion of a physical presence that they all clung to.

As the room settled down again, Sam thought about illusions. Perhaps that was what he was dealing with—illusions. Well, this was a great group to talk about that idea. After all, they were used to them.

"Okay, Sam," Sarah said. "We settled in, and are ready to talk."

Hannah, once again, had been asked to make sure that Lex and Johnny were not within listening distance. On her way out the door, Hannah gave them all what Ava called 'the look,' but obeyed and went looking for Johnny and Lex in the family room. However, as she was leaving, she said, "Someone better tell me what you guys talk about." Seeing her dad's face she added, "I mean could someone please tell me what this is about later?"

Ava smiled at her and said, "Since you asked so politely, and you are so helpful, I promise."

After Hannah was gone, Sam asked, "Is Valerie still asleep? I don't want to upset her further right now."

Leif drifted off the couch and came back a few seconds later. "Yes, she is still asleep. I agree, best to let her sleep and rest as much as possible. I have a feeling, Sam, that you have a theory that, if true, would be extremely upsetting to her."

"I do. And it is just a theory at this point. Before you start thinking I know who, or how, those women on the hill were killed, I don't. I just have little pieces of information. I think if I share them with you, some of them will fit together."

Sam took a deep breath, and said, "Okay, here goes. Not in any particular order. First, although there obviously hasn't been an autopsy of Harold yet, the theory is that there will be no physical evidence as to how he died."

"Like the women on the hill," Mandy said.

Sam nodded. "Like the women on the hill."

"So a working theory," Mandy added, "is that they were killed by the same person?"

Sam answered, "That's the working theory. Which means that not only is the person still alive, he or she is probably local."

Holding up his hand before anyone spoke again, he added, "Let me throw it all out to you at once before you start talking again."

"First, if Harold died by the killer's hand it would rule Harold out as the killer. Even though I understand that there was a theory that Harold was the killer, it is doubtful he killed himself. That rumor began once everyone noticed how upset he had become when he discovered that Emily was building on the hill."

Mandy interrupted again. "Sorry, Sam. Gotta talk. However, that doesn't mean he wasn't part of it. And perhaps the killer wanted to get rid of him before he gave something away. Especially considering how visibly upset he was and how erratic he was behaving."

Before Sam could answer, Grace added, "Which would mean that they knew each other, which would mean your theory of being local fits right into this scenario."

Sam gave up and sat down beside Mira. "I am obviously not going to run this the way I used to run FBI meetings."

Everyone laughed, and Sarah answered, "Sam, I think you will find collaboration works better, and that is what you have here. A group think-tank. So let us think along with you. Keep adding what you need to say, and let us all mull it around. And thank you for bringing this to us, Sam."

A round of agreement broke out, and Sam smiled as he said, "You're right, of course. Your way will work much better. I don't have a choice anyway, do I?"

A smattering of "no you don't" statements went around the room along with a symphony of head nodding.

"So," Sam continued, "We know that Harold grew up here, and then came back. We did some research. Harold left town about the time we believe the women died. Which suggests that he knew about it, or maybe, since we don't think he killed them, helped the killer?"

"Then he came back?" Mira said. "Why would he do that? Did he think it was all over and done with, or just that he would be safe, or was he still helping the killer?"

Grace spoke up and said, "Maybe he just wanted to come home. Valerie told me he loved it here, and once they got married, he wanted to bring his wife and children back to where he grew up. Maybe the love of place overrode what happened. Or perhaps his involvement was so small, and so much time had passed, he thought it was safe."

"Until Emily started building on the hill," Hank said.

"Which means he must have known that there were bodies," Pete added.

"And that he knew the bodies were buried on the hill," Grace agreed. "So what else, Sam?"

Sam looked around. "So everyone thinks Harold knew about the bodies on the hill?"

When everyone nodded, yes, he continued. "Now that could mean he heard about it, either on purpose, or by accident. Or he participated in it."

"Does it matter which?" Hank asked. "Whichever scenario it is, rumor or participation, he probably knew the person who is responsible for the deaths."

"You might as well come out with the whole thing, now Sam," Hank said. Seeing Sam pause, he continued, "Oh never mind, I'll tell it. What Sam has discovered is that Grant—yes that Grant," he said as everyone looked at him with disbelief, "could be part of this."

"What do you mean, Hank?" Ava gasped. "How could Grant have anything to do with this?"

Hank looked over at Sam, gesturing for him to continue the story.

"Well, while we have been looking at all things Doveland, the FBI has been going through all of Grant's old files and trying to piece together his life. I got a phone call yesterday telling me that they discovered that Grant used to come here every summer to visit an aunt who lived in Doveland."

"I knew it!" Evan said. "I always wondered why Doveland was where Grant had Hank burn down a house. He must have known the area already. So either he could have killed those women, or had them killed, or knew who did.”

"But that doesn't make any sense," Mandy said. “Assuming he was part of it, he’s dead now. What difference would it make if someone found out he killed those women? Let me repeat. He’s dead!”

In the doorway, Valerie, shoes off, looking dazed, asked, “Who’s dead?”

FORTY

"Valerie," Ava gasped as she rushed to Valerie's side. "Why are you up?"

"I don't know. I heard voices, so I came out to see what was going on. Who's dead? Were you talking about Harold?" Valerie said, shaking her head in a daze as Ava led her to a seat on the couch. The one where Leif had been pretending to sit.

If this wasn't such a horrible moment, there is levity in watching Valerie almost sit on Leif's lap, thought Grace.

As Mira headed into the kitchen to get Valerie a glass of water, Sarah put her arm around Valerie and said, "Yes. We're talking about Harold. Are you sure you want to be here?"

Valerie looked around the room. Concerned and compassionate friends surrounded her. She nodded, "Yes. I need to know. The more I try to make up what I think happened, the more confused I get. Didn't I know Harold at all? And if I didn't, how can I trust anything that I know?"

Mandy and Ava looked at each other. They were both thinking about the people they thought they knew before they discovered the truth about them. They both knew that it hurt more not to know.

After getting the affirmative nod from everyone in the room, Sarah briefly told Valerie what they had found out so far. As Grace watched Valerie take it in, she realized her friend was much stronger than they had been giving her credit for. Valerie didn't fall apart. She sipped her water and listened.

When Sarah finished, Valerie remained silent for a minute, emotions playing across her face, but her hand had stopped shaking.

Finally, she spoke in a soft but calm voice. "I know Harold wasn't perfect. He had a big ego, and he used his charm to get what he wanted. But he wasn't a killer. That I know for sure. He once was a kind and generous husband, and he wanted to be a good father to the boys.

"However, I agree that he knew something terrible happened here when he was young. That explains why he got progressively more and more worried and frustrated once we moved back to Doveland. He turned into his worst self.

"I think he thought he could forget what happened and move on. But I believe the past eventually comes back up again to be dealt with in some way before it can be released. Perhaps he was getting there. I wish he had told me. I think I could have helped.

"I hope he has found peace wherever he is now, but when Emily started building on the hill, he remembered something, something that terrified him."

Valerie paused to take a sip of water. Taking a deep breath, and holding Sarah's hand for support, she continued, "I agree that he knew about the bodies buried there. But instead of talking about it he ran away from it, and look what happened.

"That is what I don't want to do. I don't want to run away from it. I don't want my children to run away from it. I want to be part of what you are doing. No, not want, need. Please help me help Harold now by bringing the truth to light.

"I think Harold knew who killed the women. And if he knew, so does someone else."

Pausing again for another drink of water, Valerie added, "He said something before he died. He said, 'tell them I'm sorry.'

"I'm not going to be able to tell anyone he's sorry until I know who he meant. Would you let me do this for him? And for my boys and me?"

There was really no need for Valerie to hear the word yes, their faces told her everything she needed to know. Instead, Sarah gave Valerie's hand an extra squeeze, and Sam asked the next question. "Since we all think that Harold knew the killer, and perhaps assisted him, assuming it was a him, perhaps what we need to do next is see who else Harold knew."

"Yearbooks!" Valerie said. "Perhaps yearbooks?"

"Great idea," Sam said. "Did Harold have any?"

"No. But I am the principal of the school, even though it seems like a million years since I was last there. If there are yearbooks or records to be found, I can find them."

"And if Grant used to come visit an aunt here, isn't there a list of people who lived here in the Seventies in the files we pulled from the library in Pittsburgh?" Evan asked.

"Plus, we know that in the files we brought back from Pittsburgh, Evan found the name of a trust that owned Emily's hill before Dr. Joe bought it. So far, we haven't been able to trace anything to that trust, so it is probably going to take interviewing people and then piecing the bits of information together."

"Doesn't Dr. Joe know who he bought the land from?" Grace asked.

"No, he said he worked through an attorney, and he never found out who the actual owner was. That attorney died years ago, and we haven't been able to track down any of his records," Sam answered. "Speaking of Dr. Joe. Since he has been the doctor in this town for so long, and claims to know everyone, wouldn't he know who Harold's friends used to be? It seems he would also know who Grant was, too, since he probably knew the aunt," Sarah said, looking at Craig.

"You're right, of course. But when I bought the practice, Joe explained that he was a terrible record keeper. It is only recently that he started keeping good records.

"I think it was when Joe realized that if he wanted to sell his business, he needed proper documentation to pass on to the next doctor. Joe mentioned that in the past he and his secretaries would destroy patient records after they died, or moved away.

"Joe said that they did that because of client confidentiality, but also because the old country practices didn't need so much paper. He knew his clients so well he didn't need to look at a file."

"Then that proves my point. With or without records, Joe knew his clients well. So unless he is losing his memory, he might be the best source of information about town residents that we have," Sarah said.

"And then there's Melvin," Hank piped in. "He keeps telling me that there is something he is trying to remember. Perhaps if I fill him in on what we have discussed, it may help his memories return."

"We also have resources in Tina and Emily. Emily because she has been doing some research, and Tina because didn't she and her husband, Frank, grow up in Doveland?" Sam said.

"Wait," Sarah said as the whole group recognized the implication of what Sam just said. "I know that we are talking different generations since Frank and Tina are much younger than Harold. But did they know each other?

"Did Harold know Grant? Were they all working together all this time? How long has this been going on?"

Hank sighed. "Always, Grant. But even if all this is true, that they all knew each other, who would have killed Harold? We are missing something."

Ava glanced at her phone and said, "It's getting late. I need to get the kids to bed. They all have school tomorrow. Perhaps everyone can work on their part, and we could meet again?"

Hugs were exchanged, and goodbyes said as everyone but Valerie grabbed their jackets and shoes and headed out the door, agreeing to check in with each other the next day. Leif and Eric walked with their wives to the car, waved, and faded away.

Evan checked on the sleeping Ben while Ava and Valerie corralled the other children into bed. Lex and Johnny were somber and withdrawn. Both of them had questions Valerie said she couldn't answer yet. Valerie told them they would be going home after school the next day, and she would share with them everything she knew.

As she kissed them both goodnight, she whispered that she loved them. Lex hugged her back. Johnny didn't. Valerie understood. He had to work this out in his own way, but she would ask Hank and Pete for extra help. Dealing with Harold's death and the ensuing investigation was not something she could do by herself. But she would and could do it with the help of her friends.

In the bedroom Ava had given her, Valerie sat on the bed and prayed for help. She prayed to understand. She prayed to have the strength to confront what had to be done and to be both strong and loving while doing it.

Having done all she could do, she breathed out a prayer of thanks for her children and pulled the covers up over her shoulders.

Once again, she thought she saw a light in the corner of the room. I'm not afraid, she said to the light. She thought she saw it spin before Valerie drifted off to sleep, smiling in spite of everything, and grateful that she had hope in her heart.

FORTY-ONE

Hank never got the chicken dinner for Melvin; the meeting at Ava's ran too late. Melvin had assured him it was fine, he could have the chicken another time. By the time Hank got home that night, Melvin was sound asleep. Melvin was still in bed the next morning when Hank got up at four, having hardly slept at all. The thought that Grant was back, even though he was dead, kept rolling around in his mind. It was a waking nightmare.

Hank left Melvin a note saying he had a lot to share with him and to get the barbecue ready around five. To make up for not being home for dinner the night before, he would bring back some steaks, and they could talk over a good dinner out on the picnic table.

Hank texted Sam and asked if anyone was going to the prison to speak to Lenny. He thought that as Grant's second-hand man after Hank, Lenny might have some answers. Perhaps they could trade a favor or two to get him to talk.

Sam answered right away, proving he wasn't sleeping either, and said that he would go himself. Lenny knew him. Perhaps that would buy him some points.

Instead of making breakfast, Hank headed to the Diner. They opened early and stayed open late. Basic good food and friendly service had made the Diner a favorite spot for most everyone in town. Hank knew the members of his construction crew were often at the Diner this early, so he thought he would buy them breakfast. Plus, pick up some gossip.

Grace and Mandy's coffee shop across the street from the Diner offered a different atmosphere and a different kind of gossip. Both were useful. Hank wanted Diner type food and information.

Pete smiled in delight when Hank came through the door, just as he was unlocking it. Behind him, the Diner still didn't have all its lights on, but Hank could smell the bacon and eggs cooking on the grill.

"Couldn't sleep either?" Pete asked.

Hank shook his head and slid onto a stool at the counter.

"Barbara and I talked long into the night. We are the newcomers to this town, which means we don't know much of its history, but we do get to hear things going on that might be helpful," Pete said.

"That's what I was thinking, Pete," Hank said. "Anything that seems at all out of place, take note of it."

"I have also been thinking about Johnny. I know what it feels like to get your life completely turned upside down. First, his dad dies, and then the whole town is eventually going to be talking about the fact his dad had something to do with the women on the hill," Pete said.

"Yes," agreed Hank. "We need to give him every kind of support possible. The kind that will help him turn this into something that strengthens his resolve to be a good man, and not tip him over into following the easy path."

"That's right. Johnny worked with Grant last year. That will make it even worse, won't it?" Pete said.

Hank nodded. "My guess is that Grant targeted Johnny knowing he was Harold's kid. That was Grant through and through. Evil. Doing evil because it was fun for him. He could have left Johnny alone, but he didn't.

"Probably helped increase Harold's anxiety. He couldn't tell us he knew Grant, and he knew Grant went after Johnny on purpose."

"Damn," Pete said.

"Hon, what's got you so upset," Barbara said coming in from the kitchen. Both men looked up and smiled at her. She was a breath of fresh air.

"We need to ask the women," Pete and Hank said together.

"Well, whatever you are going to ask us, it's about time you all learned to do it," Barbara said, smiling and hugging both Pete and Hank.

"Let me get my apron on, so I can be ready for customers, and you two can tell me what you want me to bring to the council."

• • • • • • • • • • •

Emily sat in her living room moping and feeling lost. She knew there had been a meeting at Ava's the night before, and she knew she hadn't been invited. The logical part of her brain understood that it was a group who knew each other, and she was the new girl in town.

But she still felt hurt and left out. After all, this had to do with her. It was her aunt that had died on that hill. Besides, she thought she had found some information that might be useful.

As she was trying to decide whether to call someone or not, the decision was taken out of her hands when her phone rang. Glancing at the phone, she saw it was Sarah.

For a split second, she thought about being petty and dismissing the call. Instead, she answered and was happy to hear that Sarah wanted to know if Emily could come to coffee with her that morning. Although Sarah lived north of Your Second Home and Emily lived to the west, they were about equal distance away.

It was early, but both of them were already dressed for the day, so they agreed to meet in fifteen minutes. Emily grabbed the information she had found in her searches, slung her purse across her body, and walked out the door into a beautiful late April morning.

She tried not to think about the fact that they were weeks behind in getting the center ready for the summer camp. There were worse things going on than that.

Emily was surprised to see that all the women in the council were already at the coffee shop seated around some tables that Grace and Mandy had pushed together. Emily's heart did a flip-flop. She wasn't left out. She was part of a group that promised to help her and here they were.

Sarah stood up, smiled and hugged Emily, motioning to the empty seat beside her. "We thought we'd all have coffee together this morning," Sarah said. "Kinda informal because Grace and Mandy also need to be minding the store, but we wanted to hear how you are and share what we learned last night."

"We also invited Valerie and Tina to have coffee with us too. You three need the council for different reasons, but we need you too. We think that together we can solve this mystery, and then all three of you can move on with your lives."

Ava jumped in, "I was the one in need last year, Emily, and Mandy too. Grace and Sarah need us more this year. So it's equal. We share. Is it okay with you that Valerie and Tina are included today?"

Emily clapped her hands together in delight. "Absolutely!"

Sarah sent a text on her phone, and a few minutes later, Valerie and Tina walked in the door together. Everyone, including Emily, got up to hug them. Both women were in tears by the time the hugs were over, and Emily was beaming. She had a mission. She had help.

"Okay, ladies," Sarah said. "Let's see what we can do about this mess."

They all lifted their coffee mugs into the air and said, "Hear, hear!"

FORTY-TWO

Emily passed the picture around. Going through the files again, she had found it stuck to one of the other papers. At first, she didn't think much of it, but looking at it again she realized what she had found.

It was a faded photograph from a newspaper article she had stumbled across while looking for news of her aunt. It showed a group of people posed in front of what appeared to be an A-Frame house. The caption was hard to read, but using the magnifying glass Emily had brought with her, the word "Doveland" could be made out.

"See that tree in the background," Emily said. "I think that's the white oak that is up near what will be the parking lot on my hill. Much smaller of course. And down at the bottom of the picture, it looks like the edge of the stone that I love to sit on."

The picture made the rounds until it came back to Emily, accompanied by a slight hum from each person as they squinted at it.

"Of course I could be making this up because I want so much to find the answers, but what do you think?"

"Well, the masthead looks like it says Doveland, and the date is June 1972, so it's possible it's your hill," Sarah said. "Let's assume that it is. Do you recognize your aunt?"

"I wish I could say that I do, but these faces are so blurry. They must have made microfiche of the paper when it was already old, and then printing it out made it worse.

"The thing is, there are two men in this picture. Maybe one is younger? Could that be Harold, Valerie?"

"I don't know. I met Harold when he was over forty, so I have no idea what he looked like as a young man. He didn't have any pictures of himself or his family. Now I realize how strange that was, but I just accepted it. When I asked him why he said his family never took pictures."

"Okay. Let's assume that is Harold. Who is the other man? And what are they doing in front of that house? It was the Seventies. We know that there were communes around here then, maybe that was one of them," Tina said.

"I know the other person couldn't be Frank since he wasn't born yet. But it made me wonder. Do you think Frank and Harold knew each other back then, Tina? Did you ever hear Frank talk about him?" Sarah asked.

"I knew Frank since grade school and I don't remember Harold at all. Harold was probably gone by the time we were growing up here. To answer your question though, no, Frank never mentioned Harold."

"That's the thing about this. It spans a few generations." Grace said. "If the killer is still here, he was probably here when Frank and Harold were both growing up. And Grant was visiting here too, so that may be how he and Frank met. A long time ago. Not only last summer."

"And that might mean that Frank knows who the man is, even if he doesn't think he does." Tina paused, looked around at the circle of women and said, "I guess I am going to have to do something I really, really don't want to do. Go talk to him."

There was a moment of silence while everyone thought on how hard that was going to be for Tina and then three women spoke up at once. "I'll go with you," said Grace, Mira, and Valerie.

Tina looked around the table in astonishment. "Why? Why would you all go with me?"

Sarah laughed and reached across to hold Tina's hand. "Welcome to what women do together, Tina. We need to plan this out, so let's meet together at Grace's tonight and go over what you are going to say to him. I'll let Sam know so that he can set up an appointment for you.

"Let's review one more thing before we break up this morning. Barbara was asked to bring something to us by Sam and Pete."

Barbara beamed at the group. She was still getting used to having a circle of friends who did things together and supported each other. She kept telling Pete that the best gift he ever gave her was bringing her to Doveland so she could be part of it.

It was odd to think that it was actually because of Grant that it happened. If he hadn't arranged to have Pete pick up Ava when she was hitchhiking to Los Angeles a few years before, none of this would have been possible. Hank and Pete started off on opposite sides, and now they were the best of friends.

"Barbara?" Sarah prompted.

"Oh, sorry. I was thinking about how it was Grant's actions that resulted in my being here with you. It's true isn't it, that people do find each other if they pay attention."

"It is," Sarah agreed.

"Well, this is about you, Valerie, because it involves Johnny. No, not a bad thing," Barbara added as the color started draining from Valerie's face. "It's just that Pete and Hank said they want to be even more involved in Johnny's life as he works through this. I think they also mean Lex too, but it was Johnny who met Grant last summer.

"Anyway, they asked me to bring the question to the council about how to do that without being too obvious or doing the wrong thing. Does anyone have any ideas I can take back to them?"

The group had just started buzzing with ideas when Mandy looked up and noticed that Dr. Joe had come into the shop and was standing at the counter looking for coffee.

Seeing that Mandy had work to do and the shop was starting to get full, Sarah said, "Let's break this up for now, but keep thinking about ideas to answer Barbara's request and the other things we discussed."

As everyone returned their chairs to other tables, and Sarah and Grace pulled the two tables apart, Grace whispered to Sarah, "What's up with you and Dr. Joe? Every time he's around, you get weird."

Sarah laughed. "You are such a nosy busy-body. Do you think anyone else notices? I don't know what that's about, but thank you for calling it to my attention. Shall we be at your place tonight around 5:30?"

Grace said, "Perfect." Sarah grabbed her purse off the back of the chair, and as she turned to go, she stopped and went back to Grace.

"I know I don't have to say this to you, seeing how you can't keep your nose out of anything, but will you watch him and see what you think? I know the town loves him. He's handsome and very charming. So it could just be me."

As Sarah left, Grace looked over at Dr. Joe talking to Mandy, who was smiling back at him. *I don't think it's just you, Sarah,* she thought. *Maybe we just aren't easily charmed anymore.*

Forty-Three

Joe thanked Mandy for the coffee and headed to his favorite table, thinking how much he loved this coffee shop. He knew that Mandy and Grace had designed the store, and he admired them for it. With its walls lined with books and the quiet feeling of the room, Joe thought it was precisely what a coffee shop should look and feel like.

Sipping his coffee, Joe watched the store fill up. Many people were picking up coffee to go, but others stayed. He saw people with laptops working. He knew Grace was hoping that a few books would be written in the store. There were couples sitting close together on the benches, whispering things to each other.

Others were reading while drinking their coffee, and a few had set themselves up to watch out the window at the unfolding day. The summer table and chairs had been brought out a few days before and set out on the sidewalk, but no one was in them yet. Still a little chilly in the morning for that, he thought.

When Joe was younger, he used to practice his art in places like this all the time. It wasn't art that was visible. To Joe, the fact that no one could see his art made it even more enticing. If no one noticed what he was doing, but he could see the result of it himself, he marked it a success. Entirely invisible and yet it changed things. Like the wind.

Over time, Joe had stopped practicing in public unless he was in a new town. Years before, when he was first starting out, everyone seemed to respond well to what he was doing. But over the years, he heard people say that when he came into a room, it felt weird.

It was a good warning sign, and he was smart enough to stop what he was doing in places where people knew him. He had become a master at his art by then, so there was no need to gratify his ego by practicing unnecessarily.

Doveland had been off limits for a long time. He had learned that lesson years before. The fact that he had to start again worried him. It bothered him that both Grace and Sarah acted differently around him. They did their best to hide it. Probably thought it was impolite not to treat him like everyone else did, so they attempted to be normal.

But part of Joe's art was reading people. In fact, it was the basis of his art. And he was confident that the two of them had a feeling that something was wrong. He would have to do something about that. Not with them. He knew they were probably not easily manipulated. It would have to be something else that caught their attention and moved it away from him.

At that moment, Grace stopped by his table and asked him if he would like a refill. He nodded, "yes," and smiled up at her. It was a smile as real as Joe could make it. He let everything go and let himself be as transparent as he knew how to be. Grace smiled back and patted his hand.

Anyone else would have thought it had been a warm and friendly exchange. Joe was sure Grace tried to make it feel that way. But it wasn't. Without meaning to, Grace had warned him.

The question now was, what to do. It was more than Grace and Sarah, and that worried him. It was the whole community they had formed. What if they shared their feelings with them? Joe knew they were a quietly powerful group, with gifts and talents that they kept to themselves as much as possible. Much like his art, most of it was invisible.

When they started moving into town a few years before, they brought a breath of fresh air. Somewhat too fresh for some of the old residents. But it was hard to complain when they did so much good. They did most of it as invisibly as possible, but gossip would leak out about what they were doing. They had funded, and were building the bike path, renovated the church, and gave money to the city for needed repairs. Never taking credit, just being part of the community.

It was when Joe noticed that they seemed to know things they shouldn't know, he started thinking about retirement. When they took care of Frank, Lenny, and Grant last summer, he knew it was time. Joe didn't even have to use his art of mental suggestion, or manipulation, on the doctor in the group. Craig already wanted to move to town. So a few apparently random meetings, and a few simple statements that he was ready to retire, brought the discussion to a head right away.

Joe thought Craig would be the perfect doctor for Doveland. It pleased him to know he was leaving the town in such good hands. Joe loved Doveland. He loved that Doveland loved him. Joe didn't want to do anything that would disturb his legacy. Perhaps I don't need to do anything at all, he thought. I'm already packed. I could go at any time.

Satisfied that he had found the answer, Joe left money on the table for Mandy and smiled at Grace on the way out. He would meet with Craig later and tell him he was tired and he was going to leave this week. He knew Craig would understand.

Mandy and Grace watched Dr. Joe until he turned the corner towards his home. Neither spoke until he was completely out of sight.

"Something is wrong, isn't there?" Mandy asked.

"I think there is. When Joe comes into a room, something else comes in with him, and it doesn't feel right," Grace answered.

"Should we say anything?" Mandy asked.

"Well, Sarah has already noticed, too. Maybe it has nothing at all to do with what we are working on right now. Maybe he is just slightly creepy."

"Maybe," Mandy said. "But I am watching out for him, and I am going to mention it to Tom, just in case."

After leaving Your Second Home, Joe turned the corner to his house, and then turned around and came back. Without being seen, he watched Grace and Mandy as they stood at the window.

He sighed. He had wanted to let it go. But it didn't look like he could. He didn't like it, but something would have to be done. The choice was up to him what it would be. The choice as to how bad it would be was up to that group.

Turning, he started home again. He had some plans to make.

FORTY-FOUR

Hank kept his word. He stopped at the grocery store and bought two huge steaks and a packaged salad. Before pulling away from the store, he called Melvin to remind him to get the barbecue started and to tell him he had some information to show him.

Melvin had merely grunted and said, "I haven't forgotten. Already primed and ready to go." And then before hanging up he said, "Drive safe, boy."

Hank laughed at being called a boy and hung up, seeing the picture of Melvin standing in his kitchen talking on that old phone. Hank wondered if he would be able to get Melvin to use a new smartphone, or at least a simple flip mobile phone. Hank made a mental note to look into one for Melvin. He could guilt him into it. Tell Melvin that it gave him peace of mind knowing Melvin had one. Hank sighed. He knew Melvin was thinking about his own death all the time now.

Sarah had made copies for him of the pictures that Emily had shown the council that morning. He also had notes about the trust that Sam and Evan had discovered. Hank was hoping that something would trigger Melvin's memory.

Hank thought that Melvin, in his own way, was a gatherer of information the same way that Grace was, and that he probably had a wealth of information and memories tucked away that just needed to be teased out.

As Hank pulled into the driveway to Melvin's, he smiled at the sight. Melvin was sitting on the front porch swing, a beer beside him, and a cooler on the porch. It wasn't that warm out yet. Although it was late April, the air still had a touch of chill in it. But Melvin was in full summer mode.

Hank picked up the cooler and the two of them headed behind the house to the picnic table and the barbecue that was heated up and ready to go. After seasoning the steaks, Hank slapped them onto the grill, set a timer, grabbed a beer and settled down across from Melvin.

While the steaks cooked, Hank caught Melvin up with what had been discussed the night before at Ava's. Melvin listened and drank his beer. Telling someone else helped Hank hear the patterns in what he was saying, so it was good for both of them.

During dinner, they chatted about Johnny, the bike path, how the work was going on Emily's hill, and what was going to be planted in the vegetable garden now that it looked as if spring was going to stay around. For dessert, they made s'mores. They had everything already to make them because when Hannah came over it was her favorite thing to do.

After dinner, they stayed at the table, and Hank brought out the pictures that Emily had found. Melvin stared at them, and then pushed them back to Hank.

"I can barely see the people in there, so I don't think I can help you with who they are for sure. But still, this could be a picture of that commune that Emily's aunt belonged to. And now that I see that picture, I agree that it was probably located on Emily's hill.

"Isn't that strange? After all this time, Emily buys the very land where her aunt was buried. It's almost as if she was led there. Well, okay, your friends are going to say that she was led there, that all of it was waiting for you to discover it and bring it to light."

Hank thought about it. "A few years ago I would have laughed at such an idea. Life was so chaotic, and I had no hope. But now I can look back on all of it and see how it led to this. To my friends. To meeting you, Melvin."

The two men laughed and clinked their beer bottles together.

"Right now, a lot of this might be solved if we knew who owned the hill before Dr. Joe bought it, " Hank said. "All we know is that it was owned by a trust, no names of the people in the trust, though, and we haven't found anything to point us to who they were."

Melvin humphed and asked, "What did you say the name of the trust was again?"

"Not sure I did." Hank pulled out the papers Sam had given him and read the name. "It was Turtledove. Strange name for a trust."

"I thought you were going to say that. I don't know why, but that name kept coming to me all day. I was waiting to see if the word came up somewhere. It's weird though."

"Melvin," Hank said, "what's weird? Tell me now before you forget it."

"Hey, it's not that bad, young man. But okay, it's weird because Turtle Dove was what Dr. Joe's wife called their son when he was a baby."

"What? Dr. Joe was married. He has a son?"

"Yep. And that's what Joe and his wife, May, called him. It was kind of a code between the three of them. His real name was Edward. He ran away a long time ago. Never came back. His mom died a few years before that. People said it was because she was an alcoholic. I don't believe it though. Never seen her drunk. But what are you going to do, when that's what Dr. Joe and the autopsy said? They were the experts. We were just farmers."

"Did anyone else know that name for Edward?" Hank asked.

"No, I don't think so. Only Dr. Joe and May called him that. I doubt that anyone knew it outside the family except for Sally and me, given that May shared it with her. They were quite close, which is why we both never believed the story that she drank too much."

"So you are saying that Dr. Joe bought the land from a trust he already owned?"

"That's what it sounds like," Melvin said. "Weird, right?"

FORTY-FIVE

It could have been a depressing meeting, but Grace and Mandy were determined that it wouldn't be. In fact, they went the opposite way. They made it into a celebration.

When the rest of the women's council showed up at 5:30, they were greeted with a party. Balloons hung from the ceiling and sparkle lights draped down the wall. Mandy had worked her magic and turned Grace's living room into a fairyland. All the curtains were pulled to increase the effect.

Barbara, with Pete's help, had made four different kinds of pizza, and their aromas filled the space and wafted down the stairway. Pete was experimenting with recipes. He wanted to get a pizza oven, and this was one way he was pushing the project forward. First, he needed the approval of the council on his pizzas, then he could work on approval from Barbara for the pizza oven.

Ava, Mira, Sarah, Valerie, and Tina all arrived at the same time and ended up clumped at the top of the stairs, oohing and aahing over the transformation. Sarah had to gently nudge them forward so she could see what they were looking at.

"Wow." Mira finally said. "What happened here? And why?"

Grace came out of the kitchen, wiping her hands on her new apron that sported lace and flowers. "We thought that a shift of perception about what was happening might be helpful. Instead of thinking of all this as a problem, we are going to celebrate that we are finding the answers."

No one needed to be convinced of the wisdom of a party. They each grabbed at least one kind of pizza, their favorite drink, and headed into the living room where even the most humble of chairs had been transformed into something new.

Some of the chairs were wrapped in fake furs. Others had what might have once been a tablecloth stylishly pinned over them. The couches were wearing some shiny net material. The whole effect changed everything from something they knew to something they had never seen before.

Sarah had to smile at the brilliance of the move. That was precisely what they needed to do. Not see themselves in a place of confusion, but one of awareness. Transforming a space was a perfect symbol and impetus towards the perception shift that they needed.

Once everyone was finished eating, Sarah asked Tina to tell them about how she met Frank. Tina complied by giving them the short version of the story. They met in grade school. Yes, the same school where Valerie was now the principal. She told them that she thought that Frank would eventually grow up and be a good man, but that was wishful thinking on her part. She foolishly didn't pay attention to the clues of what life would be like with him until it was too late.

"But now, I want him to tell me what we need to know," Tina said. "And we haven't said a civil word to each other in so long I don't have any idea how to start the conversation. Let alone get information from him."

"Well," Valerie said. "I understand everything you have said, but I think if it was Harold that was in jail, even if he was furious with me, he might be willing to help just to keep his children safe."

"That's true," Tina answered. "He wasn't a great father, but he did seem to love his children at one point. I'll try that first. What if it doesn't work?"

"I say you lie then," Mandy said. "Tell him he'll get something for helping. Perhaps get you back. Maybe he'll think he can control you that way. Or feel as if he won in the end. Or tell him that Sam will get him a lax sentence. Maybe extra privileges. Well, maybe those won't be lies. Maybe Sam can pull some strings to get that done."

"So, Sarah," Mira asked. "Is lying a good intent or a bad intent?"

"Don't you have the answer to that, Mira?" Sarah asked.

Grace said, "Well, personally I think that is the kind of lie that produces good and doesn't hurt anyone. Well, maybe it would hurt Frank, but I doubt it. Tina wouldn't have to lie to him if he was acting with the right intentions in the first place."

"That's what I mean," Mandy said.

"Okay," Tina said. "I can do that. But I am going to appeal to his goodness first."

"We vote for that too, Tina," Grace said. "Either way, we are on your side."

"Well, I vote for an early bedtime," Ava said as she pushed herself off the floor where she had ended up sitting.

Everyone agreed that it was going to be a long day and sleep was a good idea to prepare for it. Barbara and Mandy stayed and helped Grace clean up the food and dishes, but Grace said she wanted to keep the room as it was for a while. After the mystery of the bodies on the hill was solved, they might need another night of a magical experience. In the meantime, she was going to enjoy it all by herself.

Snapping off the lights, and heading down the hallway to her bedroom, Grace caught a glimpse of Eric. She knew that he would be watching over her as they solved this mystery. And really, what more could she want. Love is love in whatever form it occurs, Grace thought as she drifted off to sleep dreaming of a magical fairyland.

• • • ● ● ● ● ● • •

It was a long walk to the phone with leg and arm chains on, but it was worth it. Lenny hadn't had a phone call for so long he was happy to hear from anyone. Except for Grant. He was delighted that he would never hear from Grant again. Not because he didn't like Grant, but because he had killed him. As he shuffled through the jail towards the phone, Lenny remembered that day in the field.

It had been easier than he thought possible to kill Grant. Everyone's attention was on him as he ran towards Hank shouting, waving a gun. No one was looking at Lenny as he stepped out of from behind a tree and shot Grant in the back. At the same time, Grant had fired at Hank, hoping to kill him. Instead, Jay had stepped in front of Hank and saved him. Now that was a friend, Lenny thought and wondered if anyone would do that for him.

Later, Lenny wasn't really sure why he killed Grant. Grant would have been captured, and Lenny could have continued to run the organization that Grant had built. Instead, Lenny became a fugitive. And without a well thought out plan, he was quickly caught.

Lenny had hopes that someday he would be paroled. Then he could start up his business again. So, Lenny was a model prisoner. It was curious, Lenny mused, that none of his cronies, business partners, or so-called friends, had ever tried to help him get out of jail, or even tried to help him while he was in prison. He had been banished. He would get back at them someday.

On the other hand, Lenny thought, perhaps this phone call is the beginning of the help he needed. Full of curiosity and hope, Lenny answered the phone. He listened and didn't say anything.

In fact, there was no one on the other line. It was a recording. If someone had been listening in on the call, they would have heard a series of gibberish words with no discernible meaning.

To Lenny, there was a meaning. He understood what he needed to do. After hearing the recording the whole way through, he said, "Okay," and hung up.

At the same time, across the state, Frank got the same phone call. He too listened, said "Okay," and then hung up.

Later, when the authorities researched what happened, the two untraceable phone calls became just one more piece of a mystery that no one understood.

FORTY-SIX

Sarah didn't turn on the lights in the house. She knew every inch of her little bungalow by now, and could easily make her way around her home without lights. She loved the silence of the predawn and turning on lights took some of the magic away.

In her little kitchen, Sarah made a cup of coffee and, still in the darkness, made her way out into her garden. Winter had finally breathed its last breath and spring had once again come to Doveland.

The air was still chilly in the morning, so she was dressed in layers of clothes. As the day progressed, layers would come off. A slight breeze brought the scent of daffodils and lilacs to her, the harbingers of summer.

As she sipped her coffee, Sarah thought about how different her life was now. Last year, she had Leif, and Grace had Eric. If Leif were still here, Sarah would be sitting with him in their garden in Sandpoint now, looking out at a forest.

Instead, this year, she had a tiny backyard, which she had grown to love, and she was sitting alone, which she had decided to accept. After all, there really wasn't much else she could do other than surrender.

She and Grace had been forced to learn a new way of living, and the easiest way to do that was to let it be okay.

One of the essential things Sarah had come to realize was that with Leif's physical absence, she needed to become more practiced at what he had been doing before he left. Listening and protecting. They went together. She needed to take up the practice of that art with more diligence. Her friends were busy today, taking care of what needed to be done. She would be here protecting them.

Most people thought protecting was taking some kind of physical action. Sometimes it was. But only after the inner listening and protection had taken place. Protection wasn't a reaction. It was state of being.

Sarah knew that too often, she, like most people, reacted instead of pausing to listen. And in doing so gave away their authority to people, places, things, and ideas. Instead, Sarah wanted to take action based on listening and acting from the ultimate authority of the Infinite One. Sarah changed her mind all the time about what to call that authority or One, but the name didn't matter. The power of it did.

Sarah had always known that there were forces of evil that claimed to have power and authority. Sometimes she found herself frightened by that knowledge. But Sarah knew that they only got their power by taking, manipulating, confusing, and distracting. It was imperative that she not let herself become manipulated or distracted. It was so easy to forget, especially in today's world which is set up more than ever to distract and manipulate.

Sarah knew there were many people who worked diligently to combat visible evil, and she was grateful for them. But what about the invisible evil?

It took much more awareness to stop its action, and that was what Sarah thought they were dealing with this time.

Grant had been terrible. He lived and acted from an evil intention. They had all suffered from his relentlessness in attacking them. But now there was an invisible evil present. Aimed at them. It had turned its eye towards them because it knew that they were searching for it. She could feel its presence in the town. Perhaps it had been there all along, but lying dormant. Now the discoveries of the bodies on the hill had awakened it.

Someone was practicing the evil arts of mental manipulation, and Sarah was afraid that they had been doing it for years. In secret. A shadow was walking through everyone's lives, without anyone seeing it. Invisible, except for the outcomes it caused.

Mentally manipulating anyone, even through prayer, was always dangerous. Human will and plans are a determination to keep control, instead of letting divine Love take over.

Instead, true prayer is the affirmation of a higher power always in charge, no matter what the human picture looks like. Prayer breaks the blindness of human perception and opens thought to the ultimate authority of love and allows us to see what is really going on, Sarah thought.

But someone practicing mental manipulation on purpose was more dangerous than Grant had ever been, and that was what Sarah was afraid was happening. Someone was getting what they wanted, all the time. Invisibly.

As Sarah sat in her garden, she let herself become empty. She let the hundreds of thoughts that drifted through her mind go by without attaching to them in any way. She practiced letting go.

Then she imagined the light of the divine encompassing everyone. She saw her friends and family in the light where darkness could not enter. She imagined light filling every space, flowing over and around first her and then expanding into space. She felt the warmth and safety of that presence.

When she felt that she had turned everything over to that light-filled presence, she breathed out and opened her eyes ready to do what needed to be done. Bring the invisible darkness into the light.

· • • ● • ● • • ·

Sam didn't like that the women were going to see Frank by themselves. But he was on his way to see Lenny so he couldn't go with them. When he called the prison to set up Tina's visit, he asked to speak to the warden who was a friend of a friend. He promised to look out for them.

Even so, as he hugged Mira goodbye, he asked her if she was going to use her spidey senses to stay safe. She laughed at him and told him she would.

Mira was the designated driver. Even though Mandy had wanted to go with the women, someone had to stay home to take care of the coffee shop. It was probably better anyway. With Mira, Ava, Grace, Valerie, and Tina in the car there really wasn't any more room. Sarah said she needed to stay home and do some quiet thinking.

Everyone knew Sarah meant that she needed to listen and protect them using prayer and meditation. She could do that best at home, in the silence.

Sam hugged Mira goodbye, closed her door for her, and then flinched as Leif said, "Don't worry, we'll watch over them."

"Damn it, Leif. When will you stop sneaking up on me like that?" Sam said.

"I didn't sneak. You just weren't paying attention, Sam," Leif responded.

Sam paused and looked at the two men standing by the car. "You're right. I am distracted almost all the time. Keep doing that until I can feel you coming."

"Not to worry, young man," Leif said. "I will."

The three men waved at Mira as she pulled away, and blew kisses at the three of them.

As they drove away, Sam turned to the two men still standing there. "Is it a bad thing that I don't get how you travel to other places, or where you are when you aren't here? I mean, I'm getting used to it, I guess. After all, here you are so I can't deny that it happens.

"But being here and there, you both not having a body, and yet I can still see you, is so strange I can't wrap my head around it."

"Honestly, Sam," Eric said. "I don't know if we understand it either. I keep getting told it is dimension shifting or traveling. We are all here at the same time in the same place all the time. Just in different dimensions.

I think that the reason that we can be where the women are going without having to travel physically to get there is because we aren't moving a body. We are just moving an idea of ourselves."

Sam shook his head. "Don't get it. But I am happy that it is real. Otherwise, you two wouldn't be in our lives anymore, and no one would like that. And Leif, thank you for reminding me to be more aware."

Leif and Eric nodded and then faded away. Sometimes it seemed they blinked out, and sometimes it was a slow fade. Sam had no idea why. Just something else he didn't understand.

Sam's phone pinged, reminding him that Pete would be picking him up in a few minutes. When Pete heard that Sam was going to speak to Lenny, he asked to go along with Sam. At first, Sam had said no. There was no reason for Pete to get involved. But Pete had assured him that Barbara and Alex could manage the Diner and that Sam needed to be free to think on the drive.

Pete was right. This whole thing was confusing. Sam was used to having concrete things to pin down. He could track suspects, bug rooms, and follow people. But with this, there were so many pieces of the investigation that Sam didn't understand, he felt constantly confused. He needed to get the timeline straight. He needed to figure out if it was true that Grant, Frank, and Harold, and maybe Lenny, had known each other in the past. That would help them find the missing person in the scenario. There had to be someone else, but how did they fit in and who were they?

And then there was the information that Hank and the women's council had brought to him. Dr. Joe bought the land from his own trust. Why did he do that? Why didn't he tell them? What about the fact there was a commune on the property in the Seventies. Who went there? Who managed it? Were the women murdered because of the commune or because of something else? Did Dr. Joe know those women even though he said he didn't? There was evidence he had taught a class or two there. Were those women there at that time?

How did it all fit together? Did Lenny have an answer for them? Or Frank? All they needed was something that tied all of the pieces together so that it made sense. Sam hoped that by the end of the two meetings, they would have a key to use to unlock the mystery.

Even he, Sam, Mr. Unaware, could feel the pressure building. He needed to release that pressure before it was too late. The problem was, they had no idea who was causing it.

On the way to the prison, Sam got a phone call from the local police. They were giving him a heads up. An anonymous tip claimed that it was Valerie and Tina that had killed Harold. There was no proof, but it meant they needed to question them again.

Sam agreed to bring them into the station on Monday morning. Neither he nor the police thought there was any validity to the claim. But it muddied the water. It built up more pressure. Someone was manipulating him. Sam didn't like that at all.

FORTY-SEVEN

Craig was doing something that made him incredibly uncomfortable. He felt sleazy and dishonest. On the way to pick up Johnny and Manny and take them to the construction site with him, Hank had stopped by to see him and share what Melvin had told him about Dr. Joe.

Craig knew he was being defensive. But it bugged him that Hank had questions about his friend. No, he hadn't known that Dr. Joe had been married. Craig didn't think that it was a big deal. It had been a long time ago, and probably a hard subject for Joe to talk about. Besides, it was none of their business.

Still, Hank wouldn't give up the idea that there might be something they needed to know that would help them with the investigation. Craig assured Hank that he had Dr. Joe checked out thoroughly before he bought the practice. Dr. Joe was a highly respected doctor, with no record of any wrongdoing anywhere.

Hank asked Craig just to do one more check. See if Craig could find out more about Dr. Joe's wife's death. Look into her autopsy. How did she die? When exactly was it?

Out of a long-standing friendship with Sarah and her friends, Craig agreed.

So that meant Craig was in his office making calls and trying to find out who was the attending physician for Joe's wife, and could he get a copy of the death certificate? So far he was not getting anywhere, but then it was many years ago. Melvin said it was in the late Seventies that she had died.

Under any other circumstances, Craig would ask Joe. But Hank told him not to, and Craig hated that even more. Joe was his friend. This sneaking around didn't seem right. Once he found the information and proved to Hank that Joe was just what he appeared to be, he would feel better.

He glanced at his watch. He had a patient coming in soon. His client load was growing, and he knew that he would soon need to hire an assistant and a full-time nurse. Craig wondered how Dr. Joe ran his practice by himself all these years.

Or did he? Craig thought. I never asked him. There must have been assistants and nurses through the years. Who were they? Perhaps they knew about Dr. Joe's wife.

Craig felt better already. Perhaps he could solve two problems at one time. Find himself an assistant and get Hank off his back. He knew just who to call to get the answer, Melvin.

· · · · ● · ● · ● · ● · ·

Mira took the nearest off-ramp, pulled into the back of a Wal-Mart parking lot, and switched off the engine, breathing heavily.

"Whoa, Mira what was that?" Grace said from the passenger seat.

Instead of answering, Mira opened her door and practically fell out of the car.

"Get out. Everyone, get out now," Mira yelled.

Within seconds all the women were out of the car. They followed Mira until she sat down on the curb about twenty feet from the vehicle.

"Something is wrong. I don't know what it is, but something isn't right. Sarah always says to follow your internal voice, and I knew I had to stop the car and get out," Mira said.

Everyone's phone pinged. It was Sarah asking if everyone was okay. When Grace texted back "yes" Sarah called.

"What's going on, Sarah?" Grace said. "Mira scared the crap out of us all. She decided that something was wrong, pulled the car into a parking lot, and then made us all get out."

Grace put Sarah on speaker so everyone could hear the answer. "Good girl, Mira. You knew something was wrong, and you did what needed to be done. Although you gave me a bit of a fright when you pulled off the road."

Valerie mouthed, "How did she know that?" to Grace, but Grace just shook her head and whispered, "Later."

"It was scary," Mira said.

"Yes, I know it was. But before we talk about that, I need to tell you something else. It's about Frank and Lenny," Sarah said.

"What about Frank?" Tina yelled.

"I'm sorry to tell you this way, Tina. But it is best that all of you know this right away.

"At the same time, in their different prisons, Lenny and Frank attacked a guard, and in defense, the guards shot and killed them." Sarah paused and added, "I'm so sorry, Tina."

Tina gasped and fell back against Valerie who put her arms around her.

"Wait," Ava said. "They both were shot and killed? At the same time? Isn't that impossible?"

"Yes, it would seem to be—except that it happened. And yes, at the same time, and in the same way. Sam got a call from both prisons and then called me to get in touch with you. He wants you to all turn around and come home. Carefully. Do you know why I am saying this, Mira?"

"Yes. I understand," Mira answered.

"There is someone working hard to make people do things they would normally never do. Sam told me that before he died Lenny kept whispering, 'He said they were coming for me.' So, what was it that you heard, Mira?" Sarah asked.

"I kept hearing a loud voice telling me to ram the car in front of me. When I didn't do that it became an insistent whisper that kept saying, 'Do it, just do it, you'll be glad you did.' Instead, I paid attention to that other voice inside of me that told me to stop the car safely and get out."

Everyone stared at Mira, and then slowly sat down on the curb beside her, Grace still holding the phone.

"Mira, thank you," everyone said at once.

"I was never going to pay attention to it, but it was really scary," Mira answered.

"Shows what a wise woman you are, Mira. Please come back. We'll meet at Ava's. Everyone will be there," Sarah said.

"On the way home, each of you say thank you for every good thing you can think of. That will keep that voice away. We'll deal with what happened when we are together. Once again, I am sorry, Tina," Sarah said.

Tina nodded and put her head on Valerie's shoulder, tears streaming down her face. After Grace hung up with Sarah, Tina said, "I have no idea why I am crying, I hated him for so long."

"But you loved him before that," Valerie said, understanding exactly how Tina felt.

On the way home, they sang, laughed, and took turns talking about all the beautiful things in their life. It was a ride filled with joy. Exactly the opposite of what was intended by whoever meant for them to be harmed.

At her home, Sarah stood outside and let the sun shine down on her face. As she looked up to the sky she said over and over again, "Thank you. Thank you."

FORTY-EIGHT

"Intention is the key." Sarah said. "Ask yourself, what is the intent behind this request or demand? Is it intended to hurt and harm, or help everyone? And that's the tricky part. Is it couched in a way that looks like it is meant to help, but it would only be for a few people, and other people would be hurt? What is the long-term damage of the request?

"Sometimes it looks just like something good. That's a dangerous resemblance because that is when we can be fooled. We think we are doing the right thing, when in reality we are working against the good of ourselves and others. However, if we check the intent we can spot if it comes from love, or from something else."

Sarah was answering the question of how to tell if what they heard, thought about, or planned was something they should listen to, or not.

"Mira did what she did instinctively. She knew that hitting the car in front of her, or driving the car into a tree, was wrong because of the intention. Someone who is less aware might have been tempted, or distracted enough to do what that voice was saying. We can see this in our society now. People are flipping out and doing something terrible or nothing, or entire groups of people are committing acts of terror and horror against fellow humans. Mental manipulation has become more and more sophisticated, subtle, and dangerous. And it is always invisible. To find it, we have to look at the result, and the intent.

"For us, right now. Someone is attacking this group. On purpose. To make us stop looking into what they have hidden. However, they have now discovered that they can't be so blatant about what they want you to do. You know too much. You are defended against any authority other than good. Now, they will try more subtle things. Now they will go after the most vulnerable, and the most distracted."

"The children," Ava said and looked around in terror.

"Yes, the children are vulnerable. But you just made yourself vulnerable too, Ava, because you became afraid, and distracted. Understandably. So forgive yourselves right now for anything you think you have or will do wrong. Once again, it leaves a door open."

"This is so hard to do," Valerie said. Tina nodded, holding Valerie's hand. The two of them sat together on the couch looking as if their whole world had flipped upside down, which in many ways it had.

Everyone was there, except Pete and Barbara who were on their way and bringing Johnny with them. The rest of the children were once again in the family room. But this time they were told that they would be included in the meeting later on because they needed to know what was happening.

Leif and Eric were also present, leaning against the back wall. Tina and Valerie were told about Leif and Eric being there so that it wouldn't seem as strange that people were talking to what looked like air. But it had added to their perception that perhaps they had entered another world of some kind.

Sam looked at the two of them and said, "I know how you feel about how strange this is, but after a while it becomes more normal. I couldn't see Leif and Eric until recently. Just know that everything about this group is here to help. Even if they are all a little weird," he added, looking slyly at Mira.

Mira gave Sam a playful punch and said, "It's actually fairly new to all of us. But, Sam is right. We are a group of people who want to do what's right."

Looking at Sam, she asked, "I understand how much we need to pay attention, so could we talk about what we know so far? We need to stop this person. Like now."

Sam nodded and then told them about what happened with Lenny and Frank, saying, "Obviously it was to stop them from talking to us."

Hank looked over at Craig sitting in a chair by himself looking very unhappy.

"You look like you lost your best friend, Craig," Hank said.

Craig straightened up and cleared his throat. "Well, thankfully I haven't lost any of you, even though I may have screwed this whole thing up, and you may all change your mind about me after this."

"What did Sarah just say about forgiveness and non-judgment, Craig?" Grace said. "I think she was serious about that."

Craig looked around the room at all the friendly faces, gave them all a weak smile, and continued. "Hank asked me to look up how Dr. Joe's wife died. It pissed me off that he asked me. I reacted in a way I would never think I could.

"I started hating Hank for the asking, and almost didn't do it. But because of my loyalty and love for all of you, I did it anyway. Now I recognize that I wasn't behaving like myself because someone didn't want me to start researching anything to do with Joe. My friend. A respected colleague."

Craig sighed and waited until he felt he could talk again. Everyone did their best to be patient and send him love, but there was an unspoken question. They wanted to know if he had found anything of use to them.

Finally, Craig found his voice again. "No. I couldn't find anything at all about Joe's wife's death. Nothing. Anywhere. None of my contacts could either. That was weird, of course. There should have been a trail or breadcrumb somewhere. But, no. Nothing.

"Since I couldn't find anything about his wife, I started searching for people that worked with Dr. Joe to see if I could track them down and get answers from them."

Sam smiled at Melvin sitting in his favorite chair beside Hank. "Melvin pointed me towards Joe's first assistant. He also gave me names of other assistants, or nurses, Dr. Joe had employed through the years. Melvin remembered them because he was a patient of Dr. Joe, and his wife Sally had kept their numbers in a little book that Melvin still had, in his kitchen drawer."

"That's my Sally," Melvin said proudly, and everyone smiled at him. Hank gave him a fist bump.

"Yes, thank you, Sally," Sam said.

Valerie and Tina looked at each other, and Tina asked, "Is Sally here too?"

Melvin shook his head, "I only hear her voice sometimes. I don't see her, yet."

Sam nodded at Melvin, who motioned for Sam to go on. "The first assistant was a woman named Wanda James. She is no longer alive. Nor are any of the other assistants, or nurses that worked with Joe. None of them.

"Yes, that's telling, I know. I was quite distressed by then. It was my friend I was researching, someone I trusted. But I kept on going. I gave Sam Wanda's name to run by the people who are researching Grant's past. Turns out that she was Grant's aunt. Grant Hinkey was really John James. Now that we know his real name, Sam says that information is starting to flow about his early childhood."

The room became deathly silent as everyone brought all the pieces together.

The driveway beeper went off announcing the arrival of Pete, Barbara, and Johnny. Valerie stood up to hug her son, but when Pete and Barbara came through the door they were breathless, white as a ghost, and Johnny wasn't with them.

"It's Johnny," Pete gasped. "We can't find him. He's gone!"

FORTY-NINE

At that moment, Hannah rushed into the living room and grabbed her mom's hand and pulled her down so she could whisper in her ear. "Mom, I know we are supposed to wait, but I had to come get you. Everyone started getting a headache, and now they all say they don't feel well."

Ava grabbed her husband's hand and rushed out of the living room. Once she saw what was happening, a room full of children looking ill and complaining about a headache, she sent Evan to get everyone to help.

Within a few minutes, every child had someone holding them while cold cloths were pressed to their foreheads. Ben was quietly sobbing while being rocked by Evan. Valerie clutched Lex to her, trying not to cry. She had one child not well, and another missing.

Sarah looked out over the scene of adults in a panic and children crying, and walked out of the room, motioning for Grace to join her. Leif had already followed her. Outside in the hall, Sarah asked Grace to go back in the room and get everyone to start singing. Something uplifting. "Make everyone sing. Make it as loud as possible. I'll be back in a minute," she said.

Back in the room, Grace had to get Melvin to whistle for her to get everyone's attention. "Sarah said she would be back in a minute. In the meantime, she wants us to sing. Something happy. Something loud."

Eric stood next to Grace and said to those that could hear him, "Let's sing If You're Happy And You Know It." Everyone looked at him as if he had lost his mind. "She was serious about this. Let's do it," Eric said and started singing. Within seconds, everyone joined him, even Tina and Valerie who thought everyone had lost their minds.

Leif and Sarah stepped outside into the late afternoon sun. Nothing was said for a few minutes, and then Leif said, "You can do this Sarah. You can block him. We'll help. And when you go back into that room, you can get everyone else to do it too."

"And Johnny?" Sarah asked.

"Johnny is a smart kid. He could tell someone wanted him to hurt Pete, and he knew right away that couldn't be right, so he left the restaurant and hid. He is blocking Joe's thoughts which means he is also blocking me, only because he doesn't know if it is safe to let anyone in. We just have to find him before Joe does."

They could both hear the rowdy singing going on in the other room, and Sarah started laughing. "What a song to sing. Perfect. Even the kids know that one. And it's working."

"Yes, it is. You go take care of the group, and I'll see what I can do," Leif said as he faded away.

Sarah took another moment to gather her thoughts and returned to the room. When she opened the door, everyone was laughing at Eric trying to clap his hands and stamp his feet, and no one looked sick.

FIFTY

Johnny stumbled in the dark. Branches grabbed at him, and roots tripped him. He fell to his knees and started sobbing. He was terrified. Of himself.

Back in the Diner, something horrible had happened. Pete and Barbara were closing up shop so they could all go out to Ava's. Johnny was looking forward to seeing his brother and his mom. He knew that Pete and Hank were keeping him busy, so he couldn't wallow in how bad he felt about his dad. That's when it happened. Something terrifying.

Up until that moment, the day had been fantastic. Hank had taken him and Manny, Tina's son, out to the job site on Emily's hill. They spent the morning helping the crew. The crew members were great. They'd call him over and show him how to use a tool, or hold a board properly. Johnny even got to run the bulldozer for a minute with Hank sitting beside him to make sure he didn't run into anything. It was the perfect morning.

Hank's crew had finished the outside of the barn and were nearing completion on the inside. Hank said not to tell Emily yet that they had also started working on her deck. It was a surprise. Johnny thought Emily could use the good news right now, but he kept that thought to himself. He didn't want to ruin the morning. It was just too perfect.

And then Hank got a phone call, and everything got weird. Hank told the crew to take the rest of the day off. They said they wanted to finish what they were working on, so Hank put one of them in charge and said he would see them on Monday.

Hank dropped Johnny off at Pete's. He told Johnny it was because Pete had called and needed help. Johnny didn't believe it for a minute.

Hank took Manny to Ava's instead of taking him home. All the kids were at Ava's because the women were going with Tina out to the prison. Johnny wished that they would get over themselves and tell him what was going on. It was his life too. It was his dad that died, and he knew they were going to the prison to get some answers about that.

Johnny was pretty sure that Pete had given him the job just to keep him busy and to keep him from asking too many questions. Both Pete and Barbara were distressed about something, but once again they thought they were doing him a favor by not telling him. Johnny felt that not knowing was worse than trying to figure it out. Besides he would be eighteen in June. It was time for them to treat him like a young adult. That's what he was thinking as he chopped vegetables. Normal stuff.

And then without warning, he had the worst thought. He started thinking about taking the knife and stabbing Pete. He could see himself doing it. He could see himself enjoying it. He could imagine how Pete would grunt and then fall to the floor with the knife sticking out of his back and blood seeping out over the tile. Johnny imagined how good that would feel.

It was terrible. It was like looking at a horror movie inside his head. Like he was a puppet, and someone was pulling his strings. There was no one in the Diner at that moment except him and

Pete. Barbara was upstairs changing clothes, and the last customer had paid and had wished them a good Friday night.

"Now is the time. Do it now," the voice kept saying. Pete had his back turned to Johnny. It would be easy.

So Johnny ran. He went out the back door without even grabbing his jacket and started running to get as far away from Pete as possible, ignoring the voice that told him to go back and do it because there was still time. Johnny ran until he was out of breath and then hunkered down behind a house in a grove of evergreens. He had no idea how long he stayed there. It had gotten dark. Then the voice found him again. It asked him why he was running. It suggested that if he didn't want to use the knife on Pete, he could use it on himself.

And that's when Johnny woke up and realized that it wasn't him having those thoughts. It was someone else talking to him in his head. With that realization, he heard his mom's gentle voice reminding him that he wasn't his bad thoughts, he was his good ones. Last summer, Grant had done the same thing to him. Told him it was good to set off the fireworks. He said no one would get hurt. Someone did though. The next year Grant had killed Jay. All because Johnny had helped Grant escape.

"Think good thoughts," his mom had said. "Think about who you love. Think about how much I love you."

That's what Johnny started doing. Thinking of his mom telling him she loved him. Of the nights she cuddled with him and Lex on the sofa as they watched their favorite movies together.

Slowly the other voice faded, and Johnny imagined slamming the door on it and locking it so it couldn't get back in.

Once the voice was entirely gone, Johnny realized he still had the knife clutched in his hand. While turning in a circle to orientate himself, Johnny noticed a trash can in the back of someone's house. He dropped the knife into it, promising himself he would get Pete a new one. But there was no way he was keeping it.

At first, he didn't know where to go, but then he remembered the bike trail. It was finished up to Ava's house. He could find his way in the dark, and in case someone was looking for him, he could stay just a little way off of it. He had a tiny light attached to his keychain. That would keep him on track.

Johnny quickly found the trail. But staying on it in the dark was harder than he thought it would be, and when the memories started flooding back, he couldn't stop himself from crying. Was he that person? Would he hurt the people at Ava's if he went there?

He sat in the middle of the trail and sobbed. And then Hannah stood in front of him.

"What are you doing here?" Johnny screamed. "Is that really you?"

"Oh, silly. I'm not here. I'm at home. And yes, of course, it's really me. Hannah, your friend. I came to tell you to keep moving. No one is after you right now, everyone knows what is happening, and they have blocked that bad man from sending bad thoughts."

"You're not here?"

"No. See." Hannah reached out and touched Johnny, and he saw her hand go through his shoulder. He shuddered and backed away.

"Now don't be a scaredy cat, Johnny. Just come to Ava's, and you'll see what's happening. Just follow me until you see Leif. He's waiting around the corner.

You are going to be able to see him now 'cause he said it was necessary. I have to go. Mom is going to wonder why I am not paying attention if I stay here too long."

Johnny stood up looking dazed. "How do I know you aren't coming from that bad place. You could be pretending to be Hannah."

"Hum. Good question. Okay, could a bad person do this?"

Within seconds Johnny felt an overwhelming rush of pure love. For everything. The forest came alive. The roots that tripped him and said they were sorry they had only wanted him to slow down.

He heard the thoughts of trees and knew what the bird had said as it sang its last note for the day.

When it was over, he was speechless. And changed.

Hannah smiled at him and motioned for him to follow. Still basking in the glow of that feeling, Johnny wasn't afraid. He was ready to stand up to that voice, to whoever was hurting his family. But he wouldn't stand up in fear, he would stand in that feeling of love, and that would banish the evil.

Around the corner, as Hannah promised, Leif was waiting for him.

"Good job, Johnny," Leif said. "The world can use a man like you."

Tears leaked down Johnny's face. This time not from fear or pain, but from joy.

FIFTY-ONE

Sarah closed the door of her little home and dropped onto the deep mauve, soft couch in her living room that looked out into her garden. The sun had just started peeking up over the back fence, weaving its way through the morning glories that snaked up the trellis mounted onto the fence. As the sun's rays touched each bloom, they opened to greet the day. It was Sunday morning, the perfect day for rest and reflection. Mostly rest. She was exhausted.

It had been a long night at Ava's. They had stayed together through the night, taking turns with the children and then staying with them until they fell asleep peacefully. Even then, someone remained in their room as they slept. Everyone knew that they would need to find a way to teach the children how to stop attacks like that.

How to do it without scaring them would be the subject of a discussion among the grownups. On the other hand, they knew that it wasn't the children that had been attacked. The attack was aimed at them. The children were being used as instruments against them. What did the person want them to do? Stop investigating? Would they?

When Johnny found his way to the house, Valerie was overcome with tears and couldn't speak. They sat together for a long time silently crying together and holding hands. Sarah knew that a bond had been forged that night between the two of them. Johnny had become a man who understood that his heart and his actions were always going to be on the side of good. For a time, he had doubted his ability to know the difference. After his experience, he didn't question that anymore.

The grownups sat with Johnny listening to what happened and then answering his questions the best that they could. No, they didn't know for sure who was trying to take control of his thoughts, but whoever it was didn't succeed, and that was what he needed to remember. Now he could practice.

Johnny's question, "Practice what? Practice how?" led into a lengthy discussion of the need for sitting in silence in whatever form most worked for him and the situation. Practice moving slowly. Think before reacting. Only respond. Practice choosing to focus on what is good, and not be seduced by the claims of quick money, revenge, or easy distractions.

Tina and Valerie had never heard that kind of talk before, so like Johnny, they drank it in. Holding Johnny's hand, Valerie asked if perhaps there could be a training, or class, that she and her children could attend. Valerie said she wanted help and thought that others like her also needed a community to practice within.

And that question led to a discussion about the details of that kind of training. By then, everyone was drooping, running out of ideas, and ready for sleep.

Ava offered to house everyone for the night if they wanted to stay. They had plenty of room. The younger children were already asleep, so both Tina and Valerie knew they would stay with them. Hank and Melvin headed to their rooms in the bunkhouse. Everyone else said they needed to go home, and yes, they would be careful driving. Hugs were exchanged all around as goodbyes and whispered words of "be careful" were exchanged. Craig barely participated, which he thought no one noticed, and yet everyone did.

After everyone else had gone to bed or gone home, the only ones remaining were Johnny, Pete, Barbara, and Sarah. Johnny had asked Sarah to stay while he talked with Pete and Barbara. She agreed, but sat in a chair away from the discussion. She knew she could support Johnny, but couldn't do it for him. He needed to do it himself.

For a moment, Johnny just sat in front of Pete, trying to gather his thoughts. To Pete's credit, he didn't rush him, just waited patiently with as open a heart as he knew how to make it. His heart, Barbara knew, was as wide as a heart could go.

Finally, Johnny said. "Pete, you have taught me so much this past year. About what being a man looks like. What responsibility looks like. What belief in someone else looks like. You, Sam, and Hank gave me a chance to walk a better path.

"But you didn't just support me. You and Hank are teaching me physical things to do, too. I can cook now. I am learning how to build things. I am becoming useful.

"If you wouldn't have been there, I might have been sucked up into the life that Grant was offering. And I would have been lost. Maybe forever."

Taking a deep breath, Johnny continued, "So you must know that I would never have been able to hurt you, or anyone else, but especially you. But that is because of what I learned from you. A year ago, I might have thought I was that other person. The person trying to get attention any way that I could. The boy reacting against the world instead of looking for the good and protecting and encouraging it.

"The best way I can thank you, Pete, is to be more like you."

Pete, big man that he was, burst into tears and grabbed Johnny and hugged him tightly. Barbara's arms went around the two of them, and they stood together for another minute until Barbara pulled away and handed them both tissues.

"You do us proud, boy," Pete said. "You are always family to us. Whatever you need, we're here for you and your mom and brother."

Yes, it had been a long night, Sarah thought. Actually, it had been a long couple of months. Sarah dropped sideways onto her couch, closed her eyes, and was asleep within minutes. She hadn't even taken off her coat. Leif leaned over and whispered to her that he loved her and that she had done well. "Sleep my love," he said. He knew that her work had only just begun.

FIFTY-TWO

Hank and Melvin didn't stay for breakfast even though they knew that despite everything, Ava would make Sunday morning crepes. They wanted to go home. Both of them had slept for a few hours, which was enough rest to get them back to the farmhouse.

They thought everyone else was still asleep, so as they walked down the new gravel path to the back patio, they were both startled when Evan whispered, "Hey, want coffee before you go?"

"Couldn't sleep, either?" Hank whispered back.

Evan just shook his head and gestured towards the kitchen. "I left two to-go cups out for you. Figured you both would be up and leaving and could use coffee to help get you home."

All three men knew they had done enough talking the night before, so Hank squeezed Evan's shoulder on his way to the kitchen, and Melvin and Evan exchanged nods.

Evan remained outside, with a cup of cold coffee on the table, staring into the distance.

Hank knew that Evan was wondering the same thing that Hank was running over and over in his mind. How could he protect the ones he loved when he couldn't see what was coming at him? It was an invisible and powerful enemy. Was there a defense? What was it?

Neither Melvin nor Hank said anything on the way home. If Melvin could have found the desire to speak, he would have explained that there were too many emotions tangled up inside of him to make sense of anything.

They didn't talk when they got home, either. They both headed to their bedrooms and quietly shut the door. Hank lived in Jay's old bedroom now, the one that used to be Melvin's son's room. Now it was Hank's. He had no time to think about what any of that meant. He barely had time to take off his boots before sleep took over. It was a relief from thinking.

Melvin didn't go right to sleep. He needed to talk to Sally. After being around Hank and his friends, Melvin no longer thought it was strange that he spoke to his dead wife, or often heard her voice. He used to think it was his imagination, wishing she was still with him.

After the last year's events with Jay, Melvin had opened to the possibility that he didn't just wish it to be true, but that it was. Lately, he heard her more often, and once in a while, he could swear he saw her standing there smiling at him, wearing his favorite dress. Perhaps it was because he was closer to the door to whatever came after death. Melvin never was afraid of death, but now he thought of it as a trip he was going to take, and at the end of it he would be once again united with the love of his life.

Or if his friends were right, she was the love of many of his lives. Something he now believed to be true, too. Either way, she was the one he wanted to see. He knew he would. She was waiting.

She was waiting for him tonight, too. As he knelt by his bed in prayer, he heard her voice telling him not to be afraid.

"I'm not afraid for myself, Sally," Melvin said. It's for my friends and their children. I am afraid for anyone that is within the sight lines of someone like Dr. Joe. Because it is Joe, isn't it?

"I can't tell you." Sally said. "However, no matter what, there is still no reason to be afraid. Surround yourself and everyone you think about with light. You can hide from darkness in light, and when darkness touches that light, it dissolves."

"Is it that simple?" Melvin asked. "Not that remembering to do that, or doing it well is simple, but is light always the answer?"

"It is," Sally answered. "It's the visible expression of Love. And Love is always more powerful than what claims to be another power. Evil. Which is only the belief in the absence of Love."

Melvin crawled up into his bed and sank into it in relief. He knew about love. Love was something he understood and knew how to do.

• • • ● • ● • ● • • •

Both Hank and Melvin slept until noon. Something neither of them ever did. However, they both knew that rest was one of the best recovery tools, and they needed every ounce of strength they could gather.

They both stumbled into the kitchen at the same time, noticed the clock, and without talking about it made sandwiches, grabbed a beer, and headed out to the picnic table. Hank broke the silence with the simple question, "Want to talk?"

Melvin stared at his beer for a minute before answering. "Yes, but not now. Let's talk about the schedule for Emily's hill. In fact, I would like to see it. Can we take a trip there? And I would like to see the bike trail."

"Sure," Hank said. "I'd like that. Let's go to the hill first."

"Okay," Melvin said as he grabbed the last of his sandwich and stood up. "Let's go."

Startled, Hank laughed, grabbed his sandwich and headed to his truck. Melvin stopped at the house to get a few bottles of water and lock up. He never thought it necessary to do that before, but Ava had given him a scolding last summer when she found out he didn't bother, so now he did it for her.

"Do you want to go through town or take the bumpy shortcut," Hank asked.

"Give me some bumps!" Melvin answered, surprising even himself. "I'm on a mission of some sort, so I guess I'll go with the flow, or in this case, the bumps."

Hank looked at his friend and thought he must have done something right somewhere to have ended up with a friend like him. Melvin's eyes always twinkled, and he never lost his patience, or ability to listen. "Melvin," Hank said, "you are the man. Whatever you want, I'll do it."

Melvin reached his wrinkled and spotted hand out and touched Hank on the shoulder. Hank looked over and knew what Melvin was telling him. They smiled at each other, started laughing, and kept on laughing the whole way to Emily's hill. Enjoying ever bump along the way. At some point, Melvin started saying, "Whee," as they flew off the bumps, and when Hank joined him, they filled the cab of the truck with laughter.

"Now that is the perfect way to hide in the light."

"Did you hear that?" Melvin asked Hank.

"Hear what?" Hank answered.

"Oh. Must have been Sally," Melvin replied.

Hank didn't need an explanation. He just kept laughing.

FIFTY-THREE

Craig thought maybe they had it all wrong, and he was going to prove it. Just because Joe knew Frank, Harold, and Grant when they were younger didn't mean anything. Plus, there was nothing wrong with buying property out from a trust. People did it all the time.

As for all Joe's assistants being dead, well all the records showed them as natural deaths. It was just a string of unfortunate circumstances. If you looked at it that way, Dr. Joe was the victim.

Then there was the case of not having any records for his business. Joe was old. He had been running his practice for a long time. Things get lost, floods happen. And as Dr. Joe readily admitted, he was a terrible record keeper.

As far as Craig was concerned, too many assumptions were being made. It was time for Joe to set the record straight. Craig intended to let Joe know that strange ideas were being floated around about him, and give Joe a chance to refute them.

Craig also knew that a search warrant was being issued, along with a request to dig up Joe's wife. And that just proved Craig's point. There was a grave.

So what if the papers that registered her death were missing? He would ask Joe for them, and that would clear that up.

He had texted Joe earlier to let him know he was coming. Joe texted back that he would have the coffee on. He was looking forward to seeing Craig, he said. He remembered some information about the commune that might be helpful.

Dr. Joe greeted Craig with a big hug, looking fit and spry. The house smelled like a good brew of coffee and a hint of lilac fragrance coming from the bush growing outside the open window. It was homey and welcoming, just like Dr. Joe.

They each poured themselves a cup of coffee and chatted about the beautiful Sunday morning. Craig followed Joe into his office with a smile on his face. Everything felt normal. He knew that the pieces weren't pointing them in the right direction.

"So, young man," Dr. Joe began. "You look like something is troubling you."

Craig paused and put down his coffee, leaned forward and said, "Some people are confused right now. Some of them are my friends. In researching the bodies on the hill, you keep popping up. I think they are making a bunch of assumptions that don't point to you, but to someone else. Perhaps, someone you might know.

"So I am here to get some help from you. And to let you know about these assumptions. The police are working on a search warrant right now. I'm sorry."

"Oh dear, boy," Joe said patting Craig on his knee. "I've been around long enough to have many charges leveled against me for the same reasons. I was a common factor in something that went wrong. None of them have been proven true. As for the search warrant, the judge is a friend of mine. Don't tell anyone, but he gave me a heads up that he was issuing one for later today. It won't be the first time. And as long as I live here, it won't be the last."

Craig gave a little a laugh and looked at Joe in amazement. "I see I have a lot to learn from you about letting things be."

"Well, you might have to learn them from a long distance," Joe said. "I plan on leaving as soon as possible. I know my patients are already comfortable with you, so you don't need me here to convince them to use you as their doctor."

"Of course, Joe," Craig said. "I can handle it even though I will miss our talks. But is there a reason you want to go sooner?"

"Honestly, those bodies on the hill have disturbed me quite a bit," Joe said. He paused and leaned back in his chair, as if afraid to say more.

"I think I need to tell you something I have been keeping to myself. I know I did wrong. I should have told you and the police when it happened."

Again, Joe paused, and Craig took a deep breath afraid to hear what Joe was going to say.

"I knew those women," Joe said. "It took me a little while to put it together. But I used to go up on the hill to teach a little self-healing, and basic first aid. It was a long time ago as you know. But as I thought back on that time, I realized those women were part of the group.

"That was a strange group. They were studying mind healing, which of course I am very interested in. Mind over matter kind of thing. A little woo-woo at the time, but now it seems to be part of the culture.

"Anyway, it was a small group of women. I think there were more than four, maybe eight or so? Sometimes when I went there to teach, I brought Harold with me. He did chores for them.

"Poor boy. I hope he didn't have anything to do with those women's deaths." Joe paused and took a deep breath before continuing.

"I guess he wasn't a boy anymore, was he? But to me he was always that boy I watched grow up. I couldn't help feeling terrible when he got sick. Does anyone know how he died?"

"Not yet. The idea keeps floating around that Harold might have been poisoned, but so far nothing has been found.

"About the women," Craig asked, switching the discussion back to the bodies. "Did you know them well? Didn't you wonder where they went?" Craig asked.

"I did, actually. But Harold told me that everyone on the hill had packed up and left. They had only built a few A-Frame houses and hadn't done that very well. The buildings started rotting away within a few years, so I had them cleared off the land. I loved looking out the window at that beautiful view. Just as I do now."

They both looked out Joe's office window at what everyone now called Emily's hill. In the distance, Joe knew if he had binoculars he would be able to make out the barn and the beginning of Emily's dance deck. Joe would have had a perfect view of the commune when it was there. Of course, he would want to clear rotting homes off the land and let it return to nature.

Joe looked back at Craig. "By then, I had purchased the property from the trust. I dismantled the trust to make it easy to get to all the different pieces of land held within it. I realized that over time I would probably sell them off to fund my retirement. Which, as you know. I have done.

"So to answer your question, I'm leaving because I am tired of all of this. I am ready to lie in the sun, and maybe write a book."

"What would the book be about, Joe?" Craig asked.

"I think I would like to take the idea of mind over matter to the next level. It's an interesting subject. I've been studying it for a long time. Trying out ideas. If we can learn how to heal just using thought, think what could be done."

Craig nodded. Joe answered all his questions, even ones he didn't ask. It was almost as if he knew what was being used against him. Which, Craig mused, would be natural. Joe knew how the community worked, and how people thought. As Joe said, he has been around a long time, and this kind of awareness is something he had been studying and practicing his whole life.

Although Craig smiled at Joe and they continued to chat for another half hour or so, Craig couldn't shake the feeling that Joe hadn't told him everything, or perhaps Craig had forgotten to ask him something. It didn't matter really. Sadly his friends were wrong. But Craig knew they would listen to reason. It was someone else. Now they needed to point their attention elsewhere.

As the talk petered out, Craig rose and shook Joe's hand. "Thanks for everything," he said. "When are you leaving?"

"If all goes well," Joe said opening the front door, "tomorrow morning. No reason why it won't go well. So it might be a while until I see you again. Perhaps a hug this time?"

As the two hugged in the open door, across the street, Sam was watching and thinking that things were not as they appeared to be.

FIFTY-FOUR

Joe watched the last of the police leave his house. It had been a long day, and he was dead tired. Much more tired than he would ever admit to anyone. A lifetime of doing for others, now he had to ask himself if his work was done. Could he let himself rest? Had he done everything he had set out to do?

Joe thought back to the first time he had the feeling that he would do great things in the world.

He was only eight years old, and his mom was sick. She had been ill for almost a week, and instead of getting better, she was getting worse. He did his best to do all the things for his mom that she did for him when he was sick, and it always worked. He always got well. He couldn't figure out why it wasn't working for her. He was terrified that he would lose her.

The day she took sick had been a beautiful sunny day and the two of them had just come back from the park. They often went places together. Both of them never said why they didn't stay home, but Joe thought it was probably because his dad was always angry. Whatever the reason, Joe was always happy to have his mother all to himself.

They had a special bond. They created a world for themselves where all things were good. And then that day she had stumbled in the door, held her head and said, "I need to lie down, Joe. I don't feel well."

He had helped her to her bed and then sat beside her holding her hand and singing little songs he made up, just as she did for him.

When his dad came home, he was angry that his wife was sick. Joe remembered him yelling that he wasn't going to spend good money taking her to the doctor, she could damn well get better on her own.

After one day of not having his wife make him dinner, and wash his clothes, he left, slamming the door behind him after yelling that she was useless and that he wished Joe had never been born.

That week, Joe had lots of time to think while he held his mother's hand, helped her to the bathroom, and got her water when she asked for it.

He didn't know what else to do for her until he had an idea. What if he could convince her that she wasn't sick? He had no idea why people got sick. He imagined that some monster came along and told them they didn't feel well. That monster gave them reasons why it was true. That's what he believed had happened to his mother.

Joe had never learned any other reason for people not feeling well so he decided that if that was true, he could be a superhero like the ones he saw in the comic books that his dad sometimes left lying around.

So Joe pretended he was a healing superhero and he was stronger and smarter than the monster. He started telling his mom that she wasn't sick. She was strong. She was beautiful. She was his mom. She didn't want to be sick. She wanted to play with him.

He sang those ideas to her. He said them to her over and over again. He talked aloud, and when he got tired of talking, he just spoke to her in his mind. He didn't know how long he did this, but he had only fallen asleep once before his mom opened her eyes, and said she was hungry.

She was well. Joe never told her what he had done. But he knew even then that he had found power, and he was never going to let it go.

He practiced it everywhere. He said things to people to see if he could convince them of something. Even stuff he made up.

His ability to make people think what he wanted them to think and see what he wanted them to see, became more and more refined. It helped him raise him and his mom out of the cycle of poverty that his dad had put them into.

Joe decided to become a doctor once he learned what they were. He would learn the traditional and accepted ways of healing because it would provide the perfect cover to practice healing by suggestion. His suggestion. That would give him the license to heal, and people would love him for it.

By the time Joe reached high school, he had discovered that he could do more than heal people with his suggestions or make them do what he wanted them to do. He could also harm. It fascinated him. What thoughts would people accept as their own? How far could he take it?

Healing and harming became the same to him. The only thing that pleased him was watching the outcome of what he was doing. When he became a doctor, he allowed people to see the healing he did. It was expected. He just never told them how.

However, if he didn't like someone, he used this art to hurt them. It all felt the same to him. It was the power that motivated him. It resulted in people loving him, and believing everything he said. It was a legacy that he was leaving. A legacy that no one was going to take away from him. Including the people that Grant had called the do-gooders.

Joe knew that they suspected what he was doing. And, unlike most other people, they were able to block his suggestions.

Actually, everyone could if they were only paying attention and knew that there were people like him purposefully manipulating events and people just because they could.

Oh, yes. Joe had met them. They always recognized each other. Usually, it was because they would feel someone else inside their mind, and then realize that the man standing across the room was trying to make you do something. You'd stop him and give it right back. When that happened, they would merely nod at each other and go their own way. There was plenty of opportunity for all of these mental malpractitioners. It was an unwritten agreement to stay away.

Someday Joe thought that there would be someone who didn't follow that rule, and then perhaps all of them would need to unite against him. He hoped it wasn't while he was still alive. However, if there was someone like that around, he wasn't too worried. Joe thought he would win anyway. He always did.

· · · ● · ● · ● · · ·

The search at Dr. Joe's house was revealing nothing. Joe was kind and gracious. He had even provided food and drinks for everyone. Some of the police took him up on it. No one expected to find anything. The judge had been upset about being bothered on a Sunday. No one was happy. Did I really think this would work? Sam thought.

After all, it was Dr. Joe. What were they looking for anyway? Did they expect to find records that somehow he had killed four women and buried them on the hill? Murdered them in a way that no one knew how they had died? And got away with it for forty-five years? And to keep his secret, killed his wife and all his assistants without anyone knowing it was even murder? *It sounded ridiculous,* even to Sam.

Then there was the question of how would he have killed Harold? And why? And what about Frank and Lenny? How did he get to them? Assuming, once again, that it was Dr. Joe that did all of that. Without a single shred of evidence.

Sam wondered why they even bothered. There would be no records. Joe knew they were coming. If there were any evidence at all, it would have been destroyed. Every single thing they had that pointed to Dr. Joe as a killer was circumstantial. Not even that. It was a suspicion. A feeling. If there was anyone who knew what Joe had been doing or could do, they were dead. Yes, suspicious. However, not something that could convict him.

How do you find and convict someone that can manipulate what you see, feel, or think? Sam asked himself. *Even if he had proof, was there anything he could do about it?*

On the other hand, would it be better if left untouched? Joe was retired and moving away. Sam was beginning to think that maybe it would be best to let him go. Messing with someone like Dr. Joe could be more dangerous than anything he had ever done before.

However, it burned inside of Sam. He had always needed to speak out against injustice. If he could find a way to prove what had happened, he would do it, no matter how long it took. Nevertheless, for now maybe he needed to stop pursuing Joe. That might be the better way to protect his friends. Perhaps the council would be able to help him decide what to do next. Assuming he had a choice about what would happen next. Sam wasn't so sure that he did. That's what made it all so terrifying.

FIFTY-FIVE

Joe watched Sam during the search. He knew that Sam believed that he was responsible for all the things that had happened, and was frustrated with not being able to prove it.

It pleased Joe to no end that Sam was frustrated. He might not be able to manipulate Sam's thinking, but he could frustrate him.

Sam, like most people, could not fathom how people could be made to believe things that weren't true. *Yet,* Joe thought, *it happens every day.* Commercials peddle products for diseases no one had until the products came to market and people are sold the symptoms. The spread of lies and gossips that occupied so much of everyone's life. Group mentality. Perception blindness. These terms were everywhere.

However, people didn't have time to worry about them. They were busy. Why were they busy? Because they were distracted and believed in the need to acquire. They believed in false authorities. Companies, medicines, religions, money, politics, the stock market. All manipulated. All an agreed upon perception.

It made Joe laugh. He wasn't doing anything that the culture hadn't already promoted. It was just that Joe did it so much better. And he was awake to it.

Joe knew that people were astonished at the synchronism of Lenny and Frank's deaths. Ridiculous, he thought. It wasn't synergistic. It was planned. Perfectly. Joe had decided that he might as well see if he could manipulate both of them even when they were so far apart. He didn't see why not. Distance doesn't mean a thing to thoughts. And he proved it.

The timing was perfect. It might have been sloppy on his part to do it that way, but he wanted to try it out. What a thrill it had been to pull the timing off so succinctly.

The suggestion to rush the guards even though they knew it would get them killed was buried within what they heard. Lenny and Frank didn't have enough mental discipline to overcome his suggestions. Besides, it had been programmed in them years before when they were young and unaware. Add the fact that they were both filled with fear which made them very easy to manipulate.

Neither of them had Grant's innate ability or willingness to learn. Joe wouldn't have been able to pull that stunt off with Grant. He was much too brilliant of a thinker. Grant had been a genius of manipulation and distraction.

If Joe missed anyone, it was Grant. However, last summer Joe realized that Grant was going to be a liability. He was letting his personal feelings and his need for vengeance get in his way. Joe thought that it was interesting that Grant had hated the do-gooders because they had gifts. Gifts that were in the same realm, although not the same motivation, as Joe's. He supposed that Grant was afraid and didn't recognize his drive to destroy them as fear. But Joe did. If he had regrets, it was that Grant had to go. Grant's reign was over.

Joe didn't have to manipulate Grant to do stupid things, like focus on revenge. He had done that to himself. All Joe had to do was kill him. Which was easy. Grant believed that Joe would never hurt him.

Of course, Joe wouldn't kill Grant himself. He used someone else. Lenny. Lenny was a handy tool to get the killing done. Lenny wanted Grant dead anyway. At least that is what Lenny thought he wanted. That idea had been planted in him by Joe.

Joe sighed again. He didn't want to leave Doveland yet. He had been looking forward to spending the next year with Craig. Joe didn't have any hopes that he would swing Craig entirely his way, but Craig wanted a brilliant friend like Joe so much, it made him easy to deceive. Joe sighed. *They would have had some great talks together. But it was not to be.*

However, the main reason Joe didn't want to go away was his son. Even though Edward had been gone for forty years, Joe kept the hope alive that he would return someday. Joe knew it wasn't because he loved Edward. Other than his mother, Joe knew that he had never experienced the love that other people talked about, nor did he want to. It was a distraction and a weakness.

No, he wanted Edward to respect him. That's what he wanted. And Edward never gave that to him. He was a mommy's boy. It didn't dawn on Joe that his son was like him. Joe had loved his mother. Hated his dad.

Joe finished his scotch and left the glass on the desk. The housekeeper would clean up after him. It was time for him to go. And time for him to stop thinking about the past. He was going to leave it all behind the minute he stepped out his door.

Still, he was a trifle irritated. He wouldn't have to leave if Harold had done his job. That was a mistake Joe would have to own. He had made a mistake in trusting Harold.

The women had died because they believed what Joe told them. He practiced different words and suggestions on each of them. They died one by one because Joe told them they were sick. He tried out a variety of suggestions to observe what the outcome would be. They had different symptoms. Different reasons. Different illness. Same suffering.

He had eight canvases. It was beautiful. He was an artist.

Then there was Harold. He had recruited Harold when he was just a boy looking for someone to act like a dad. Joe was happy to do that. However, Harold didn't have the aptitude for what Joe had to teach the way that Grant did.

So Joe gave Harold simple jobs. Harold helped with chores, and building the houses. However, once the women started dying, Harold stopped obeying without question. Still, Joe thought he could trust him. He put Harold in charge of taking the bodies away, explaining that it was a way that he could show the women respect.

Joe told the remaining women he was sending their friends home to their loved ones. Instead, Harold was supposed to take them out into the deepest part of the lake and drop them overboard weighted down with concrete blocks.

This is where Joe admitted that he had made a mistake. He hadn't checked up on Harold. Four women never made it to the lake. Harold had taken the easy way out and buried them. He had just been a teenager. Joe should have checked on him.

Still, it wasn't Joe's fault. All of the extra deaths could have been avoided if only Harold had come clean and told him. Harold would still have had to die, but no one else would have been harmed.

After the women, Joe had kept most of his killing out of Doveland. He was preserving the town for his son. Now that everyone who knew anything about Joe's past was dead, he could leave Doveland alone again, so Edward would see the beautiful town his father had helped to make.

Yes, Joe was tired. It was time for him to go while he was still loved. People might have their suspicions of him, but there was nothing to prove what he had done. He was not a serial killer. He didn't collect trophies. He was a healer. His research into healing was helping people all over the world.

Craig would convince his friends to let it go. Joe was safe. That meant they were too. For now anyway.

Joe picked up his overnight bag and turned back to look at the home that he loved. He had already sent everything else that he would need ahead to his house in Morocco. Anything else, he could buy when he got there.

The car he had hired to take him to the airport was waiting. He locked the house and put the key under the mat. There was nothing for anyone to find in the house that meant anything to him. The housekeeper would look after it for him. If his son ever came home, he would know to look under that mat for the key.

Opening the app on his phone, Joe checked the cameras one last time. He would be watching and waiting.

FIFTY-SIX

As Hank and Melvin drove up the recently graveled driveway, neither of them were surprised to see Emily sitting on her rock, her ever-present backpack beside her.

On the other hand, she was surprised to see them. She was even more surprised to hear them laughing as they drove up. Her heart lifted at the sight of two of her favorite men.

Before they were even out of the truck, she had raced across to meet them, practically knocking Hank over as she hugged him, and then Melvin, and then back to Hank. As Hank hugged her back, she burst into tears burying her face in his soft flannel shirt.

"I'm so sorry, Hank. I am just so happy to see you both. These aren't tears of sadness. Really."

Hank took out his handkerchief and dabbed at her tears, trying not to cry himself.

With a voice rough from emotion, he said, "It was Melvin. He had a bug up his butt to get out here. Fast. Like now."

Emily went back to hugging Melvin, who took it all in stride, in spite of the fact that he had little or no experience at being embraced by young women.

"You must have heard me wishing, Melvin," Emily said pulling back and looking at his kind face.

"I wished for company, and here you are. Oh. I just realized that you have never seen the hill. Well, at least not like this."

"Nope, I haven't," Melvin answered. "And I want you and Hank to walk me through the whole thing and tell me what you are planning to do with it all," Melvin said, sweeping his arm to take in the whole hill.

"Yes!" Emily said, pumping her arm. "But I need Hank to fill in details. Besides, I think you have a small surprise for me, Hank?"

Hank's face turned red as he looked down at his boots. "Wasn't expecting you to be out here so soon given what was happening. I thought we might be further along, but yes. I do have a little surprise for you."

"Well, let's get to walking," Melvin said. "Tell me what is happening here."

For the next hour, Emily and Hank took Melvin through the whole project. Hank's surprise of the partially built deck made Emily happier than Hank could have imagined. She told him that now she could plan an outdoor dance to be performed on the deck for the town during the summer camp week.

She thought she would get Valerie and Tina involved. It might help take their minds off of what had happened with their husbands. She knew that Tina's daughter Lynn had decided to take dance with Hannah, and perhaps the boys would come to class too.

When Hank and Melvin guffawed at the suggestion, she reminded them that dance was no longer considered sissy. It had never been. But at least people were starting to wake up and notice. Had they watched "So You Think You Can Dance" lately? "Or even Dancing With The Stars?" Gone to a performance of any dance company? Any at all? When they said they hadn't, she made them promise to come to her house and watch some dance shows with her that she had taped. They would change their mind after they watched the men and boys dance. After a few hems and haws, they agreed.

When Emily asked Hank when he thought her house on the hill would be done, he assured her that they would finish the outside before winter set in. If she wanted to, she could then move in while they finished the interior over the winter. He suggested that Emily get Mandy in on the project because her sense of design would add just the right touches on the project.

After the tour of Emily's dream, the three of them stood near her rock and looked back towards the village. Emily pulled a pair of binoculars from her backpack and handed them to Hank. Looking through them, he could see Dr. Joe's house from where they stood. It was distinctive, with its slate gray tin roof.

"What are we going to do about him?" Emily asked.

It was Melvin who answered, "Stand together in love," he said.

Emily and Hank looked at Melvin and nodded in agreement.

If Dr. Joe had been looking up at his hill, he might have seen them, standing together, Emily holding hands with Hank and Melvin, and realized that perhaps he might not win after all.

But he didn't see. He had already left town.

• • • • • • • • • •

Emily asked if she could go along to see the bike path. By then, the three of them were hungry, and even though Melvin wouldn't admit it, Hank could tell he needed to rest.

They decided to stop in at the Diner for a late-afternoon meal. Emily would drive her car home and meet them there.

On the way to town, Hank asked Melvin if he was sure he wanted to see the bike trail today, or perhaps wait until another time.

"I know. I'm tired. But I do want to see where it starts, and then where it ends. We can walk the first part for a short way, and drive to the end because isn't that back in Concourse?"

Hank looked over at the old man and tried not to let his concern come through as he asked, "Is there a reason you want to do both these things today, Melvin?"

Melvin looked over at him and didn't answer, and Hank wisely didn't pry any further.

Emily had told Hank what she wanted to eat, so by the time she came in the door, her portobello burger was waiting for her along with a side of fries and a diet Dr. Pepper.

Over the winter, Barbara had worked with Alex until he had perfected the burger just the way Emily liked it, and it had become a hit among some of her younger customers. Even a few old timers had decided to try it and had given it a thumbs up.

"Man, I am happy to see you," Pete said to the three of them. "It was a rough night. We need some bright faces around here, and the three of you look pretty happy right now."

Emily laughed and told them what they had been doing. "We are planning to do good, Pete. That has to have an effect, doesn't it?"

Before Pete could answer, the bell over the door dinged, and Sarah walked in. Without talking about it, everyone picked up their food and moved to a booth so that Sarah could sit with them. When Alex came to take her order, she pointed at Emily's plate and said, "That please."

As Alex went to put in her order, Sarah added, "I didn't feel like cooking today. I'm beginning to see the value of living close to town. There is always great food and even better company just a few blocks away."

As they ate, no one talked about the night before. They chatted about the weather and Sarah's garden. She needed some garden work done and asked if she could hire Johnny to help her. Pete and

Hank said that was what they wanted for him. Work that made a difference.

Before Emily left with Hank and Melvin, Sarah said, "Sam wants to meet with the council tonight. Emily, would you be there, please?"

"What about the rest of us, Sarah? Shouldn't we all be there? I think Sam is going to ask the same questions that we all need to have answered," Pete asked.

Sarah glanced up at Barbara, who had come into the room as Pete asked the question. Barbara nodded in agreement.

"You're right, Pete. Would you gather the men, and I will gather the women. Instead of meeting at Grace's, we'll meet again at Ava and Evan's. There's a bit more room, and that way we can watch over the children at the same time."

Seeing a cloud of concern come over everyone's faces, Sarah added, "Be joyful, please. There is nothing to worry about right now."

As the booth was being cleared, Sarah walked over to Barbara, who was leaning against the counter, looking downcast.

"I'm still worried," Barbara said.

"We can be vigilant and not be worried," Sarah replied. "It's a big difference. Have you ever watched how birds behave? Always vigilant. Always joyful. In fact, all of nature provides that example."

Barbara thought for a moment, then leaned over and hugged Sarah. "Vigilant and joyful. I understand."

As Sarah walked home, for the first time she felt at peace about her move to Doveland. She would always miss her home in Sandpoint, but her home now was just around the corner from everything that she needed.

FIFTY-SEVEN

Tina put the sign out in front of the gas station on her way over to Valerie's. Yes, it was a little strange to send people to a different gas station. But she had something more important to do than pumping gas. She had a friend to support.

A new gas station, with shiny new tanks and the standard tiny store, had opened. It was down the road that led to the lake. It was only a mile out of town, so Tina wasn't worried that someone would run out of gas just because she was closed. She made the sign herself and taped it onto a sawhorse. It said: "Closed. Gas One Mile That Way." An arrow pointed the way.

Tina could see herself in the gas station window as she placed the sign. There she was in her baggy jeans and fly away brown hair that had seen better days. Plus, she was too thin. She had always been thin, but now she was not looking good. The last month had been more stressful than she thought was possible. Years of hiding from Frank had taken a toll. Then Harold's unwanted attention, which ended in both Harold and Frank dying, increased her stress level.

Add to that, she and Valerie had briefly been suspected of killing Harold. As if. If she were a killer, she would have done away with Frank years ago.

Tina hated what had happened to Harold and even to Frank. She hoped that they would catch who did it. Although Tina believed that it was Dr. Joe, she knew that there was no proof. She was open to being wrong. Besides, she didn't want to spend any more of her life worrying.

She pulled her sweater closer as she crossed the street to Valerie's Bed and Breakfast, thinking that as terrible as it had been, she was now free. She did not need to mourn either man. But Valerie did, and that's why she agreed to go with her today.

Valerie was waiting at the door for her. She and Tina were dressed almost the same. Jeans, t-shirt, sweater. They were both thin, for all the wrong reasons. And although Valerie could have been Tina's mother, they looked more like sisters. What surprised them both was that they had become good friends.

Common disasters could do that, Tina knew. But it was more than that. It was Valerie's heart. Valerie had looked past the circumstances of their meeting and had seen what they had in common. They understood each other. Both widows. Both with children to raise on their own. Both married to men that they didn't really know.

Tina followed Valerie to the back of their house, each grabbing a bottle of water on their way through the kitchen to the garage. Valerie was driving. She knew how to get where they were going, and had the nicer car.

The cemetery was south of town. Tina had never been there before. There had been a funeral for Harold, but Valerie had kept it private. Just her and her children. Neither she nor Harold had a family. All they had was each other. In the midst of all the allegations of who and what Harold was, Valerie didn't want to bring more attention to his death. But her children had a right, and a need, to mourn for their father.

Tina had Frank cremated. She and the children had released his ashes into the field where Jay had been shot. She thought it a fitting tribute to them both. A symbol of what she hoped for Frank. That he was now free.

Valerie had chosen a plot for Harold near the edge of the cemetery. It was close to the forest that embraced the grave sites. There was a small bench that she had brought and placed in front of the grave, and that's where the two friends sat.

"Thank you for coming, Tina," Valerie said, touching the back of Tina's hand.

"Thank you for asking me to, Valerie. I haven't been able to give back to anyone for a long time. I was too busy running and hiding. You could have shut me out, and you didn't."

There was nothing either woman could say to make it better. They sat on the bench and let the sun wash over them.

They sat so still a squirrel walked over Valerie's foot, causing them both to laugh out loud, which turned into a full-blown giggling fit. After it calmed down, Valerie said, "Wow. I needed that!" Wiping the tears from her face with her sleeve, she asked, "Are you still selling the gas station and moving?"

Tina paused, looking up at the beautiful blue sky, and watched a fluffy white cloud that looked like a sheep drift by.

"This is a beautiful town. I know I will always love it, but it was Frank's town. Even when I was little, it never felt like mine. I want to find a place that is mine. So yes, I'm still selling the gas station.

"Grace helped me find someone who does that kind of thing. He didn't think I could get much for the station itself, especially since that new station has been built. But the land right there in town might be worth something.

"Plus, when Frank and I first married, we bought small term policies on each other. I never stopped paying the premiums on Frank's, even when it was a struggle. Given who he was, there was always the chance that he wouldn't live that long, and in life, he was never going to support us. So in death, he is. That money, and whatever I get for the station, will get us all started on a new life.

"Do you know where you are going?" Valerie asked.

"Not far. I think we'll move closer to Pittsburgh. I would like to come back and visit from time to time, so I didn't want to go too far away. Pittsburgh seemed like a good choice. A city, and yet close to Doveland.

"I am checking out school districts and that will determine where we go. We don't need a big place. After all, we have been living in one room rentals or tiny houses like the one behind the station. Anything will be better than that."

Turning to face Valerie, Tina added, "Then I am going to do something I always wanted to do. Take night classes. I can do that while working a day job."

Valerie reached over to Tina and hugged her. "I am so proud of you, Tina! And I'm thrilled you will be so close. We can spend more time together. I'll come there, and you can visit me here."

"So you aren't moving?"

"I thought about it. But even though this was where Harold grew up, as soon as we moved here, I fell in love with it. I love my job. The school has been so forgiving of my not being present very often this past month. Now that things have settled a bit, it's time for me to see what I can do to make sure every child around here has the best education possible.

"And then there are my friends. Grace and her friends have become my friends, our friends," Valerie said, looking at Tina.

"I don't know if I can run the Bed and Breakfast by myself though. I don't want Johnny to feel that he needs to help me so that he doesn't go off to school. That's something I have to decide. But it does mean that I have a big house to put friends in when they come to visit."

Tina smiled at her friend and wondered if she could learn to be more like her. "And Craig?"

Valerie stared at Harold's grave for a moment before answering. "You noticed?"

"Well, it was kinda hard to miss. Craig has been so attentive and concerned. I don't think it was just about taking care of a patient."

Valerie paused. "We didn't talk about it at all. I loved having his support, and I felt my heart leaning towards his. But it's too soon. And now. Well, he has pulled back. Not just from me, but from everyone. I don't know if that rift will ever be closed."

"His loss," Tina said, grabbing her friend's hand.

Valerie nodded, thinking that if the door had closed on that possibility, it was her loss too. But she wasn't going to mourn something that never happened.

She stood up and said, "Come on. Let's go get something yummy to eat before the kids come home from school."

"Aren't we eating at Ava's tonight at the meeting?" Tina asked.

"Oh, yes. But look at us. This may be the one time in our life we can overeat and not care what kind of food it is either. We can go with our taste buds instead of our logic. For once!"

Laughing, they linked arms and strolled back to the car.

Leif watched them go. He had chosen not to be seen this time so that they could have their time together. He could report back to Sarah that yes, they were doing fine. For them, life had gotten better than it was before. Whatever they still needed to go through, they had each other to lean on.

FIFTY-EIGHT

"So we just let him go?" Sam asked.

They were all outside Ava's house, sitting around a fire that Evan had made for them. It was a warm May evening, but the blazing logs gave them a focal point. It reminded Sarah of the fires they used to gather around in Sandpoint. It was a much smaller group then. And Leif was sitting beside her then. No, she shook her head, not going there. Besides, he was still right beside her. Perhaps not physically, but she could see and hear him. That was enough.

The silence dragged on. No one spoke. Everyone knew how Sam felt.

Finally, Sarah said, "No, we are letting go, Sam. It's different."

"But he is going to fly away and go unpunished? We'll never know for sure that it's him. Well, I know it's him, but I can't prove it."

Craig grunted quietly, but everyone heard him. He sat with the group, yet slightly apart. His chair just a bit out of the circle of light the fire created. He had made it clear that he didn't believe that it was Dr. Joe who had killed the women on the hill, let alone Harold, Lenny, and Frank. As they said, there was no proof. None at all.

"Who do we need to prove it to? Will it make you, or us, heroes in someone's eyes?" Mandy asked.

Mira reached across and touched Sam's hand. "You haven't failed, Sam."

"Well, then why do I feel that I have? All those deaths with no one to blame for them. No one is going to be punished."

"That always brings up an interesting question," Sarah said. "Who is responsible for punishing people? Our justice system is set up to punish. Even to the point of killing. On purpose. Yes, we all need to look at the wrong that we do and rectify it. But we often punish instead of helping.

"Why does someone become a criminal? Look at Hank. He was a criminal. He did evil things. And yet today, his life is dedicated to helping. What if he would have ended up in prison, punished? Would he have gotten better, or worse?"

Hank squirmed in his chair and added. "It's true. Without your help at changing, I probably would have seen myself as evil my whole life."

Emily, sitting beside Hank, bumped his shoulder and smiled at him. They could all see him physically relax at her assurance that they understood.

Everyone, including Valerie and Tina, was at the meeting. Everyone except Melvin. As Hank had thought, Melvin had worn himself out.

After walking the bike trail for about a half a mile, they had gone back to the truck and followed the trail to Concourse. Sometimes the finished part of the path could be glimpsed through the trees. As they drove, Hank pointed out where the trail would continue, and finally where it ended in Concourse—on one of the side streets that led into the center of town. The dream was to connect

Doveland and Concourse. Melvin told Hank it was the best idea he had ever heard.

When Hank dropped off Melvin, he made sure he was settled for the night, before heading back to Ava's. He worried about him, but at the same time, he knew that Melvin understood and accepted what was happening.

"I'm not saying that we don't need to keep people off the streets who intend to hurt others, in one way or another. But should we punish them, or help them?" Sarah said.

"Not everyone is going to get better. Some people have no desire to be anything but evil," Sam answered.

"You're right. And those people need to be stopped. Joe is probably one of those, I agree," Sarah rushed in, as Sam started to speak again. "And if it were possible to catch him, he would have to be put somewhere that he could do no more harm. Not an easy task given his skills at manipulation and mental suggestions."

"But those criminals are not the majority of people that we end up punishing. And even some of those hardened criminals can be helped to find their way back to the infinite presence of Good.

"However, Sam, in this case. We can't even prove who committed these killings. Or how he did it. Plus, we know that our friend Craig doesn't believe it is Dr. Joe."

Everyone turned to look at Craig who simply nodded and looked away.

"Besides," Leif added, "Joe has already left town. He flew to Morocco this morning. There is no way to get him back here unless he wants to come back."

"That doesn't mean we are safe from him though, does it? Thought travels. What if he targets us, or the people of Doveland again?" Mandy asked.

"Oh, for god's sake!" Craig yelled. "You keep convicting him and you know it's not Joe. It can't be Joe. Look at all the good he has done for this town! For everyone. I can't believe that none of you are thinking clearly. Stop blaming him. Look elsewhere!"

Everyone looked at each other. No one knew what to say. Craig just kept staring. "Sarah, tell them!" Craig yelled.

"Craig's right in that Joe has done much good in this town, and we can't prove that it is him. Craig is also right in another way. We can't divide ourselves this way. That separation would make us vulnerable. Whether it is or isn't Joe isn't the point right now. We need to learn how to protect ourselves, the town, and then spread out from there. We need to stick together.

"We also need to remember that evil, or moral wrongness, is not real. It's an illusion. One we can, and will, dissolve. First within ourselves. And it will be much easier if we do it together.

"Agreed?"

"Agreed," was the answer, with a few scattered "Amens," and "So Say We all," mixed in.

Mandy went back into the kitchen and brought out a cake she had baked that day, and fixings for s'mores. "Tonight," she said. "We celebrate!"

"What are we celebrating?" Pete asked.

"May! We are celebrating May. It's Sarah's favorite month of the year. No other reason is necessary."

As everyone laughed and started helping themselves to the food, including all the kids who were asked to join the grown-ups, Sarah and Leif stood off to the side and watched.

"Is this enough?" Sarah asked.

"It's enough for now," Leif answered. "Eric and I will keep watch over Joe. If he turns his sights back to town, we'll let you know."

Sarah stood alone for a while after Leif and Eric faded away, wondering if she knew what she was doing. How much danger were they in, and what would they do if Joe returned?

Grace joined Sarah and looked at her friend. "Stop it."

"Stop what?" Sarah laughed.

"I think you said to be vigilant and joyful. Not vigilant and worried. Besides, you aren't alone."

Grace pointed to the woods surrounding the house. A light blinked. Sarah looked at Grace in wonderment. "You see that?"

"I do. And I happen to know that means The Forest Circle is here too."

Sarah sighed. A weight she didn't know she was carrying slipped off her shoulders. Grace was right. They weren't alone.

FIFTY-NINE

I miss all the other kids being here," Hannah said to her mom as she sank back into her bed after saying her prayers. She looked around the room, thinking how lucky she was to have such a pretty bedroom. She still loved it, but now that she was almost eleven, Hannah thought that perhaps soon she could design a new bedroom that was more grown up. Besides, she always added an extra eight years on to her age since she still kinda, sorta, remembered her lifetime before with her past-dad, Jay, and her mom, Maggie.

Ava told her it was okay to let the past slip away, but if she wanted to remember, she would help her. So they had established a secret time together to talk. Once Hannah was in bed, they would sit for a while and tell each other private things about their lives. They couldn't tell anyone else what they shared unless they had been given permission.

Hannah loved their secret time together, which delighted Ava. Ava knew that she was the one who received the best gift in the world during that private time. It was a privilege to hear all her daughter's little secrets and fears about growing up.

One night, Hannah shared that she had a small crush on Johnny. She was sure that Johnny didn't know, and didn't feel the same way about her because he saw her as a little girl.

Ava just smiled to herself thinking that Hannah only had to bide her time. When she was older, Johnny, and any other boy she liked, would be flocking to her like bees to honey. Not that Evan would be happy about that. Ava was pretty sure that Evan would be keeping a tight rein on his daughter. Plus, Eric was continually checking on his adopted, granddaughter. Hannah would always have a chaperone, like it or not.

On another night, Hannah told her mom that a girl in school had been mean to her. With this news, Ava had a private talk with Valerie about what was going on in school. Ava never gave away Hannah's secret, but the bullying issue immediately became a focus of the school and was resolved. Not just for Hannah but for everyone else who had been at the mercy of a child who had only been reaching out for help and now was getting it.

Hannah often shared about missing Jay. She would always add that she loved her dad Evan too, and Ava would assure her that it was okay to be sad and to love both of them. There was no limit to the number of people she could love.

Ava knew it was a privilege to listen and hold those secrets that Hannah shared sacred and close to her heart. Ava hoped that as Hannah got older, they would continue to keep their private time together and share their secrets. Ava made sure that she also shared with Hannah little secrets from her own life. It was a simple way to teach Hannah lessons she had learned, usually the hard way, without being preachy. They were sharing stories. Ava knew that Hannah was getting to know her mother in a way Ava never had a chance to know her mother, Abigail.

As Ava kissed Hannah goodnight with a butterfly kiss, she said, "I miss having the kids here too, but I love this little secret time that we share. Sometimes it's a little busy when all of them are staying here, and we don't get a chance to share. But we can plan a sleepover soon if you like."

Hannah nodded, and as her eyes closed, she whispered, "You don't have to worry about Dr. Joe, mommy. At least right now. He likes his new home, and doesn't care about us anymore."

"That's good to hear, sweetie," Ava said, thinking that Hannah probably did know that to be true. How she knew didn't matter.

Out in the hall, Evan was waiting, holding a sleepy Ben. "He didn't want to go to bed until you kissed him goodnight," Evan said. Ava looked at her little boy in his fire engine pajamas and Evan, who became more handsome every day and said a silent prayer of thanks for all their blessings.

She knew the practice of gratitude would help keep them safe.

SIXTY

Six weeks had gone by since Dr. Joe had left town, and once again, it was the summer solstice in Doveland, Pennsylvania.

This time, there were no threats of poisoning, nor fear of killing. The miasma of fear had lifted, and for those that were paying attention, it had happened when Dr. Joe left town.

Valerie had used the preparing of the solstice as a time of healing. She was her best while running things. The school had welcomed her back, saying that chaos had begun to take over when she was gone. Within a week, Valerie had everything running smoothly again.

With Valerie at the helm, the solstice went off without a hitch. Face painting, musicians playing, dancing, fireworks, and food all happened. Perfectly.

But this year they didn't celebrate in the village square. This year the celebration was held on Emily's hill. The whole town had voted. They wanted to celebrate what Emily had brought to their village, and although the discovery of the four women had brought heartache, it had brought joy and freedom, too.

Almost every family with young children had become involved. Emily had even added adult dance classes in ballet and hip-hop, and within a few weeks, they were the most popular classes she had ever taught. She was still using the town hall for her big classes, and teaching the children in the house she was renting.

But a week of summer dance classes at the hill would start right after the July 4th holiday. Melvin said he would drive the little school bus Emily bought to transport her students to and from town. Just this year, he assured her. Next year, he wouldn't be around to do it. No one wanted to hear him say that, but they had all learned to respect what people knew, and Melvin was determined that he was right.

The finished dance barn hosted all the food. Gleaming mirrors and sturdy ballet barres lined the walls, ready for students. Some of the little girls from the town were holding on to them, pretending to be ballet dancers. No one shooed them off. After all, this was a celebration of dreams come true.

In the center of the barn, long tables held every kind of picnic food imaginable. Hank had thought ahead and installed a refrigerator in a small pantry in the back of the barn. When Emily asked why she needed a pantry and a fridge in the barn, Hank reminded her she might want to hold small celebrations there from time to time.

Emily had agreed, having no idea that the first celebration would not be small and would be in her honor. It would be a whole town arriving at her dream on the hill to wish her well.

As Emily helped serve food, she couldn't help but wish that Aunt Jean would have been there to see it. Looking out across the hill down towards town, Emily thought that perhaps Jean was there. Her spirit was anyway.

Emily and her friends had held a small, very private ceremony in the stone church in town. Afterward, they had scattered Jean's ashes around Emily's hill. And then they buried the urn under the white oak tree by the parking lot, not far from where Jean's body had lain for all those years.

Four large stepping stones led the way from the parking lot to the paths that led through the property. Each stone had one of the women's names carved near the top, and their favorite flower engraved into the middle of each stone.

Hank had the stones made as a gift to Emily, but Emily knew it was also for the town. Although the investigation had stalled and was moved to the back burner, no one wanted to forget what happened here. The three other women were returned to their families. Emily had called each one of them and shared tears and memories. Each of the rooms in the barn were named for one of the women. Their families were grateful to finally know what had happened to them, or at least where they had ended up. Only one person knew what had happened to them, and he wasn't telling.

At least he is gone, Emily thought, and then felt guilty for the thought. Craig kept insisting that Joe was innocent. As if to prove Craig's point that Dr. Joe was a good guy, Joe had mailed a large manila envelope to the town hall. They had received it a few days after he had left town.

In the envelope was a last gift to the town. Although he kept his house, Joe had given the rest of the land he still owned to Doveland. A note was clipped to the deeds saying he was grateful for all the business and friendship he had received in his years of living at Doveland. His only stipulations on the gift was that no shopping centers be built on the properties and that as many of the trees and as much of the natural lines of the land be preserved as possible. One piece of property he designated only for a public park, which made almost everyone happy.

Emily received her own envelope. Inside she found the deed to her land, along with a copy of what she still owed him. Across the top he had written, "paid in full." He had included a nice note saying it made him happy to know that there would always be a celebration of art on the hill. There was also a copy of a trust he had set up to fund scholarships for students who wanted to take classes but couldn't afford it. In memory of his wife May who loved the arts, he had written.

At first, she didn't know what to do with it. Joe was evil, she knew it in her heart. But turning down the gift that would benefit so many seemed stupid and in a strange way selfish. So she said, thank you. Not to Joe, but to the universe. She accepted the gift in the name of her aunt and her mom, and Joe's wife.

Once everyone had eaten, the crowd ambled up to the seats above the dance deck. Hank had kept his promise and finished it in time for summer camp and the celebration. The seats were set back into the hill, rising with the gentle slope of the hill.

The deck was stunning. It jutted out from the hill, A vast open expanse, reaching out into the space between the hill and the town. To keep dancers safe, there was a chest high clear Plexiglas barrier that ran the whole parameter of the deck.

It was more beautiful than Emily could ever have imagined, and she couldn't stop thanking Hank for it. He just blushed and mumbled, "You're welcome." After the children performed, everyone was invited onto the deck to dance, music provided by Emily's musician friend, Shawn. Emily laughed to herself. She knew that people thought there was something going on between her and Shawn. But no, she wasn't his type. Besides, she had her eyes set elsewhere.

It was a glorious sight. As Emily watched the town dance on her deck, she breathed out a prayer of thanks. Silently Ava, Mandy, Mira, Grace, Barbara, and Sarah joined her to watch the dancers, and the moon rise.

"Thank you," Emily said, smiling at all her new friends. The seven of them joined hands and headed to the dance floor. It was a night of celebration. They would let nothing take that away from them.

EPILOGUE

A few months later, in a small town on the Oregon coast, Edward pushed back from the computer. Every week for years, he had logged on and checked for news. Now, after all these years of faithful watching, his patience had been rewarded.

It seemed to Edward, given how momentous of an occasion this was, the world should have tilted or done something unusual. After all, everything was entirely different for him. The sky should have turned purple, or clouds could have rained silver stars. But no. Outside, nothing had changed.

It was only Edward's world that had drastically shifted. No matter how much he had wanted it to happen, it was still a shock to realize that it finally had.

Edward leaned back in his chair, trying to decide what to do next. Within minutes, he heard the command. "Just go."

Following directions, Edward picked up the backpack that sat beside him at the coffeehouse. Without a glance behind him, he began the last leg of his long trip. This time he was headed towards a place that probably didn't remember him.

In many ways, he had never existed there. But the village had lived in his dreams for a long time. He often wondered how much of what he remembered was accurate, and how much he had made up. Yes, he had been patient. He had patiently waited for the secrets to be revealed and for evil to give up and leave town.

Both had happened. Now Edward was free to go home. And he was taking his mom with him.

He patted the letter and tape that he had kept safe since his mother gave it to him. She made him promise never to show it to anyone until it was safe to do so. For all these years, it had never been safe, so he carried them with him wherever he went.

They were never out of his sight. They were copied to the web. Copied to thumb drives. Hidden many places, with hidden instructions where to find them. Just in case he didn't make it. The truth would still come out. Someday, someone would discover what he had kept safe for all these years.

But now it looked as if it just might be him that brought what everyone was looking for, proof. And something else. Something that would change the lives of more than one person.

AUTHOR'S NOTES

All characters in this book are fictional. Some are composites of people I have known. Most are entirely made up. As this series goes on, the characters and situations come more and more from my imagination.

Some places are real, others, like Doveland, I imagined. However, I grew up in State College, PA, and now we live a few hours from Pittsburgh, so these places and scenery are part of my DNA.

In today's political landscape—although I am not sure it has ever been much different—there is so much throwing around of personal authority that I wanted to write about what, for me, is the authority that overrides all human authority. I found the word Exousia, and it meant exactly what I was looking for.

And, I love that women are the ones that are speaking up and that men are supporting them. Women taking their place in the world has been a driving force for me my whole life.

As part of that drive, I have been guiding a women's council for almost fifteen years. They are just like the women in this book. Kind, generous, brave, and there for each other, all the time, in all ways. Being part of this council has changed my life. Although a few members have come and gone, there are a few that have been in the council the whole time. The council knows themselves as a Karass. Thank you for finding me!

And for my larger Karass, may I ask a favor of you? If you have a second, please review Exousia.

All authors ask the same thing. We love your honest reviews. With millions of books in the world, this is one way that people find us. I thank you in advance for taking the time to tell others what you think.

I hope you are enjoying the *Stories From Doveland*. The next one in the series is called *Stemma*. Read it to learn what happens when Edward returns home to Doveland. — Beca

PS

Be the first to know when there are new books when you join my mailing list at becalewis.com/ and choose a free book or two.

Also By Beca

The Rivers of Time Series: Women's Lit, Friendship, Small Town, Mystery, Magical Realism, Small Town Fiction
The Returning, The Awakening, The Rising

***Follow Me Here:* Women's Lit, Friendship, Small Town, Mystery, Magical Realism, Small Town Fiction**

The Ruby Sisters Series: Women's Lit, Friendship, Mystery, Small Town Fiction
A Last Gift, After All This Time, And Then She Remembered, As If It Was Real, Almost Innocent

Stories From Doveland: Women's Lit, Friendship, Small Town, Mystery, Magical Realism, Small Town Fiction
Karass, Pragma, Jatismar, Exousia, Stemma, Paragnosis, In-Between, Missing, Out Of Nowhere

The Return To Erda Series: Fantasy
Shatterskin, Deadsweep, Abbadon, The Experiment

The Chronicles of Thamon: Fantasy
Banished, Betrayed, Discovered, Wren's Story

The Shift Series: Spiritual Self-Help
Living in Grace: The Shift to Spiritual Perception
The Daily Shift: Daily Lessons From Love To Money
The 4 Essential Questions: Choosing Spiritually Healthy Habits
The 28 Day Shift To Wealth: A Daily Prosperity Plan
The Intent Course: Say Yes To What Moves You
Imagination Mastery: A Workbook For Shifting Your Reality
Right Thinking: A Thoughtful System for Healing
Perception Mastery: Seven Steps To Lasting Change
Blooming Your Life: How To Experience Consistent Happiness

Perception Parables: Very short stories
Love's Silent Sweet Secret: A Fable About Love
Golden Chains And Silver Cords: A Fable About Letting Go

Advice / Journals
A Woman's ABC's of Life: Lessons in Love, Life, and Career from Those Who Learned The Hard Way
The Daily Nudge(s): So When Did You First Notice

About Beca

Beca writes books she hopes will change people's perceptions of themselves and the world, and open possibilities to things and ideas that are waiting to be seen and experienced.

At sixteen, Beca founded her own dance studio. Later, she received a Master's Degree in Dance in Choreography from UCLA and founded the Harbinger Dance Theatre, a multimedia dance company, while continuing to run her dance school.

After graduating—to better support her three children—Beca switched to the sales field, where she worked as an employee and independent contractor in many industries, excelling in each while perfecting and teaching her Shift System and writing books.

She joined the financial industry in 1983 and became an Associate Vice President of Investments at a major stock brokerage firm. She was a licensed Certified Financial Planner for over twenty years.

This diversity, along with a variety of life challenges, helped fuel the desire to share what she's learned by writing and speaking, hoping it will make a difference in other people's lives.

Beca grew up in State College, PA, with the dream of becoming a dancer and then a writer. She carried that dream forward as she fulfilled a childhood wish by moving to Southern California in 1968. Beca told her family she would never move back to the cold.

After living there for thirty-one years, she met her husband, Delbert Lee Piper, Sr., at a retreat in Virginia, and everything changed. They decided to find a place they could call their own, which sent them off traveling around the United States. They lived and worked in a few different places before returning to live in the cold once again near Del's family in a small town in Northeast Ohio, not too far from State College.

When not working and teaching together, they love to visit and play with their combined family of eight children and five grandchildren, walk, read, study, do yoga or taiji, feed birds, and work in their garden.

www.ingramcontent.com/pod-product-compliance
Lightning Source LLC
Chambersburg PA
CBHW071457110726
47908CB00003B/639